Sally's Shadow

Sally's Shadow

Kinky Companions 1

Alex Markson

This paperback edition 2020.

First published by Parignon Press 2017

ISBN: 979 8 61 677963 2

Chapter 1 – Marcus

That went well …

It was only the second time I had been to the book club, and here I was, leaving the bar after half an hour, shortly after Karen, who I had offended so much she walked out.

Thinking back, I was still surprised at myself. I am normally very calm, and nothing much angers me. But blind prejudice is the red flag to my bull. The book we had been discussing contained a gay affair. It was a minor part of the story, but you wouldn't have known that from Karen's critique.

At the previous meeting, Karen's had been the dominant voice. She had to have the first, last and most other words on any matter. While I listened to her lecture us, I had looked at her closely. I was going to call her middle-aged, but she was probably not much older than me, just seemed it. Part of me was thinking of her living alone with two cats, and in need of someone to love, but that was unfair.

Probably …

This time, she'd carried on where she left off last time. But instead of offering her views on the whole book, she went straight for the 'gays', a term she proceeded to use with venom and obvious distaste.

After about five minutes, I gave up listening and looked around the group. There were seven of us. Apart from myself and Karen, there was the organiser, a friendly lady called Jane and a chap of about 60, who I vaguely remembered was called Ian. Then there was a girl probably in her late twenties called Sally, and two women who attended together, called Fiona and Beth, but I couldn't recall which was which.

I tuned back in to Karen and she was still going on and on.

"… and I don't want to read about gays in a normal book. I mean, I have nothing against them personally, but they should keep it to themselves. I don't want it rammed down my throat."

This last comment caused a few smiles and a stifled giggle from someone.

"Karen?"

She stared at me. "Yes?"

"Have you never met anyone gay?"

"No," she stated emphatically.

"How do you know?" I asked.

She looked flustered.

"Well," she said, "I'd know, wouldn't I?"

"How? Do they all look like the Village People? Or wear dungarees? Or carry convenient signs? How would you know if anyone around this table was gay?"

She sat with her mouth slightly open. She promptly closed it. One or two people around the table shuffled uncomfortably, but I heard another giggle. I stared straight at her. I'd come to talk about books, not listen to a bigoted lecture on putting anyone back in a closet. A silence fell over the group.

Jane finally said "Umm, does anyone else want to give us their thoughts?"

Karen jumped in. "I haven't finished yet!"

I'd had enough.

"Are you going to talk about the book," I asked, "or give us more of your bigotry?"

"I have a perfect right to give my opinion. I've been with this group a long time, and you're new here, so I can understand you not knowing the rules."

"I'd have thought the first rule was not to offend the other members."

"Who have I offended?"

"Well, anyone gay, for starters. Oh, but I forgot, you'd be able to detect them with your built-in gaydar."

2

She stood up abruptly. "I've had enough." Picking up her book and her bag, she headed for the door.

Now, I felt bad; I looked around at the others. Jane looked worried, Ian was studiously staring at his pint, Sally was leaning on the table looking at me sternly, and Fiona and Beth were looking at each other trying not to laugh.

"Well," I said, "I'm sorry about that. I guess I went too far. I think it's best if I leave as well, so you can carry on without further drama."

As I came out into the fresh air, I took a deep breath and headed for my car. It was a pity really; I'd been pleased when I had found this book club. I'd only been twice and already blackballed myself. Ah well, I'd always been good at …

"Excuse me."

… being on my own, so I'd …

"Excuse me."

… have to go home and do it some more.

As I got to my car, I heard someone walking quickly, and 'excuse me' again. I'd heard it before but ignored it. This time, I turned around and saw Sally coming towards me. I remembered the look she had given me, so prepared to apologise and be on my way.

"Marcus, isn't it?"

"Yes. Sally, right?" I replied. "Has the group broken up already? God, I'm sorry if I spoiled everyone's evening."

"No, they're still there, discussing you."

"Oh, really? I thought the idea was to discuss the book."

She laughed. "Yes, but it's probably the most exciting thing that's happened to them in ages. So, I thought I'd skip that."

"Sorry."

"Don't apologise. I thought it was funny. Karen was such a pain. Every time we met, she'd spout off, but Jane was too nice to do anything about it. They're hoping Karen doesn't come back."

"Ah …"

"No, what I really wanted to do was ask you a few questions about fatigue."

"Really?"

"Yes, if that's alright?"

At the first meeting I attended, I had mentioned in passing that I had suffered from Chronic Fatigue.

"Are you in a hurry?" Sally asked. "There's a coffee shop around the corner. Can I buy you something and pick your brain?"

Five minutes later, we were sitting at a table in the window. Sally briefly explained her aunt - Mary - had recently been diagnosed with Fatigue and was refusing to accept it. She was constantly overdoing it and crashing. Could I offer any advice? We chatted about my experience and the lack of support available.

"Would you meet her?" she asked.

"Well, if she won't accept the problem, then she's not going to welcome me."

"Oh, she knows she has it, she just won't face it. I'm hoping talking to someone in the same situation might help."

I agreed to meet her aunt, provided Sally thought it would do any good. We swapped numbers, and she said she'd give me a ring.

***

A week later, I arranged to meet Sally at Mary's home. Mary was depressed, and it was hard work talking to her. She was going through everything I had been through over the years – coming to terms with any chronic illness is a bit like the stages of grieving - but she seemed to be going through the stages all at once. Sally was right. Mary knew what the problem was but was in denial.

It had started after she caught a bug on holiday abroad. I explained my fatigue had a different cause – another chronic illness – but the effects were broadly similar, and a bit about how I had coped with it. She listened, was polite, but I wasn't sure she was taking it in. After an hour or so, she was clearly tiring, so I left but offered to talk again if she wanted to. Sally thanked me and I went home.

To my surprise, Sally called the next week and asked if I'd visit Mary again, as she had some more questions for me. Over the next few weeks, I met Mary a few times and realised she was a shrewd cookie. She listened to everything I said, because the next time, she'd have lots of further questions.

After the second or third visit, Sally asked if I was going to this month's book club.

"God, no. I suspect I'm persona non-grata there"

"Not at all. Karen has told Jane she's never going again, and Jane says you'd be welcome."

"If only to make up the numbers."

"Well, possibly," she replied. "Without Karen, I'm not sure how much the rest of us will actually say. We couldn't get a word in edgeways while she was there."

"Oh well, I might come along then."

**

In fact, it went rather well. Without the domineering absentee, everyone seemed happy to chip in, and we had a relaxed discussion. A couple of times during the evening, someone quietly thanked me for getting rid of 'that woman', and I couldn't help wondering why they'd put up with her for so long.

As we got up to leave, I went over to Sally.

"How's Mary?" I asked.

"She seems happier in herself. She's booked herself on one of those courses you suggested. I think it's helping, thank you."

"Not sure I've done much, but it helps to know you're not alone."

"I wondered …" she looked down briefly, and I thought she blushed slightly, "… if I can buy you lunch or dinner one day? As a thank you."

"Well, that would be nice, but it's not necessary."

"I know, but I'd like to."

"What did you have in mind?"

"Well, evening would be best for me."

"Fine. Would you like me to arrange something?"

"No, I'll sort it out. Any preferences?"

"Not really, but I prefer somewhere quiet."

"Okay, I'll book and let you know."

Chapter 2 – Sally

"Hi, Luce."

"Hi, Sal. How are you?"

I gave Lucy a big hug.

"I'm fine. Shall we go in? I've only got an hour."

"Me too."

We found a table, quickly browsed the menu, and ordered.

"Come on," I said. "How did it go?"

Lucy made a face. "Oh, don't ask."

"You can't leave it at that."

"Okay. It might have been a lovely evening if she hadn't started laying down rules before we'd even finished the first course."

"Rules?"

"Whether we could hold hands in public, how often we'd see each other's families, the list was endless. Well, it seemed that way."

"But it was only your second date."

"I know. I began to wonder if I'd missed a few months somewhere. She already had us down as an old married couple."

"What are you going to do?"

Lucy chuckled. "Already done."

"What?"

"She'd already told me how much her cats meant to her, so I casually told her I'd once eaten cat in the Far East. I was free before we got to the dessert menu."

"Oh, Lucy."

A waiter arrived with our order, and we tucked in as soon as he left.

I sighed. "We don't seem to have much luck, do we? Neither of us seem to meet normal people. I either end up with action man; fit, toned but no brain. Or Mr Wimpy; lovely guy, but no balls. And you've had more than your fair share of nutters, waifs and strays."

"Thanks."

"Sorry, but you know what I mean."

"Yeah. It's getting boring. I think I'm looking too hard. What about you?"

"I don't think I'm looking at all."

"Don't you miss sex?"

"I think I can give myself as much pleasure as anyone I've slept with."

"More, probably." Lucy gave me a grin. "After all, your lovers have all been men."

"And you?" I fired back. "How many of yours have been better than your own efforts?"

Lucy thought for a moment, staring into space. I watched her, knowing she was pausing for effect, to wind me up. Finally, she picked up her fork and played with some pasta.

"A few," she said, smiling. "Well, one or two. Possibly?"

"There you go. We're not desperate; neither of us need looking after."

"No." She stared into space again for a minute or two. "But what *do* we want."

"I've been thinking about that a lot recently."

"Any conclusions?"

"Yes. I want someone a bit different. Someone to help me explore a bit."

"Ooh, tell me more."

"No."

"Aww, go on."

"No, not now. I need to get things clearer myself."

Lucy knew not to push further. We had always been open with one another; discussing our partners, sometimes in detail. But we knew each other well enough to know when to let a subject drop.

"How's Mary?"

"A bit better actually. Well, more agreeable. There's a guy joined our book club who's had Chronic Fatigue, and I asked him to talk to her. I think he's helping."

She darted me a look. "Potential?"

"Oh, no. He hasn't shown any interest."

"Perhaps he's gay."

"Possibly. At the last meeting, he got into an argument with our resident bore when she started bashing a gay storyline. She walked out in the end."

"Ooh, murder at the book club."

"Well, it didn't get quite that far. I think we were all grateful though; she was awful and hasn't come back. I'm taking him out for a meal next week to thank him for helping Mary."

"What's he like?"

I thought for a moment.

"He seems nice enough. He's a writer, but I'm not sure what he writes. Probably in his forties. Not handsome, but with an intelligent expression, if you know what I mean."

"I thought you weren't looking?"

"Trust me, Lucy, I'm not. You know how guys look at a woman they want, and I'm pretty sure he's not interested."

"Okay, if you say so. God, I must go. How about meeting up one evening? We haven't had a night out for ages."

"That sounds like an excellent idea, Miss Halstead."

We grabbed our stuff and gave each other a hug. I offered to pay, as I wasn't in quite the rush Lucy was. She turned and was out of the door before I knew it. As I stood at the counter to pay, my mind wandered. I still had to book the meal with Marcus. I realised I was quite looking forward to it. He may not have shown any interest in me – perhaps he *was* gay – but that was no bad thing. Outside work, I hadn't had a decent, intelligent, equal conversation with a man in months. I must arrange it.

Chapter 3 – Marcus

"This is nice."

"Yes," Sally said, "it's quite simple, but it's not far from me, and I knew it would be quiet on a Monday. Do you have a favourite place?"

"Not really. Years ago, when my health was bad, I decided I'd let people down too often, so became a bit insular. Lost my confidence. The book club is the first thing I've signed up to for ages."

I had been a bit surprised when Sally had rung me to arrange dinner, thinking it had been mentioned out of politeness. But here we were in a restaurant I'd never even noticed before. I suppose you'd call it 'shabby chic'. Friendly staff, comfy little booths, and the menu looked good.

"Don't you miss socialising?" she asked.

"Yes, and no. I've never been a particularly sociable person, definitely an introvert. Dinner or drinks with one or two people, but anything larger and I instantly do a great impression of a wallflower. I've always been happy with my own company and a good book."

Our starters arrived, and we fell silent for a while as we began to eat.

"Are you going to the book club this month?" Sally asked.

"Yes, I expect so. You?"

"Yes."

"Why do you go?"

"Sorry?"

"Well, I may be wrong, but there seem to be two reasons for going to a book club. One, you're a book geek. And two, you're a sad loser with no friends and need to get out of the house more."

She spluttered slightly and laughed.

"We're both sad losers, then?"

I smiled. "Well, I think I possibly qualify, hence my question to you."

"I love books and everything about them. I trained as a librarian, and now look after all the archives at the university, so I guess I'm the geek. Books, manuscripts, documents, they all do it for me."

We chatted for a while about books; books we'd read, loved, and hated. Our main courses arrived, and I was struck by how relaxed I was. It was some time since I'd had dinner with someone I didn't know, let alone a woman who was smart and attractive. Years ago, I wouldn't have been so relaxed, probably trying to impress and probably failing. Here, neither of us was trying to impress. We were enjoying a meal with no hidden agenda, and that meant we could relax.

"Do you have a partner?" Sally asked.

"No, my last relationship ended about four years ago."

"Man or woman?"

"Woman, Claire."

"Happy single?"

"Yes, and no. I'm happy being by myself, never get bored. But there are things I miss."

"Like what?" she asked, a cheeky smile on her face.

"Yes. That. But other things as well."

"I don't know what you mean," she said with mock innocence. "What other things?"

"Well, intimacy I suppose. The hugs, the passing touches, the unspoken eye contact. And probably most of all, what I call quiet companionship."

"Explain."

"Perhaps spending a whole evening together listening to music and each reading a book. There may hardly be a word spoken, but there is a human connection, a …"

"Companionship," she completed my sentence. "I know what you mean."

"There's someone there if you want to talk about your book, or if a particular track comes on."

"Sounds good to me."

"Well, in my experience, most people find it boring."

"You just need to find the right person."

"Yes, but where? We introverts are all sitting at home on our own, wondering why we don't come across like-minded people."

Sally laughed. "I think I see the problem. What about dating sites?"

"Have you ever tried them?"

"Once or twice."

"Me too. At least, I've registered with a few. Once you can see beyond the fake profiles, there seem to be three categories. Those who are looking for sex with anyone, anytime, anyplace. Those who are desperate. And those who, frankly, are probably a risk to themselves and everyone else."

"Which category do you fall into?"

"Good question." I thought for a moment. "Well, I guess I must be a member of that rare fourth category; practically perfect."

We looked at each other and laughed. A waiter came to clear the table and asked if we wanted dessert. Sally looked at me, we nodded simultaneously, so he went off and returned with the menu.

"I'm torn," she said after a while.

"Between?"

"Pear and chocolate tart, or passionfruit roulade."

"Oh, that's good. I'm down to those two as well. Let's order one of each and we can share. If that's all right?"

"Yeah, that sounds good."

"Are you with someone?" I asked.

"Nope. Been single for over two years now."

"By choice?"

She gave me a quizzical look.

"Sorry, badly phrased question, I guess." I was surprised she had been single for so long. She was attractive. Not showy, not 'in your face'. Just natural, relaxed, and open, but with a layer of shyness underneath. The sort of girl who attracted attention, but probably didn't even realise it. She was casually, but well-dressed, wore little makeup, her hair was well-cut and worn loose. But what I noticed most were her deep green eyes.

"That's alright," she said. "My ex left me with a bit of a downer on men in general. I haven't really been looking."

Our desserts arrived, we cut each in half and swapped them.

"Which ones have you tried?" Sally asked.

"Which ones?"

"Which dating sites?"

"Oh, I've not signed up for the expensive ones. Over the years, I've looked at almost everything else from the platonic friendship ones to the more specialised sites."

She stopped eating. "Specialised?"

I suddenly wished I'd used a different word.

"Oh well, you know, for people looking for specific things."

She was watching me now and I began to feel a little uncomfortable.

"Such as?"

"Well, there are sites for all tastes," I replied. I quickly made a show of eating and having a drink.

"What?" she said, watching me closely. "Sort of fifty shades of dating?"

I looked at her and raised an eyebrow. She flushed slightly and started eating again. I put my spoon down and looked at her.

"Something like that …" I replied.

She glanced up, saw I was still looking at her, and smiled shyly.

We went back to finishing our desserts, ordered coffee, and returned to safer subjects. The evening seemed to have flown by, but it was still only half-past nine, and the restaurant didn't need the table, so we were happy talking.

"Ideally, who are you looking for?" she asked, toying with her nearly empty wine glass.

"Real world, or fantasy?" I replied.

"Both. Real world first."

"Okay, someone with similar interests who can live with my bad days, but still wants a bit of fun and laughter."

"And fantasy?"

I thought I might as well be honest.

"A book and history nerd, who's looking for someone to share her darkest fantasies with."

"You don't want much," she said, smiling.

"You did say fantasy."

"True. Will you ever find her?"

"The first? Possibly. The fantasy version? God, no. I think I've missed the boat there."

I thought I'd better move on before it became awkward.

"And you?" I asked. "Who are you looking for?"

She thought for a moment.

"Good question. I'm not sure I know, that's probably why I've been single for a while."

"Come on then, real world and fantasy."

She looked at me, a look of concentration passing across her face.

"Real world; a nice guy, similar interests, the usual stuff."

"That's not very well defined."

"I know, that's why I always seem to end up with the wrong ones."

"And fantasy?"

She flushed slightly again but deliberately held my eyes.

"Oh, I don't know. Perhaps a bookish nerd who might want to help me explore one or two fantasies."

"One or two?"

"Three or four? Hell, dozens! Depends what mood I'm in."

"Think you'll ever find him?"

"The first? Possibly. The other? Who knows? Life is full of surprises …"

Chapter 4 – Sally

I got home shattered after Lucy and I had met up for a meal. We hadn't had an evening out for ages, and it was good to relax and catch up; just gossip and reminisce.

"You know," Lucy had said, "after our chat last week, I've been thinking about what we discussed. I think I have been trying too hard, searching for the one."

"Or anyone?"

"Yeah, you know what I mean. I think I'll get on with life and see what happens."

"What, rely on your rabbit?"

"You stick to your favourite; I'll stick to my wand."

"Ooh, any good?"

"Get one. Trust me, just get one."

Lucy suggested we go on to the Forum down the road. I didn't fancy it much, it's not my scene anymore, but as clubs go, it's not bad. There always seems to be a decent mix of ages, gender, and persuasion, so it never feels like a cattle market. We grabbed some drinks and sat and people watched. We spent an hour or so critiquing everyone else in the club. It was bitchy but fun.

After an hour, Lucy had seen a couple of girls she'd happily share breakfast with, but I hadn't seen anyone who stood out. Sure, there were plenty of good-looking guys and even more who thought they were. But I'd finally worked out that looks were not important. I'd had my fair share of good lookers. They'd all disappointed in the end.

Unspoken, we'd already decided we weren't looking, and the only time a couple of guys approached, Lucy grabbed my face and gave me a kiss. They turned and tried their luck somewhere else. It was a trick we'd used before in straight and gay clubs, but not for a few years. I only realised a minute or so later that Lucy's kiss had caused a reaction I hadn't experienced previously.

As I lay in bed, I couldn't get to sleep, even though I was tired. Lots of things were going through my mind. I hadn't been looking, had I? Shall I get a wand? Why did I get turned on when Lucy kissed me? It had never happened before, but I had to admit girls appeared more often in my fantasies nowadays. I hadn't really acknowledged it.

My thoughts then turned to Marcus. I'd enjoyed our meal. He was fun, intelligent, and seemed safe, but there had been things hidden in our conversation that intrigued me. I knew all my relationships seemed doomed; the past always came back to haunt me, but I decided that after Easter, I'd dig a bit deeper.

***

Marcus seemed surprised when I invited him to dinner again, but I got the impression he was keen. I suggested he chose the restaurant, but he was happy to return to 'my local', as he called it. We agreed on the following Monday.

"You look great," he said when we met.

"Oh, thanks," I replied casually. Then realised I had thought more carefully about how I had dressed this time. No jeans and a shirt now. I'd chosen a skirt I liked with a well-fitting top, heels, and stockings. Stockings always made me feel good; I'd had some of my best experiences wearing them. But I hadn't been aware of my choices until he complimented me.

We sat down, ordered, and made small talk. He asked about Mary, though I knew he was still popping in to see her. He seemed as laid back as before, but I realised I wasn't. I felt slightly tense and nervous. After a glass of wine, I relaxed a little and over dinner, I told him about my conversations with Lucy, and about not looking for partners.

"Have you known each other long?" he asked.

"Oh, yes, since uni. So, it must be fifteen or sixteen years. Best friends."

"Is she a librarian too?"

"No. She teaches art history. Quite artistic herself as well. We've always been there for one another. We've been through a few things and talk to each other about everything. You know, girl talk."

"Ah, slagging off each other's boyfriends."

"Girlfriends, in her case."

"Oh, right. How have your experiences compared over the years?"

"How do you mean?"

"Well, are her complaints about her girlfriends the same as yours about boyfriends?"

I sat back, thinking.

"You know, I've never thought about that. But yes, I guess they are. Relationships are just relationships, I suppose, no matter who's fucking who with what."

As soon as the words came out, I froze. Not because I was ashamed of them, but because I wasn't sure about Marcus. I hadn't yet worked him out, so hadn't meant to be so explicit. But I needn't have worried. He laughed.

"Ah, is the real Sally emerging tonight?"

"What do you mean?"

"Okay, can I be honest?"

"Of course, friends always should be."

"You come across as the demure archivist, head always in a manuscript or a book, legs always carefully crossed. Yet one or two of the things you said – or hinted at – last time make me wonder."

"About what?"

"Whether there's a little kinkster hiding somewhere behind the façade."

I felt my face flush, but this was where I wanted to go, what I wanted to talk about, so I wasn't backing down now.

"Can't I be both?" I asked.

"Of course, but it generally only happens in men's dreams."

"In yours?"

He paused for a heartbeat or two and looked directly at me.

"Oh, yes."

There was a break in time. We both sat, still, looking at each other for what seemed an eternity. I sensed he was playing with me. Finally, he reached for his glass, took a sip, and leaned back.

"Shall we be open?" he said.

"Open?"

"With each other. Stop pussyfooting. If we're going to be friends, then we need to be honest with one another. I'm happy to discuss anything you want to talk about, and I'm guessing some of those things might make more sense if we don't have to resort to euphemism or medical terminology. I propose we call a cock a cock, a pussy a pussy and a fuck a fuck. Or whatever words you normally use."

He stopped abruptly, looking at me. I felt flushed but burst out laughing. A quizzical look passed across his face.

"Agreed?" he asked.

"Agreed," I replied. I felt my face flush even more. "In fact, I'd be relieved. I can be quite shy sometimes, and flush a little, but normally only when I'm nervous or embarrassed."

"Yes, I'd noticed. It's quite cute."

I looked at him. "Cute?"

He looked surprised. "Sorry, have I said the wrong thing?"

I thought about it. "No. It's just no one has called it cute before."

"Well, it is. It can also be a bit of a giveaway."

"Oh, tell me about it."

I didn't blush strongly, just a pale pink. Many people didn't even notice it, but Marcus had. I had always had to live with the fact it could give me away at the wrong times. But he found it cute?

He raised his glass.

"Here's to openness and honesty."

I touched his glass with mine and took a long, slow drink.

We once again ordered two desserts to share, and while we waited, Marcus excused himself. I had relaxed and felt much calmer now, but there were butterflies in my stomach. I took a few deep breaths and closed my eyes. How did I feel? Nervous? Yes. Excited? Yes. And then as I moved in the seat, I sensed proof of another feeling; I was a bit - warm. During our conversation, I hadn't noticed, but now? Well, we'd crossed a line, and I wasn't sure what would happen next. But my body was already responding positively, and that was a good feeling. I hadn't got seriously turned on by any man I'd met in the last couple of years. Was it Marcus? Or was it the prospect of finally talking about my desires to somebody? Or both?

Lost in my reverie, I didn't notice that Marcus had returned to his seat. I suddenly saw him looking at me with a faint smile.

"What are you thinking?" he asked.

"Oh, nothing," I lied.

"Openness and honesty."

"Okay. I was wondering what we do now."

"Do? Well, that depends."

"On what?"

"On whether you want to talk about books and culture – and I'd be fine with that - or about some of those fantasies of yours."

I looked down, flushing again. I wasn't sure how to respond. I wanted to talk about my fantasies; wanted to talk to someone who wouldn't laugh or judge. Someone who had fantasies of their own and would help me to understand mine. But we had only known each other for a few weeks; I hadn't even discussed these things with Lucy, and we'd known each other for years.

Marcus brought my attention back to the table. "Sally?"

"Yes."

"Why are you here?"

The million-dollar question. I enjoyed Marcus's company, there was no doubt about that. We seemed to share some interests, we had got along instantly and were relaxed in each other's company. He hadn't tried to impress me or hit on me. I wasn't sure if he saw me as just a friend or something more. I couldn't let go now.

"Why are you here, Marcus?"

"Answer my question first, then I'll answer yours. Fair?"

"Unfair! But okay. I think we have a lot in common, the books and stuff. We're both introverts and love peace and solitude. More than enough to be friends. But I think we might be able to help each other in other ways." I took a deep breath. "I have fantasies I want to explore, fantasies that some would find extreme or weird. If I can't find someone to fulfil them, I at least would love to have someone who I can discuss them with. Confess them to, even. Someone who won't laugh at me or judge me. I want to learn and understand, experiment, even. Is that so wrong? I may be mistaken, but I think you're in a similar position. Am I right? Or have I completely cocked this up?"

He had been looking at me intently, and I had struggled to finish the statement. I picked up my glass and took two or three large mouthfuls of wine. He laughed.

"Thank you for being honest. I think that took some courage."

"Yes."

"You're right," he said. "I'm enjoying your company. But I admit, it's the undercurrent that intrigues me. Yes, I have fantasies. Yes, many are unfulfilled. Yes, I'd love to talk about them to someone and about theirs. I promise never to judge you if you promise the same in return. I can't promise not to laugh, but I won't laugh *at* you. Deal?"

I breathed a sigh of relief. "Deal."

"Good. Do you want to leave it for another time, or shall we jump straight in?"

It had taken a lot of courage to get this far, so I wasn't going to let go now.

"Jump straight in, please."

"Right, I have a suggestion. No long explanations, no recounting scenarios. Why don't we come up with single words or phrases that crop up in our fantasies? Take it in turns. I'll go first if you like."

"Okay."

This was it. I felt the tension rise in my body. This would be the first time I'd named these things to anyone but myself. But I knew enough to know there were almost as many kinks as there are people. Would ours be wildly different? Would we have any common ground? Would he think mine were weird? Would I think his were? Oh, God …

"Spanking," he said. Phew, that was all right.

"Tying up," I replied.

"Roleplay."

"Dressing up."

"Sensory deprivation." I wasn't quite sure what that was but had an idea.

"Flogging."

"Domination."

"Sensuality."

"Anal play."

"Submission."

"Enough for starters?"

I relaxed. "Yes, for now."

"Well?"

"It would seem we have some shared interests."

"Yes, it looks that way," he said. "I have a couple more questions."

"Fire away."

"Domination and submission were both in that list."

I nodded.

"In your fantasies, are you dom or sub?"

I felt my face flush.

"Sub, I think. Mainly. You?"

"Dom. Mainly."

"Well, that's lucky!"

"Isn't it?" He paused. "Is your interest around 24/7? Living it?"

"No," I replied. "That's not me. It would be playtime. You?"

"No, me neither. How much do you know about this world?"

We spent a while explaining what we knew. It turned out we had quite a few websites in common, and we quickly worked out we both had a lot of the theory. Marcus told me about his actual experience; it wasn't a huge amount, but it was more than me. I asked him if he'd only got into this world recently.

"No. I've been interested for as long as I can remember but never had a partner who was into it too. One or two played along because they saw what it did for me. But they didn't get off on it, so we could never stretch each other. How about you?"

I told him how I'd become more interested in recent years. I'd tried to get my last boyfriend to try it, but in the end, it freaked him out, and he'd found someone else. Since then, I'd done all I could to learn the theory, so to speak.

"Boy, have I learnt the theory," I joked.

"Do you masturbate to your fantasies?" He held my eyes.

The question threw me briefly. I know we had agreed to speak openly, but I'd never really talked to anyone about what I did on my own.

I shrugged. "Yes."

"Often?"

"Are you getting off on this?" I flashed.

"No. What I mean is, do you fantasise about these things every time you do, or only occasionally?"

"Oh, I see, sorry." I thought about the question. "Not every time, no. But more than occasionally."

"So, it's a big part of your sex life."

"What sex life?" I chuckled.

"I know the feeling."

We lapsed into silence for a while, each of us thinking our own thoughts.

"Marcus," I said.

"Yes, Sally."

I swallowed hard. In recent years, I hadn't been the one to make the first move.

"Do you see us as friends who are going to talk, or as potential partners who are going to actually try?"

He looked at me; no, drilled into my eyes.

"Honestly?"

"Yes. Openness and honesty."

He smiled.

"At first, I saw us as friends. Then as friends with, what shall I say, common interests. But I'm aware of the age difference and my health."

"Oh, those things aren't important."

"They're real enough to me. I don't have the self-confidence I once had. Realistically, I see us helping each other explore – what was it you called it – the theory."

"But would you be interested in the real thing? If things moved that way?"

He smiled, and for the first time, looked away briefly.

"In my dreams!"

"Marcus," I said as sternly as I could. "Would you?"

"Seriously?"

"Yes."

"Then … yes."

"Good. Me too. Now we both know where we are."

Chapter 5 – Marcus

'Now we both know where we are.'

That's what she'd said. But I wasn't sure I knew where I was at all. Sure, I'd imagined doing things with Sally since we'd met. I'd imagined her over my knee, skirt up, knickers down, my hand raised ready to strike. I'd imagined her tied spread-eagled to the bed; naked, blindfolded, vulnerable. I'd imagined her bent over the back of the sofa, a flogger or strap in my hand making contact with her naked bum.

But I seriously hadn't thought it might happen. She was younger than me; how much, I wasn't sure, but I guessed probably fifteen years, possibly more. That was very nice in a man's dreams, but this was the real world.

Towards the end of our meal, we'd agreed to meet again the following week. In the meantime, we set ourselves homework. To complete a fetish checklist and compare the results, and to find two or three pictures that summed up what all this meant to us. We would send the lists to each other before our next meeting, so we didn't have to wade through them over dinner but take the pictures with us to show each other.

The checklist was easy. Yes. No. Somewhere in between. It would be fascinating to see how they compared.

The pictures were harder. What to go for? You can't sum up a whole world of fantasy in a single picture. Individual moments, sure, but not the whole thing. So, what to pick? After a few days, it struck me. Choose the obvious. What turns me on the most? What's guaranteed to pique my interest? Well, for me, that's always been a bum; a peachy, pert, succulent bum. Once I had that, I spent some time trawling for three perfect pictures.

One was simple; a beautiful, naked ass, its owner leaning forward, legs slightly apart. Secondly, a girl dressed in holdups and nothing else, strapped down over a bench; her ass glowing pink, with four darker red lines across it, a cane laid across her hips. Finally, a black and white image of a naked couple cuddled together in a fetal position, the man almost enclosing the woman with his arms, holding her tight. I put them on my phone, sent her my checklist, and waited for our next meeting.

***

"How's the course going?" I asked Mary.

"Well, it's okay. I am learning a few things." She handed me the coffee. "But there aren't any answers, are there?"

I shrugged.

"No, I'm afraid not. It's not a treatment. It's all about learning to manage it."

"How long did it take you to come to terms with it?"

"I don't think I ever did. At the moment it's not a problem, but if it comes back, I do know what happens if I don't listen to my body. I get worse."

"Yes, I know that feeling."

"Besides," I replied, "at least if yours was caused by a virus, you might kick it all together. Mine comes from my underlying illness, so could come back in the future."

We talked about the course she was attending. She was right. When I went, I'd felt it was a waste of time. It was a way for the doctors to say they were doing something. They couldn't do anything to help, so simply taught you how to live with it.

"I gather Sally wants to take you out to say thank you," Mary said. "I don't feel up to it yet. She'll get around to it, but she gets easily distracted sometimes." I hid my grin. "Must be her father coming out in her, it doesn't come from our side."

"Actually, Mary, she already has. We had a good meal."

"Oh good, I'm glad. I am grateful Marcus. I do feel I'm making some progress."

Marcus

***

I stood outside the same restaurant waiting for Sally. She was late. Fifteen minutes late. I began to feel stupid. Had I misjudged her? Had she been playing with me? I still felt she was the type of person who would ring me if she was running late. Besides, she'd told me she lived close by, so didn't have any distance to travel.

But she was late, twenty minutes now.

My mind wandered, beginning to imagine all the things I'd dreamed of us doing which now looked rather unlikely. Thwarted before we'd even begun. Still, the images in my head were not unpleasant.

Suddenly, I felt something touch my arm and turned quickly. Sally's face was a few inches from mine, rather flushed, and we both froze. She recovered first, squeezed my arm, and gave me a quick kiss on the cheek.

"I'm really sorry I'm late. Did you think I wasn't coming?" She took a couple of deep breaths and turned towards the entrance.

"I had begun to think I'd been taken for an old fool."

"No, Marcus. I'm not into games." She turned back to face me, a sly grin on her face. "Well, not that sort of game, anyway."

We went in, found our table, and spent a few minutes settling and ordering while Sally got her breath back.

"I'm so sorry," she said. "I couldn't find my phone. The photos were on it, and I couldn't ring you either. Finally found it in the car."

"Well, you're here now, so no worries."

"You looked miles away when I arrived."

"Oh, I'd let my mind wander."

"Anywhere nice?" She looked directly at me.

"Oh, just wondering what the punishment should be for being late."

She held my gaze.

"Did you decide?"

"No, you turned up at the right time."

"Ooh, if I'd known, I'd have given you more time. What were the choices?"

I considered my reply, this could get interesting very quickly. On the other hand, patience is a virtue. And anticipation is a powerful aphrodisiac. I didn't answer directly.

"Well, our checklists seem to give us several possibilities."

We had, as promised, exchanged our lists during the week. They were quite similar and complementary. No big no-no's either way, and enough shared interests to keep us talking for some time. Of course, our experience and ratings were different on most things, but that was part of the fun; learn together and learn from each other.

"Yeah, I had fun doing that. I've seen them before, but this is the first time I've filled one in."

"Were you honest?"

"Yes," she shot back.

"No putting down what you thought I'd like?"

"What would be the point of that? Openness and honesty, Marcus."

"Good girl," I said. It might have been my imagination, but I thought she stiffened for a moment. I knew some submissives loved those two words, but many didn't, and vanilla people might well feel patronised by them.

Food arrived, and we sorted the table out and tucked in.

"Were you?" she asked.

"Honest?"

"Mmm."

"Yes, no point messing about. I don't mind letting you know what makes me tick."

"Tick? That's a new word for it."

I could see she was in a playful mood tonight. That was good.

"They match pretty well, don't they?"

"Almost perfectly, I'd say," she replied.

"Did you imagine doing any of those shared interests?"

Sally shifted in her seat, raised her eyebrows, and a brief smile crossed her face. She picked up her glass, holding it close to her lips.

"Might have."

"Not as good as actually doing it though, is it?" I asked.

She nearly snorted into her wine and laughed out loud. She slowly put the glass down and looked at me.

"I don't know, Marcus. That's my problem. I haven't done any of them."

"But you do want to?"

"Yes," she said quite forcefully, but then looked down at her food.

The conversation stopped. I deliberately kept quiet and watched her. I could see she was suddenly uncomfortable with the silence. I wondered how serious she was about all this. Had she just read Fifty Shades, and thought it was all a big game? Or did she take it a bit more seriously? Sure, it had to be fun. Otherwise, what was the point? But you only got out what you put in. Was I wasting my time?

She toyed with a carrot, pushing it around her plate.

"Are you going to eat that carrot or fuck yourself with it?" I said.

She looked at me, colouring, momentarily surprised. Recovering quickly, she speared the carrot, and looking straight at me, put the end in her mouth and delicately began to lick the sauce off. Her eyes were smiling, and that made me smile back.

Suddenly, she bit the end of the carrot off and started chewing.

"Ouch," I whispered. The tension disappeared instantly. "I hope that's not your normal technique."

"Only to any creep who deserves it."

I looked at her quizzically. "Have you met many of those? Are you out on parole?"

"Relax. I'm joking."

I smiled and pushed my plate away.

"Besides," she said, holding my gaze. "I'm quite proud of my oral technique."

"Really?"

"Umm."

"Tease."

"When I want to be. But I don't get the chance much. Most men seem to take it the wrong way."

A waiter cleared the table, and we did our now customary option of ordering two desserts to share.

"You seem more relaxed tonight."

"Yes, I feel good. I'm enjoying the company. We both know why we're here. The possibilities are … arousing." She playfully wriggled her hips in her seat. "Aren't they?" I put my hand below the table as if to rearrange myself. "I'll take that as a yes!"

I didn't reply.

"You're still not sure, are you?" she asked, her voice stronger. "What's the problem? What's wrong with me?"

"Nothing," I replied. "From my point of view, you're damned near perfect."

"So, what's the problem?"

"Well …"

"Be honest."

"My last relationship suffered because of my health. It meant we couldn't do all the things we wanted to do. Claire ended up supporting us as well, as I had to give up work, so all the pressure fell on her. In the end, it was all too much. Now, I struggle with the thought of forming a new relationship. I don't want to let someone down again. Add to that our age difference, and there you have it.

"I know this all sounds like excuses, or as if I'm sorry for myself. But it's not that. I want you to know all this up front, so you have all the facts."

"Marcus?"

"Yes?"

"Have I asked you to marry me?"

"Uh, no."

"Or move in with me?"

"No."

"How old do you think I am?"

"Dangerous question …"

"How old?"

I looked at her.

"Late twenties. Thirty at most."

She smiled.

"Thanks. I wish. I'm thirty-five. I'm guessing you're mid-forties?"

"Forty-five."

"Ten years. Doesn't that ease that concern? None of the rest is important. I appreciate you telling me, but let's be realistic. We are both looking for someone to talk to, to learn with, to share ideas with. Hopefully, someone to play with. Ultimately, I'm looking for someone to spank me, tie me up, fuck me; all those things in my fantasies. Unless I'm very much mistaken, you want those things too. Or am I mistaken?"

She was quite flushed, a determined look on her face. Those green eyes flaring.

"No," I said. "That would do for starters …"

"So, let's put our concerns aside and see what happens. I don't know if this will work out, but it seems to be the perfect opportunity, to me, at least. You're a nice guy, I'm enjoying your company, we have shared interests. In all sorts of ways. And talking about all this with you has made me bloody horny!" I laughed. "Do you fancy me? Could you imagine playing with me?"

"God, yes. You're pretty, sassy, cute and smart. And you're prepared to tell me that talking about spanking and sex makes you horny. In a restaurant on a Monday night. So, yeah, I quite fancy you."

The serious face cracked slightly, and she paused; it was the first time I'd ever talked about how I saw her.

"Thank you," she said, trying not to laugh.

Two desserts arrived, and we tucked in.

"Okay, Marcus. I know this isn't starting like most relationships. We're not doing the usual stuff, then starting a physical relationship before trying to add other things in later. We already know we want those other things from the beginning. So how do we begin?"

"Well, we need to get a few things straight."

"Such as?"

"First, sexual health. Past, present and future."

"How about we get tested?" she said. "My ex cheated on me while we were still together, so I had it done after I walked out. It was fine, and I've not been active since, but happy to get it updated."

"I'm sure I'm clean too, but happy to prove that. I've not had a partner since my last relationship, and confident we were both fine, but it will give us peace of mind."

"Okay. That's that sorted."

"What about condoms?"

"Oh, not unless you want to. I'm on the pill, keeps me regular. Besides," she gave me a cheeky grin, "latex always leaves a bad taste in my mouth." I laughed. "What?" she asked, innocently running her finger around her glass.

"Definitely not a demure librarian with her legs crossed."

"Sometimes I am. Most of the time, nowadays. But I want to see what else I can be. I need someone to help me."

"Good. That brings me to the next question. What are we?"

"How do you mean?"

"Well, are we play partners? Friends with benefits? Or building a relationship?"

We talked around these for a few minutes over coffee. And got nowhere.

"Oh, let's go with the flow," Sally said eventually. "What does it matter what we call it? It doesn't need a name as long as we're having fun."

"True. Okay. Anything else you need?"

"Yes. No other partners while we're doing this."

"Agreed."

"I think that's it for me."

"One more from me. Feedback; all the time to begin with. Telling each other what we want and how we feel."

"Okay." She finished the last of her coffee. "When do I submit?"

"Not for a long time yet."

She looked at me with a puzzled expression. "Why not?"

"Because there are a lot of strange people around. You must have come across stories online about dangerous doms – and dangerous subs."

"True."

"We need to build trust in each other and be able to relax before you truly submit; you may find you don't even want to. If we get it wrong, it could be a disaster."

"But if we get it right …"

"Exactly. In the meantime, we can still do everything on our wish lists, learning along the way."

"When do we start?"

"Well, how about we meet up one evening in a more private place?"

"I'll come to you. How about Friday?"

"Keen?"

"Is that bad?"

"No. So am I."

Chapter 6 – Sally

When I got home, I threw down my coat and jumped on the sofa. How did I feel?

Excited.

Nervous.

And horny. Definitely horny.

I laid back and replayed the end of the evening in my head.

As we left the restaurant, he guided me through the door and brushed my arm. My flesh tingled. When we got outside, I took his arm and turned to face him. We looked into each other's eyes briefly, and he leaned forward to kiss me. It was gentle, a momentary touch; I think I closed my eyes. As he pulled away, I opened my eyes to see he was millimetres away. He smiled, put his hands either side of my face, and pulled it towards him. I could feel my breath becoming uneven, and my sex tingle. Our lips touched, and I expected – wanted - his tongue to push into my mouth.

Instead, he held my head, and somehow pulled my lower lip into his mouth, and gently grabbed it between his teeth. It was a strange feeling; not painful, but I realised I was trapped. A thrill shot through me. If I pulled my lip away, it would hurt. I felt his hand moving down my back, slowly but surely. It reached my waist and carried on until it rested lightly on my right bum cheek. He moved it slowly to cup it in his hand and squeeze. He let my lip go.

"Beautiful," he said, "and never been spanked."

"No," I whispered, "not yet."

I didn't move; didn't want to. He quickly looked around; there was no one in sight. He moved his hand around my thigh to the front, and before I knew what he was doing, he started hitching the front of my skirt up. When it was high enough, he slipped his hand underneath and found my stocking top.

"Ooh, good girl," he whispered. I was glad I had chosen what I was wearing tonight carefully. I shuddered slightly as his hand met my bare thigh, and slowly moved higher. My whole body was tense and waiting for the inevitable touch.

But he had other ideas. His hand got close enough to my knickers for him to feel my dampness, but just as my pussy began to sense the back of his fingers, he gently removed his hand and straightened my skirt.

"Anticipation is a great aphrodisiac," he whispered into my ear.

"Tease."

"When I want to be," he said, trying to mimic me.

"Touché!" I replied. My own phrase thrown back at me. He gave me another hug and a more normal kiss.

"Frustrated?" he joked.

"Yes," I pouted.

"Good," he replied, leaning towards my ear, his voice soft. "Think about me later when you're playing. Goodnight, Sally."

I felt myself blush, but fortunately, it was dark now and he couldn't see it. He turned and headed to his car.

"Goodnight, Marcus," I said, and started to turn when I heard him again.

"And no, I can't see you blushing, but I know you are."

I headed home. Every step reminded me of the swollen flesh between my legs.

Lying on the sofa, I was surprised by how much we'd moved forward. Surprised.
Pleased.
And horny. Still bloody horny.
My phone pinged. I picked it up; a message from Marcus. I opened it. A picture appeared; a picture of a girl, strapped down over a bench, her wrists and ankles tied tightly, her legs spread exposing her bare pussy. Her

31

bum was pink, and she had several red lines across each cheek. There was a cane balanced in the small of her back. Underneath,

[IMAGINE THIS IS YOU]

I smiled; at the end of our date, we realised we hadn't even looked at each other's pictures. I suggested we send them to each other during the week, just one at odd times. He'd agreed; now he obviously wanted to get in early. But two can play at that game. I quickly looked at my photo library and found the one I wanted. I tapped to send it as a reply and added

[AND IMAGINE ME DOING THIS]

It wasn't one of the pictures I had originally chosen, but he wasn't to know that. I pressed send.

I went back to his message. This was the first time anyone had sent me a picture like this. Sure, I'd come across loads of pictures like this myself, but I'd never been sent one by a man who might have me in such a position.

I was tired, nicely tired. Relaxed. But my pussy wasn't. Occasionally, it could be greedy. Occasionally, one orgasm wasn't enough. I knew this was going to be one of those times. I wasn't going to get any sleep until it was satisfied. With a smile on my face, I went through to the bedroom and opened my toy drawer. This could be a long night and I needed something that was up to the job. No fictional men in my head tonight. This time, I had someone real to fill my fantasy. I just hoped my shadow left me to it and didn't put in an appearance.

***

It only takes a brief time for someone to open the door after you press the bell, but sometimes it can seem like an eternity. As I stood outside Marcus's door waiting, random words seemed to flash through my head.

Nervous. Excited. Guilt. Fear. Shame. Horny. Definitely horny.

"Hello, Sally." Marcus interrupted my reverie. After a slight pause, he added, "Are you okay?"

"Uh, yes. Sorry. Hi, Marcus."

"Come in."

"Thanks."

I walked in, waiting for him to close the door. As I heard it shut, I realised this was possibly our first step. He took my coat, and I saw him look me up and down.

"You look gorgeous, Sally."

"Thank you."

I had thought carefully about what to wear tonight. In the end, I kept it simple. A simple red dress, tight enough to show my curves, but not tight enough to reveal what was underneath; sheer soft black bra, knickers, suspenders, and stockings. All set off with heels.

Marcus smiled at me. "Do I get a kiss?"

Leaning towards him, I looked him in the eyes as I slowly pressed my lips on his and gave him a lingering kiss. As I pulled away, he put his hands on my shoulders and pulled me gently towards him again. My pulse was racing. He watched me intently as our lips met. I wasn't thinking. Before I knew it, he had my lip between his teeth again. He left it there just long enough to make sure I remembered what had happened last time he'd done that, before releasing it – and me.

He laughed. "Come on through."

I closed my eyes briefly and took a couple of deep breaths.

"Thanks."

I followed him along the hallway into the living room. He offered me a drink, and we sat on the sofa. As I sipped my wine and made small talk, I started to relax. I could feel some of the tension drain from my body. It was only a few days since our last meeting, but I had found the wait unbearable.

"Sally?"

"Yes. Sorry, Marcus."

"I said I've done some pasta, salad and bread. Hope that's okay?"

"Yes, that sounds good."

"Are you hungry now?"

"I could eat."

"I'll finish off and serve it up."

He disappeared into the kitchen, and I took the time to look around. It was a big room, plainly decorated, as most rented places are. I noticed some beautiful pictures on the walls and an eclectic range of objects placed around the room. Behind me was a wall of books, almost from floor to ceiling. I got up and went to look along the shelves. There seemed to be a bit of everything; history, science, biography, history – lots of history. As I was browsing, he came back and began to carry bowls and plates from the kitchen to the table at one end of the room.

"Come and sit down," he smiled. "Can you bring the wine and glasses over?"

I picked them up and walked to the table. He pulled out a chair for me, and then sat opposite me.

Eating relaxed me further. We talked about everything and nothing. Books, the news, comedy, films, music. Sex wasn't mentioned.

"Have you any family living nearby?" he asked. I wanted to get this over with. I didn't want my shadow to appear tonight, of all nights.

"Both my parents are dead," I replied.

"Oh, I'm sorry."

"It's okay. But it's something I prefer not to talk about. Mary's the only family I've got now. How about you?"

"I'm one of those supposedly odd creatures, an only child. Dad died over ten years ago, and Mum is in a home. She only occasionally recognises me now."

"That must be difficult."

"You accept it. Dad had dementia as well, so I found a way to deal with it then. You visit, spend some time with them, and leave. Almost do your duty. I guess that sounds cold, but it works for me. Other people do it differently."

"I don't know how I'd deal with it. But you're right, everyone has to find their own way."

After the pasta, he brought in a plate piled high with the best profiteroles I'd ever tasted. When we had both finished, he pushed his chair back a bit.

"Are you more relaxed now?" he asked.

"Yes, much more."

"You were a ball of tension when you arrived."

"I know. I couldn't help it. I've been thinking about tonight all week."

"Nice thoughts, I hope?"

I felt myself flush, and before I could reply, he said, "Ah, I see they were."

I looked at him, with a scowl on my face.

"Sometimes, I hate my blushing."

He smiled and paused.

"I still think it's quite cute."

He sat forward and rested his elbows on the table. Running his finger around the rim of his glass, he looked up at me with a sly grin.

"Do any other parts of you blush that nicely?"

I smiled and ran my tongue over my teeth. I had wondered when we would start getting more … playful. I had already decided to embrace wherever the evening took us. We had come this far; we were both keen. Eager. I wasn't about to turn and run.

"Mmm," I replied. "Some get a much deeper colour than that." He stared into my eyes and I held his stare. "At least, they do if they're treated right."

He raised an eyebrow, sat back, and laughed.

"Ah, at last. The real Sally is emerging again."

I realised I had relaxed completely. All that was left was that nervous anticipation I felt when I wanted someone. Really wanted them. That feeling that spreads around your body from your head to your toes.

"She's been here all the time," I said. "She just needs a little … coaxing sometimes to reveal herself."

"Well, let's see how much of her we can reveal tonight, shall we?" He stared into my eyes again, and I almost felt he could sense my rising need. "How about we grab a more comfortable seat?"

We left the table and I brought the wine and glasses to the coffee table, Marcus bringing the remaining profiteroles. We sat on the sofa; close, but not close enough. I tried to work out if he was toying with me, or whether he was as nervous as I was.

"Happy with everything we agreed before?" he asked.

"Yes. Completely." We had e-mailed our test results to each other the day before.

As I relaxed – that was probably the wine – my body began to react to my anticipation. I felt the blood flow to my nipples, to my pussy lips, to my clit. They started to swell; slowly, gently, but perceptibly. Every so often, I had to adjust my position to make myself more comfortable.

"Did you enjoy our picture swap?" Marcus asked.

"They were interesting, weren't they? I think it got a bit out of hand, though."

"Perhaps. Two or three became what? A dozen or so?"

"Which was your favourite from me?"

"I rather liked them all. Can I choose two?"

"If you must."

"Right. The first one you sent me."

"Which one was that?" I asked innocently, knowing full well which one he meant.

"The one with a beautiful girl's lips wrapped delicately around the head of a rather large cock."

"Oh, yes. I remember now. And the other?"

"Probably the girl in the corset with her hands behind her back."

I remembered that one, it had been my favourite of the lot. She was beautiful and curvy, and I dared to think she looked a little like me. She was wearing a black and red bustier with suspenders, black stockings, and no knickers. A black collar. She was sitting on her heels, looking up at the camera, a cane held between her teeth. The look on her face, in her eyes ...

I realised Marcus was looking at me quizzically.

"Sorry," I said. "Yes, I liked that one too."

"Quite a lot, it seems."

"I like all the ones I sent you."

"And do they all do that to you?"

"What?" I said quietly.

"Send you off to fantasyland."

"Most of them," I admitted.

"Which of mine were your favourites?"

I thought briefly.

"Two," I answered. "The first and the last."

"Remind me?" he lied. We both knew we were toying with each other.

"The one with the girl bent over the chair with her skirt up and the paddle lying on the floor."

"Ah, yes."

"And the other where the girl was strapped down over the bench with the red and striped bum, and the cane resting on her back."

"Ah," he replied. "Sort of before and after?"

"Yes," I said softly.

He picked up his iPad and started swiping. I wondered what he was doing. Surely not looking at his email at this point? I need not have worried. He suddenly shuffled closer until we were just touching. I was feeling horny now, my pussy damp. I could feel it on my thighs, blood flowing through my sex. I could feel my face was flushed too. I looked at him briefly; he seemed in control of himself. I couldn't tell what he was feeling. Was he as turned on as me?

"These two?"

He swiped between the two I'd mentioned. Just looking at them increased my lust.

"Yes."

"Which is your favourite?"

I thought it was an unfair question but didn't have much trouble choosing.

"Right now, the 'after'," I said.

Marcus put the iPad down. He turned to look at me and slowly leaned toward me. Taking the wineglass out of my hand, he put it on the table. He placed his hands on my shoulders and pulled me to him. I melted; couldn't resist. His mouth neared mine and my lips parted slightly. But instead of meeting me straight on, he kissed the end of my mouth, then planted a line of tiny, delicate kisses all along my lower lip. Then back again, across my upper lip.

My breathing was ragged; I so wanted him. He began to rub his lips along my mouth and then placed them squarely on mine. I think I surprised him when I ferociously kissed him back, pulling him to me, as we placed kiss after kiss on each other's lips. I pushed my tongue into his mouth, and he lightly caught it between his teeth, causing me to whimper. He raised an eyebrow, but then released it.

I forgot the fantasies, the fetishes, the slow exploration. At that moment, I just wanted him to fuck me. To use me. To take me. I was hot, wet, willing. But Marcus had other ideas. He pulled away slightly, moved his mouth towards my ear, and held me there. His hands came off my shoulders and moved down to rest either side of my ribcage.

"The picture," he whispered.

"Mmm."

"Are you hoping to feel what that's like?"

"Yes."

"Have you imagined your cheeks that colour?"

He was speaking softly, intimately.

"Yes," I confessed. "Though perhaps not that dark," I added shyly.

"I think that may be a bit too much for us … at the moment."

He paused. He was speaking so softly, I held my breath, not wanting to miss anything. Nothing. Not a word. His hands moved around to my back, and he slowly moved his fingers up and down. His touch was exquisite and made me gasp.

"Relax … breathe," he finally said. I did. He let me take a few breaths.

"What colour do you think to start with? How about that lovely pink flush of yours?"

I relaxed for an instant and smiled.

"Perhaps a little more than that."

"Is that what you want?"

"Yes," I whispered.

"Is that what you need?"

"Yes."

"Now?"

I swallowed. This was it. This was the moment we had worked up to for weeks. The moment of truth. Did we both really want this? I knew my answer; my brain, my nipples, my pussy were all screaming 'YES'.

"Yes," I hissed.

"Right now?"

I gently pushed him away so we could see each other.

"Yes. Right now. I need to feel your hand on my ass. I need to feel the sting, the pressure, the pleasure. Maybe even the pain. Yes."

"Good girl." And he kissed me; softly, gently, deliciously. I felt a wave of desire warm my pussy. That did it. I was his. I knew what was going to happen, and I was desperate for it.

"Stand up." His voice was different. Still mellow, still gentle, but with a firmer edge.

I stood up. He shifted and placed himself comfortably in the centre of the sofa. He looked up at me.

"On your knees." He pointed to the floor beside him. I dropped. He reached for my head and softly kissed me; I returned his kiss. He pulled away and looked at me.

"I want you over my knees."

As he sat back up, I almost threw myself over his lap.

"Get comfortable," he said.

"I am."

"Good."

He placed an arm across my back, and I waited. Suddenly I felt his hand running over my dress, resting on my bum. I shivered at the touch.

"Sally?"

"Yes, Marcus?"

"Remember what we agreed. Feedback. Tell me if I do or try anything you don't like. Yes?"

"Yes."

He gently moved his hand over my bum. It felt so good. My pussy lips were swollen; it was delicious.

"Well," he said, "I think we need to lose a layer here."

He moved his hands down and grabbed the hem of my dress, and gradually pulled it up my legs. My breathing got heavier.

"Can you—"

Before he finished, I lifted my hips off his knees so he could push the dress up to my waist. He pushed me back down with a laugh.

"Good girl."

I let out a deep sigh. I felt his hand gently come to rest on my bum, now only covered by my sheer knickers. He ran his hand over my cheeks, gently stroking, occasionally squeezing.

"Beautiful. And so beautifully framed."

"You approve?"

"Yes. Definitely. It looks good enough to eat."

"Well, perhaps later …" I replied.

He laughed.

And suddenly, my world changed. Forever.

I felt a feeling I had never experienced before. My body didn't know what it was. A sharp, brief sensation started in my left bum cheek and spread to my thighs and my back. It made me gasp, and my mouth fell open in surprise. All this happened in an instant, or so it seemed. My mouth changed to a smile; it made me greedy for more. Marcus had struck. He had brought his hand down on my bum.

Not hard, but hard enough for now. Just as those first sensations subsided, they started all over again as Marcus brought his hand down again, this time on the other cheek. Those feelings rushed through me again. Involuntarily, I wriggled slightly, and Marcus pressed with the arm across my back. After a few seconds, a third stroke came.

Then a fourth.

Then a fifth.

Then a sixth. All spread around. Never quite in the same place. But the sensations from each always ended up in the same place. Right between my legs. God, I was wet. I could feel it. I could feel the dampness spreading out.

"Colour?" he asked quietly.

I grinned. "Green," I said.

"Good."

Before he finished the word, his hand came down again. The same feelings time after time as his hand met my bum. Perhaps a dozen strokes, and he stopped. His hand landed gently on my cheeks and caressed them.

"Colour?"

"Green," I replied.

I realised I'd been holding my breath. I relaxed and took a few deep gulps of air.

"Right, Sally," he said gently, "I think it's time to move from teasing to the real thing."

I felt his fingers grip the top of my knickers and lift them away from my skin. He slowly pulled them down, and I eagerly lifted my hips, so he could pull them free and over my thighs. He gently pulled them down my legs, and over my shoes.

"I don't think we'll need those for a while." He threw them on the floor in front of me. "Besides, they're a bit damp." He paused. "Aren't they, Sally."

"Yes."

"Are you wet, Sally?"

"Why don't you find out?" I replied. I so wanted it. I wanted him to run his fingers between my legs. To find my wetness. I wanted his fingers to explore my pussy, my lips, my clit – now engorged with blood, demanding attention. I wanted him to play with them all; to run his fingers around the entrance to my pussy and gradually push them in. I wanted him to fuck me with those fingers and make me come.

"I don't think so," he said. "Not yet."

Frustration flashed through me briefly. I needed to come, to feel that high. To feel that glorious climax flood me from head to toe. I needed that release. He gently placed his hand on my bare bum. I felt my cheeks twitch slightly.

And then that feeling struck again. My body had worked it out by now, it knew what to expect. But this time, it was flesh on flesh, and it was so much better. Marcus began slowly, gently. Alternating between cheeks; sometimes higher, sometimes catching the top of my thighs. He was methodical, rhythmical. Letting the sensations flow and bringing each stroke down just as the feelings from the last one died away. It was heavenly.

But it wasn't just the sensations. It was the thoughts rushing through my mind, competing with the physical impulses. This was me. Bent over a man's lap, bum bared and exposed. Legs apart, pussy available, vulnerable. Being spanked. And loving every single stroke. Every single feeling.

Marcus stopped.

"Colour?" he asked.

"Green," I replied, not sure if I wanted more, or if I wanted him to explore between my legs. He was gently stroking and squeezing my bum and thighs. Again, I found myself consciously taking deep breaths. My pussy was crying for attention, more strongly than I could remember for a long time. I got my first inkling of the real connection between pain and pleasure; perhaps it wasn't as obvious as I'd thought.

"Right," he said. "Perhaps I'm not trying hard enough."

"Perhaps not," I replied, instantly wondering if I'd regret my cheek.

"Well, I'm not going to spank you any harder, not this first time. Let's try upping the pace a little, shall we?"

"Okay," I replied without thinking. I soon discovered my mistake. He started spanking me again, but quicker this time. The sensations from each stroke hadn't subsided before they started again, and they built up on top of each other. The pain mounted but so did the pleasure. My breathing got faster, shallower. My bum started to sting, my pussy started to ache. Really ache. I could feel moisture spreading down my thighs. I closed my eyes, determined to take everything he was willing to give. I was one step from ecstasy; just one step.

Suddenly, Marcus stopped and rested his hand gently on my bum.

"Colour?"

I chuckled. "Green," I managed to gasp.

"But approaching a yellow?"

"Getting there …" I admitted.

"Good girl. Do you want to stop now, or shall we push a bit further?"

I thought about it as he gently stroked my stinging ass. Part of me wanted more pain, part of me needed pleasure. A thought struck me.

"I'll make you a deal," I said, in between heavy breaths.

"Go on."

"I want more, really want more. But I need some … relief too."

His stroking hand moved down slightly, catching the top of my thighs, his fingers reaching further into the space between my legs. I moved my hips up slightly in the hope of pushing my pussy up to meet them. But he withdrew his hand, and I dropped again with an audible cry of frustration.

He laughed. "Go on."

"One more spanking, then for God's sake, make me come. I don't care how. I just need to come!"

I sensed him bend towards me.

"Deal," he whispered.

He sat back up. I knew what was going to happen next. Except suddenly I didn't. Was he going to strike more firmly? Slow or fast? I soon found out. His hand left my bum and came down softly on one cheek. A pause. Then it came down on the other. A pause. Then on the first one again. A pause. He continued like this moving the landing place slightly each time. My ass was stinging now. Then I realised the strokes were slowly getting firmer, and the pace was quickening.

The feelings were coming stronger, quicker. Tumbling over one another. Racing to get to my brain. But always ending up between my legs; oh, my poor pussy. My legs started to come up as I tried to lessen the stinging in my bum, that wonderful pain. I gradually gave up trying to concentrate on each stroke and let the pain and pleasure merge; let the sensations overwhelm me.

It was peaking now. The strokes were firm, fast, and regular. His hand was delivering all those sensations every time it came down on my burning cheeks. I could hear Marcus breathing strongly for the first time and I became dimly aware of his hard cock, pressing up into my stomach. He was enjoying this, so was I. I spread my legs slightly and felt my pussy opening. Suddenly, the need for pleasure overcame the need for pain. I lifted my arm and put it behind my back. Marcus stopped.

"Colour?"

"Nearly yellow," I gasped.

"Okay," he said gently. "Just relax and breathe. We'll take a rest."

"NO!" I almost screamed. I turned my head as much as I could to look up at him. He was smiling at me. "I need to come. NOW! PLEASE!"

He stared at me. I suddenly felt his hands move down my bum. He ran two or three fingers lightly along the valley between my cheeks. But this time, he didn't stop. I gasped as they slid over my perineum. They carried on. He split his fingers and I shuddered as I felt one finger run across the entrance to my pussy, whilst another ran up each side, brushing my lips.

He ran these fingers lightly backwards and forwards a few times. I felt my whole body tense and any lingering pain sensations were rapidly joined by even stronger sensations of pleasure. As he stroked my lips and pussy, they seemed to swell even more; to reach out to his fingers. My breathing was getting uneven again and I closed my eyes and let these new sensations flood through me.

He slowly increased the pressure from his fingers, and as he did so, the one stroking my pussy slowly entered me. Just one finger. But my pussy sucked it in greedily. He slid it in all the way, and this allowed his other fingers to move forward, past my lips, and reach my …

I cried out, my body arched, and I started to shake. His fingers had reached my clit, and he was gently teasing it. With each movement, it sent tremors to every part of my body. It was now the centre of attention. He toyed with it gently, circling it, pressing it lightly. Watching how it reacted to each touch. I was getting closer. I couldn't remember needing to come like this. He took up a rhythm, stiffening his hand so as he moved it, one finger slid in and out of my pussy, and the others slid over my lips, the tips rocking my clit backwards and forwards.

That did it. I felt myself sliding into that beautiful place. What I called my perfect orgasm. Not the one you get when you're relieving some tension, or when you try too hard. But the one where your whole body works together to give you pleasure. Time seems to stand still, silence seems to descend, and you feel in a different place. You feel at one with yourself, and with your lover. Immune to everything else in the universe. And that was happening now.

I realised I was whimpering; parts of my body were twitching as I neared the moment. I pushed my bum up to him, to meet his moving fingers. Marcus was holding a steady rhythm, and when I looked up at him, he was watching me. I closed my eyes again, suddenly shy of his gaze.

Then it happened. I felt my orgasm overtake me. My clit, my lips, my pussy; all seemed to explode. Colour flashed inside my head and waves of pleasure rolled from my head to my toes. I cried out, arching my body. I gave in to it; submitted to it. Allowed my lust to take over as I rode my climax for what seemed like forever.

I gradually felt myself returning to reality, my body slowly collapsing back as my muscles relaxed. I tried to calm my breathing. I suddenly sensed Marcus again, his hand withdrawn and resting gently on my bum. I opened my eyes to see him still smiling at me.

"Are you okay?" he whispered.

I managed a smile. "Yes, I …"

"Ssh," he said softly, placing a finger over my lips. "Just relax. Breathe. That was quite something. I think you needed that."

I smiled at him again. In between gasps for air, I said, "Told you … I did … I'll be … with you … in a minute."

I watched him put his fingers to his mouth and taste them.

"Good?" I asked.

"Mmm," he said. "Delicious. And from a seemingly endless bottle."

I giggled as he put his hand back on my bum.

"Take your time," he said, and I luxuriated in his hand caressing me. "All the time you need."

In the bathroom, I looked into the mirror. My face was flushed, my hair a little messy. I lifted my dress and tried to look at my bum, but the mirror was too high. It felt warm and tingly; still stinging, but I wanted to see it. It struck me as odd that after what had happened, we were both still fully dressed.

After I had recovered, Marcus had helped me back to my knees, kissing me tenderly. My dress had dropped to cover me. I hadn't noticed at the time, but now? I spotted my reflection frowning back at me. What now?

Well, time to find out.

"I've topped you up," Marcus said as I returned, and handed me my glass.

"Thanks," I replied. I sat next to him, slightly apart, a little shy.

He sat back and looked at me. "How do you feel?"

"Marcus, I'm not sure. I'm a bit confused at the moment."

"Want to talk about it?"

I looked at him and then looked away. "Yes … No … Oh, I'm sorry."

"Has the real Sally hidden herself away again?"

"She's a bit shy, yes," I admitted.

"Well, we need to find her."

He reached out, took my glass, and put it on the table. Taking my hand, he gently pulled it, inviting me to move towards him. When I was close enough, he took my face in his hands and gently touched his lips to mine. My lust had been satisfied, and now, it just felt good. Not passionate, not urgent. Just good, and I responded, putting my arms over his shoulders.

"Now. Why don't we cuddle up, relax, and see what happens."

I moved closer, curling my legs up on the sofa, and rested my head on his chest. He kissed my head and put his arm around me and hugged me to him. We sat that way for several minutes. Silent. My mind was running through the events of the evening. He seemed to know.

"Willing to share?"

I realised that in this position, I could talk without having to make eye contact. I relaxed a little.

"Share what?" I asked.

"What's going through your head right now."

"It's a bit muddled."

"What's the strongest emotion?"

"I'm confused."

"About what?"

"About what we've done."

"Do you regret it?"

"NO!" I said, more forcefully than I intended.

"Then, what?"

I thought about how to say what I was feeling; I wasn't sure I knew myself.

"I thought it might be different. I thought we'd … I thought you'd want to …"

"Ah," he said softly and chuckled. "Are you disappointed?"

I swallowed. "Yes, a bit."

"Disappointed with the spanking?"

"No. I loved it; loved the feeling." I smiled to myself. "Still feels good now."

"Disappointed with the orgasm?"

For the first time, I looked up at him.

"NO." I dropped my gaze quickly. "No … that was the best for ages."

"Then, what?"

I tried to frame the words in my mind, to express how I felt. I sat up and knelt next to him, looking him straight in the face.

"I had an image in my head before tonight. I saw it all so clearly, dreamed about it. I saw you bending me over your knees. I saw you spanking me, thrashing my ass. I pictured us overcome with lust. I saw you rolling me off your knees, bending me over and driving your cock into me. Fucking me, fucking me hard."

By the end, I was speaking quite strongly.

"Ah," he said and smiled. I knew I was flushing, and he ran his fingers along my cheek.

"Sally?"

"Yes."

"What time is it?"

"I don't know," I replied and looked at my watch. "Nine thirty."

"Are you in a hurry to leave?"

"No."

"Then we have plenty of time yet. All night, if we want." I let my eyes drop again. "Make no mistake, I thought about it. I'd had that dream too. But what we've done seemed so right, didn't it? It seemed to work. I went with the flow. Believe me, if we play again, it'll flow differently, and you'll get your wish."

I looked up and smiled.

"I was worried you didn't want me. Or at least, only wanted to spank me. I know that's all some men want, to spank."

"No, that's not me. You should know that after all we've discussed."

He looked at me, and I thought I caught a reproving look in his eyes.

"Yes, sorry. I got lost in my own lust."

"You did. Gloriously. Beautifully. It was wonderful to see."

46

"But you sparked that lust, Marcus."

"No, *we* did. And we'll share plenty more, and it can get better and better. *If* we both want it."

He stopped and held my eyes, daring me to look away. But I held his gaze, confidence returning.

"Do you want it, Sally?"

I knew in that instant this was going to be quite an adventure.

"Yes," I whispered, and we kissed. Gently at first, gradually increasing in passion until we were almost breathless.

Relaxing in each other's arms, we cuddled up.

"Was the spanking what you expected?" he asked.

I thought for a moment.

"Yes, and no."

"Come on, give me a bit more than that."

"It's difficult to put into words. I wanted it so much but was nervous as well. No nerves now, though. It was so good. That mix of pain and pleasure. Each time your hand hit, it sent shocks all over my body."

"Were they okay?"

"Oh, yes. At first, I concentrated hard, trying to analyse every stroke, every sensation. But after a while, I let go. That was when it all clicked into place. I guess that's what submitting means. Just taking whatever your partner gives."

"That's part of it."

"How was it for you?"

"Wonderful. I loved doing it, but also watching your reactions. Hearing your breathing, seeing your body twitch and stretch. Watching your legs slowly get wider and wider apart."

"Did they? I didn't notice."

"Did you not?"

"Well, I might have."

"And I loved your orgasm. It gave me a real sense of control, as well as proof you were enjoying it."

"Yeah. I quite enjoyed that too!"

"And next time, I might throw you over the table and fuck you …"

By now, all this talk had had an effect on me; I was getting horny again. Not outright lust this time, that had been satisfied earlier. But a softer, gentler need. A need to please and be pleased.

"Marcus?" I asked.

"Mmm."

"I've had my pleasure; I think it's time I gave you some."

He smiled and kissed me.

"Perhaps we can share it."

We slowly removed each other's clothes. Slowly, kissing and caressing. I was still curious about his self-control; did he ever get really passionate? But I let the question go. He watched as I removed my stockings, leaving me completely naked. Only his underpants to go. I stood in front of him, kissed him, and slid to my knees, noticing a couple of large surgical scars on his tummy. I gripped the waistband and slowly pulled them down, releasing his cock.

It sent a thrill through me; hard and proud, purple veins standing out along its length. It was big and thick, with a slight bend to the left. I imagined how that might be interesting in certain positions. But as well as all that, something else caught my eye; no hair. Not one, completely bare. I'd not had a shaved man before, and it looked a bit odd at first. I looked up at him, and he smiled. I reached up and holding his eyes, I ran my hand up his thigh, and reached his balls. As I touched them for the first time, his cock jumped in front of me. I gently ran my hand over them, caressing them and then stroking his cock. The feeling was incredible; I quickly decided I was going to like a smooth man.

The next hour was bliss. We took our time, exploring each other's bodies. Touching, kissing, caressing, licking. We ended with me slowly riding that hard, smooth cock. Oh, it felt good, filling my greedy pussy. I was in no hurry now, and although I had a couple of delicate little orgasms, I wanted to give him pleasure. I teased him, altering my pace and angle, gradually building until he came in me with surprising force. We held each other gently and let ourselves enjoy the moment. It felt so good, so warm, so right.

***

I suddenly panicked.

"What time is it?" I asked.

He reached for his watch on the table.

"Quarter to twelve."

"Oh, thank God," I said and got up and went to my bag. I found my phone and went back to sit by him. He had a quizzical look on his face

"Sorry, got to send a text," I explained. "Lucy and I have an arrangement. We look out for one another. On occasions like this, we let each other know we're okay by midnight. I've only just made it."

I wondered what to say. Then typed three words ...

[SAFE FUCKED STAYING]

I showed it to Marcus.

"Am I staying?" I teased.

"I hope so."

I sent it and put the phone down. I climbed over him again and straddled him, rubbing my still wet pussy against his soft cock. I leaned into him, and he ran his hands down my back to place one on each bum cheek.

"You do like bums, don't you?"

"I could play with yours all day."

"I'm not going to object."

My phone pinged; I turned around and could just reach it without getting off. A text from Lucy. I opened it and laughed. He looked at me with a raised eyebrow. I turned the phone and showed it to him. Just two words ...

[LUCKY BITCH]

A while later, we were lying in bed. On our sides, my back to him. My bum pressed gently into his groin, our bodies fitting perfectly. He gently stroked my hair, then laid his arm over me, and hugged me to him. An image flashed through my mind. A black and white image he had sent me. We were lying just the same. Only in colour; full colour.

Chapter 7 – Marcus

I opened my eyes and saw Sally's dark hair flowing over the pillow. She had her back to me. I could hear her breathing slowly, still asleep. Memories of the previous night came flooding back. As I lay there, I saw her over my lap, saw her red cheeks, saw her orgasm. I remembered the later events as well, when we'd made love. She'd enjoyed pleasing me, enjoyed teasing me to my climax. We'd shared the pleasure.

I got up as quietly as I could and went to the bathroom. Then went into the kitchen and put the kettle on. I heard footsteps, followed shortly after by the loo flushing. I went back into the bedroom. She was back in bed but facing me now. I got back in, lay on my side facing her.

"Good morning."

"Good morning," she replied.

"Sleep well?"

"Yes, thank you. Can't think why."

We looked at each other for some time and I moved my arm towards her.

"May I?"

"Marcus, after last night, you need to ask?"

"Yes," I replied. "One evening doesn't equal ongoing consent."

She looked thoughtful for a moment and nodded.

"True," she said. "But you can touch me whenever you want. If the moment's not right, I'll let you know."

I moved my hand towards her, and she came to meet it. I touched her arm, and she reached out to me. We met and enclosed each other's bodies, wrapping our arms and legs around each other. Caressing each other with our hands, we kissed. Gently at first, placing little kisses on each other's faces. Finally meeting lips and slowly exploring. We drew apart, and both let out deep sighs at the same time. We looked at each other and grinned. I could feel her warm body against me, and mine was responding. She could feel it too, and her hand began to move down my tummy towards my swelling cock. I placed my hand on hers and stopped it. She pouted.

"All in good time," I said. "There's no rush. How's your bum this morning?"

"Fine … I couldn't see anything. I'm slightly disappointed!" She giggled. "Want to see?"

"Mmm."

She threw the duvet off, wriggled onto her front, and watching me, she teasingly raised her hips a few inches off the bed. I propped myself up and looked at her bum. She was right, it looked exactly as it had when I first peeled her knickers off. I reached over and gently ran my hand over each cheek.

I thought there was a slight tinge, but then, she did blush easily. Silently, I was glad; I had tried to get the balance right. Enough for Sally to feel it, to feel the sensations from a spanking. But not enough to risk hurting or scaring her.

"Hey," she said gently, touching my arm. I stopped stroking her and laughed.

"Sorry. You feel so good, I got lost in the touch."

"Well, don't stop." I resumed caressing her.

"How does it feel?"

"There's just a little tingle here and there. Particularly now you're stroking it."

"Is that okay?"

"Oh, yes. Reminds me why it feels like that."

I carried on caressing her bum, letting my hands stray wider to stroke the small of her back and her thighs. She let out a little sigh and stretched her body in response to the touch. She looked up at me.

"Want to spank me again now?"

"No, not now."

"Was this soft? Hard? It's new to me, so I don't know."

"You did well for the first time. Quite hard and quite fast at the end."

I continued to run my hand up and down her body and noticed her legs part slightly.

"You could do it harder?"

"Yes, but there's only so much strength in my arm. The real next step would be faster and for longer."

"Oh," she murmured. "You mean like you did at the end?"

"Yeah." I dropped beside her again, my face a few inches from hers. I saw that familiar flush. "Only much faster and much longer …"

"When?"

"We'll see …" I slipped my hand briefly between her legs. She groaned. "But right now, why don't you turn over? Perhaps I can do something else for you."

She shifted her weight, reached over to kiss me, and looked at my now hard cock. She stretched her arm and took it in her hand.

"All I want is this. I want to feel you in me again."

I reached between her legs.

"Seems like you do."

"I can't help it."

I pushed her gently onto her back.

"Are you comfortable?"

"Yes," she said with a wicked grin. "But have me any way you want me."

Several options flashed through my mind, but they could wait. I kissed her and moved down the bed. She spread her legs wide, her pussy opening up, glistening. I lowered myself over her, teasing her pussy with the head of my cock. She shuddered. We held each other's gaze as I slowly entered her.

***

"I'm beginning to wish I'd thought ahead and been a bit more prepared."

She was standing in the doorway, wearing her red dress, but with bare legs this morning. Holding her knickers between two fingers, looking at me.

"I can't put these on, they're a bit …"

"Crusty?" I suggested.

She laughed, shoved them in her bag with her stockings, and walked over to join me at the table.

"That's one word for it."

She sat down and picked up a brioche roll.

"Ah well," I said, watching her. "I doubt it's the first time you've gone home the morning after, wearing no knickers."

She broke off a bit of the roll, held it to her mouth, a kittenish grin on her face.

"No," she said. "It's not."

We'd lazed in bed for some time, eventually getting up about ten-thirty and having a shower together. One thing had led to another, and shortly afterwards, we'd found ourselves back in the shower; separately, this time. I had dressed and put a few things on the table for what had become brunch.

We chatted; relaxed and happy. We ate, drank coffee, and flirted with one another. Both satiated, we knew it wasn't going to lead to anything at the moment. We were enjoying the lingering effects of our shared intimacy.

"What time are you meeting Lucy?" I asked.

"Oh, no idea. She's going to call me when she's ready."

"What are you going to see?"

"Don't know, we'll decide when we get there. There's usually something to keep us happy. Then we'll find somewhere to eat and move on if we feel like it." She paused to drink some coffee. "Do you get to the cinema much?"

"Not anymore. My head can't cope with the volume now; I find it overwhelming."

"That's a shame. You've got quite a collection, though."

She looked towards the shelves lined with my films.

"Yeah, I've got a few. But I do find I'm choosier as I get older."

"Got any … interesting ones?" she asked, eyebrow raised.

"Might have."

"Over there?"

"No."

"Ooh, guilty feelings?"

"No, just don't want to corrupt the first innocent, naïve archivist who happens to come along."

"Archivist? Yes; at least, some of the time. But innocent or naïve? Can't pretend I'm that."

"No, I don't think you can, thank God."

"But next time, I'd be open to a little more corruption."

Chapter 8 – Sally

"Well …?"

I'd left Marcus's flat after lunch, and headed home. Part of me had been annoyed I'd arranged to meet Lucy that night. I could have stayed with him, perhaps for another night, perhaps another spanking. But the rest of me dismissed this. I always looked forward to going out with Lucy, it was always fun. She was the nearest thing I had to a sister, since …

We knew each other's deepest secrets; well, most of them.

I got home, ran a bath, and wallowed in it for half an hour. I went through the events of the last twenty-four hours while they were still fresh in my head. Passion was wonderful, but it had a habit of overcoming common sense. More than once, it had taken me far too long to see the real man through my lust.

Brian.

I shuddered, and laughed. No, Marcus wasn't Brian. But as I lay there, the warm water surrounding me, I realised he had been right about one thing. When I'd suggestively asked him when we'd do it all again, he'd dampened my hopes a little. But he had been right. We didn't know each other. We knew we shared some interests, both in and out of bed. That was more than enough for a one-nighter; I'd enjoyed a few of those. Quite a few when I was younger.

But they left me with an empty feeling in the morning. Not like this morning, that had been different. This morning had been as good as last night; different, but just as good. Afterwards, we'd been comfortable with each other, no awkwardness, neither of us wondering how quickly we could part without being rude. What was it he'd called it? Quiet companionship. Well, if that was quiet companionship, I wanted more.

"Well?" Lucy repeated.

"Well, what?"

"How did it go?"

"Good, thanks."

"Is that it?"

I wondered what to tell her. We were open with each other, but I'd never told Lucy about my darker fantasies. I didn't intend to; not yet, anyway.

"Well, let's say I had more fun than I've had for quite some time."

"Yeah. You do seem … relaxed. Content." She raised her eyebrows. "Satisfied?"

I nodded in reply.

"Lucky bitch!"

We grinned at each other. The film we'd chosen hadn't impressed either of us and now we were sitting in a little bistro down the road from the cinema. Fortunately, the food was proving much better than the movie.

"Are you meeting him again?"

"Yes. Tuesday."

"Sal, he must be good."

"It's not for that."

"What do you mean?"

I wasn't sure what to say. I wasn't ready to tell her why we'd got together; not yet. Marcus had explained he wanted to get to know me. Our relationship up to now had been based on our fantasies. It had been back to front. We knew about each other's desires, but almost nothing about each other's lives. He wanted to change that; I saw his point. We agreed not all our meetings would be about sex. I tried to explain this to Lucy without telling her the whole truth, but it wasn't easy.

She looked thoughtful.

"You like him?"

"Yes. There's something about him. We've got lots of shared interests and ideas, but there's something else."

"Like what?"

"Not sure I can describe it. He seems to radiate a calmness, and when I'm with him, I feel … safe."

"Safe?"

"Yeah. You know, from the past."

"Ah."

"I know it could all go wrong again, but I want to try."

We enjoyed the rest of the meal, catching up on our news. We went on to the Forum, but it was Saturday night, and we were probably the oldest ones there. We found a couple of stools, grabbed some drinks, and happily watched the action. Some things never change. Small groups of lads trying to look cool and mature. Mostly failing. Elsewhere, small groups of girls trying to look wan and sophisticated. Mostly failing. Occasionally someone would peel off one group, approach someone from the other. Sometimes they were successful, sometimes not.

"Brings back memories, doesn't it, Sal?"

"Oh, yes."

"Aren't you glad we're not that young anymore?"

"Yes. Although, if I were that age and knew what I know now, I reckon I could have some fun."

"God, you'd eat any man who came near you!"

"Ooh. Now there's a thought."

I saw Marcus in my head. My mind's eye worked down his body.

"And what would you do, Luce? That age, but the experience you have now?"

"I'd probably stick to looking at the girls rather than the boys."

When we'd first met, I couldn't quite work her out, I had been a bit naïve then. In the first year of our friendship, she seemed to have boyfriends and girlfriends; I soon worked it out. But for nearly fifteen years now, it had been strictly girls.

"Okay, who would you pick?" I asked, and motioned towards a group of a dozen girls, mulling around a few feet in front of us. I suddenly felt my age, as I caught myself wondering if I'd ever gone out wearing so little. Yes, of course I had.

"What?"

"Who would you pick?"

She scanned the group.

"Can I wear gloves?" she asked.

"Come on," I said. "And tell me why."

I listened as she went through the group telling me what she thought. I found myself appraising girls in a way I'd not done before. It was interesting.

***

"So darling, I hear you took Marcus out."

"Oh, yes. It was … fun."

She heard my hesitancy. She knew me too well.

"Fun, darling?"

"Yeah."

"How much fun?"

She looked at me with a mock disapproving look.

"Oh, Mary. Behave!"

She chuckled.

"Enough to take him out again, then?"

"Already have," I replied.

"Oh, Sally," she said. "And here was me wondering how I might snare him myself."

***

When I arrived at Marcus's, he gave me a hug and a gentle kiss. His touch was warm. I had wondered what to wear; wondered if I could change his mind. But I already knew him well enough to know I couldn't, not yet, anyway. Not until I got to know some of his weaknesses. I remembered Friday night when he had concentrated on me. I'd wondered then if he really wanted me. But he did, he'd been prepared to wait. He seemed to have infinite patience; that could be frustrating but boy, I could think of times when it might be heaven. Eventually, I'd just thrown on a pair of jeans and a jumper.

We had a leisurely meal and talked. He was happy; he'd been commissioned to write another series of short stories for a magazine.

"Have you always been a writer?" I asked.

"God, no. I worked for years at a variety of things, eventually getting into IT by accident. But I had to give up when my health got the better of me. After Claire and I split up, I needed to try and do something that would fit around my good and bad times. I'd always been an avid reader, so thought I'd try writing."

"Do you enjoy it?"

"Yes; more than I thought I would. It's endlessly frustrating but very satisfying."

"Have you got an agent?"

"No. I haven't managed to snare one of those mythical beasts yet. I've got a few regular places that take my short stories, and I self-publish the novels. At least that gets them out there."

"Do they sell well?"

"They give me an income, but I'm never going to be rich."

"Does that matter?"

"Not really. I'm past dreaming of riches. Being happy is more important now."

"Are you?"

He thought for a while and smiled at me.

"Well, I think my happiness score may be on the way up."

"Oh. Why's that?"

"Something to do with corrupting an innocent librarian."

"Ah …"

We smiled warmly at one another.

"I just hope my health doesn't interfere."

"How does it affect you?"

"At the moment, it's not too bad. But if my Crohn's plays up, then I have to take some fairly aggressive drugs. It's the disease and the drugs together that seem to cause my fatigue. When it's bad, I can't do much at all. It's not so much the physical things, although my energy levels can be low. It's more the brain fog. My brain doesn't work. I feel dizzy, my vision goes, and I can't do anything that requires even a moments concentration."

"Not good for a writer."

"Exactly. It's frustrating."

"Do you know what triggers the Crohn's?"

"Ha. The million-dollar question. No, not really. It's generally completely unpredictable. I can go for ages without any problems, then, sometimes for no reason, it strikes." He looked away. "And the drugs affect my libido. Sometimes it means things don't work. And that could be frustrating for both of us."

I decided to take control of the issue. I didn't want it to become a problem.

"Oh, Marcus. That means we use our imaginations. Just think what you did with your fingers last time. What about your mouth? Your tongue? Toys? Do they go limp?"

He looked at me a bit startled and shrugged.

"No. There are ways around it."

"Of course there are. And besides, I'm not horny all the time, either. Sex isn't everything. We've got lots of other things in common. You were the one who said we should spend time getting to know one another. If things don't work, we do something else instead."

I paused, looking for a response, but he stayed silent.

"Marcus, are you trying to put me off?"

"No, I want you to know up front."

"I know and I appreciate it. I wish a few other men had been as honest. And no, I can't fully understand how you feel, although I've seen how it's affected Mary. But it doesn't bother me, and I don't want us to focus on it. Let's concentrate on what we can do, not what we can't do. Deal?"

He smiled, and I thought I saw a hint of relief on his face.

"Thank you, Sally. Yes. Deal."

We left the table and settled on the sofa. Relaxed. Comfortable. Warm. Not quite 'quiet' companionship, because we talked.

"Did you always want to be an archivist?" he asked.

"Well, no. I did English at uni, but while I was there, I became friendly with one of the librarians. I got interested and decided to follow that path."

"Right decision?"

"Yes. I've loved every minute. And as I've gone on to work with old documents and manuscripts, it's got even better. David encourages us to keep expanding our knowledge and experience."

"David?"

"He's my boss. Runs the libraries and archives. I've learnt a lot from him. Now, I work mainly in the archives, and over the last couple of years, I've learned to read a lot of these old scripts. I also do some research work for academics I know. In return, they help me with some of the stuff I'm still finding difficult."

At some point, it dawned on me he was a listener, a good listener. He didn't just let me talk. He engaged with what I said. That was refreshing. For a man. I ended up curled up next to him, my head against his shoulder, his arm around me. It felt so good.

"I'm going to have to go," I said eventually, looking at my watch. "Work tomorrow."

"Free anytime this weekend?"

I looked up at him, grinning.

"Yup. All weekend."

"Want to meet up?"

"Oh, yes. How about I come around Friday evening … with a spare pair of knickers or two."

He smiled, lowered his lips to mine, and we shared a long slow kiss.

"Perfect," he said. "Any thoughts as to what we might do?"

"Yeah. One or two."

That weekend was wonderful. I arrived Friday evening as planned; I left Sunday afternoon. In between, we enjoyed one another. At times releasing our lust; he gave me a second spanking, longer and firmer than the first. And even better. This time it did end in him bending me over and using me for his pleasure. Mine too. At others, gently loving. Taking it in turns to please each other, joining together in mutual delight.

It wasn't all sex, of course. We took leisurely meals, played each other some favourite tracks, watched a couple of films. Went for a stroll around the park on Saturday afternoon. When I got home, I closed the door, leaned back against it, closed my eyes, and let out a deep breath. Wow! Could it get any better?

***

"I've got some news."

"Good, I hope," he said, topping my glass up.

"I've been offered a new job."

A look of alarm crossed his face, and I laughed.

"Don't worry, I'm not going anywhere. Same place."

"Phew. We've hardly started. Haven't finished corrupting you yet."

"As long as I can corrupt you as well?"

"As much as you like."

"Tonight?"

"It's a weeknight." He looked at me with a twinkle in his eyes. "We agreed."

"Beginning to wish I hadn't."

"What's the new job?"

"I've been asked to do some work with the team in the History faculty. They're revamping one of their courses and want my input."

"Is that full-time then?"

"No, probably a couple of days a week for a few months. They want me to start putting together reading lists and stuff. Suggesting themes and texts, that sort of thing."

"I'd have thought the academic staff would do that."

"Oh, they'll make the final decisions, but some are highly specialised. They only know their own bit. And a lot of them couldn't organise the proverbial brewery piss-up. They want people with a wider outlook, it wouldn't just be me. Probably three of us."

"How would that fit with your current role?"

"They're going to see if the library can agree to a job share."

"Will they?"

"Don't see why not. David's usually okay about these things."

"You want to do it?"

"Yeah. It sounds interesting. I like a change now and again."

"And here was me thinking all a librarian did was stamp a few books, put others back on the shelves, and say 'Ssh!' a lot."

"Marcus!"

I knew I was lucky to work where I did. It was a little different to your local council library. We had masses of source documents dating back hundreds of years. They were my speciality. I looked after them, maintained them, catalogued them. Well, three of us did. But most of all, I loved reading them, analysing them.

Analysing …

Over the weeks since Marcus and I had become lovers, I had realised he was an analyst too. To begin with, I found the constant feedback a bit distracting. Everything we did, we talked about, sometimes while we were doing it. It wasn't that we didn't enjoy it – boy, did we enjoy it - but it seemed a bit … clinical. But I quickly saw the benefits. He asked me what I wanted, what I needed. Nobody had done that before, and I hadn't offered. How many times had I lain there after sex, thinking about how much better it would have been if …?

Marcus wanted the 'if'. He wanted to know what turned me on, down to the tiniest little detail. He wanted me to tell him everything I knew about my body. He watched me turn myself on, make myself come. Several times. I was uncomfortable the first time, I'd never let anyone watch before. But he was clearly enjoying it, so I relaxed, and began to enjoy it too.

From then on, I realised he picked up everything. He was trying the things he'd seen me do. Where to touch, and when. When to speed up, when to slow down. Which buttons to press. He had plenty of his own tricks too; I was soon discovering new things about my own body.

This encouraged me to explore him, to see what turned him on. I watched him masturbate, I'd never done that before either. In the past, I think I would probably have felt insulted, but now, not only did I watch, I did it for him. Watched his reactions, learned what he liked.

We talked about the other things too. For me, it was warmth, hugs, a word, a tone of voice. But I also craved restriction, control, vulnerability, surprise. Marcus was more visual than me; he loved to look at me, to watch me. He loved me to dress up. I was still a bit self-conscious about this side, but the response it generated soon built my confidence. He loved me to tease, to be playful. We were both tactile, loving to touch and be touched. I soon learned he could melt me with one finger. I had a few tricks of my own, too.

We watched porn, from the sublime to the ridiculous. Some went further than either of us wanted to go. We told each other which bits worked for us and which bits didn't. We even tried to copy them. But that often ended in fits of giggles, wondering how many takes the scene had needed, or even if some things were physically possible.

It wasn't all we did, of course. We were new lovers and the passion and the lust often overtook us. We were eager to try new things, to exhaust our known repertoire before we explored the unknown. Marcus had been firm on this. Yes, spanking was a part of that repertoire now, but he didn't want to introduce anything else until we'd spent time learning what made each other tick. We hadn't even used any toys. Well, I had, but only after our weeknight meetings. A girl's got to get to sleep somehow.

After a few weekends, it all came together. Now, we just needed a nudge or a gesture to tell each other what we wanted. We'd often tease each other by not doing it, but it had been worth it.

"When will you know if the job's going to work out?"

In truth, I already as good as knew. The department had made me a formal offer, and I felt sure I could work it out with David.

"Not sure yet; soon, I hope. I'm looking forward to a new challenge."

It being a weeknight, we'd spent a relaxing evening enjoying being together. Even so, by the time I got home, I knew I'd need some help to get to sleep. As I lay there afterwards, the beginnings of an idea developed in my head. I'd need to do a bit of shopping before the weekend.

Chapter 9 – Marcus

My phone pinged.

[JOB SORTED FANCY CELEBRATING @ WEEKEND? S]

That was quick.

[GREAT CONGRATS YES WHAT U WANT TO DO? M]

[WAIT & SEE S XXXX]

I'd had a busy week. Writing had gone well; it seemed to flow. I'd written a few chapters of the novel I was working on, as well as some blog articles, and a couple of short stories. Not being able to work full time, I relied on my writing, and it could be unreliable. I had to make hay while the sun shone.

After I'd eaten, I made myself comfortable for the evening. When I'd had counselling after my dad died, my counsellor had kept on about the importance of having 'joy' in your life. It had been one of his buzzwords. Sally was certainly bringing some joy to my life for the first time in ages. I hoped I was doing the same for her. I thought back to that first night, remembering my apprehension. I had wanted to make it work, but I had still doubted her motives. Fearing she'd run when she realised the reality of her fantasy. But she hadn't. She'd wanted more. My doubts had disappeared after that night, and now we both wanted more.

The weeks since had been a bit of a dream. We knew more about each other than many established couples. She was a delicious mixture. An intoxicating blend of lust and reserve; of confidence and reticence. I still wasn't quite sure what prompted these varying elements, but we were having fun finding out.

At times, she could be bashful about what she wanted, things she wanted us to try. But when she relaxed and got into the mood, she was completely uninhibited, demanding, even.

She'd picked up a few tricks over the years, too. One evening early on, we'd been talking about being selfish. Not worrying about your partner's pleasure, just satisfying your own desire.

"What single thing gives you the most pleasure," she asked.

"A really good blowjob," I replied. "Occasionally – and it has only been occasionally – the experience can be overwhelming. Sometimes, I think it's the closest I get to a female orgasm."

"How do you mean?"

"Well, when a man comes, it's largely centred on his cock and balls. At least the physical part is. But sometimes when I see a woman come, really come, it seems to engulf her. Take her over for a brief time; consume her, head to toe."

"Oh yeah ..."

"And that's what I've felt from a few blowjobs. Complete ecstasy."

"Only a few?"

"Yes. A handful in my entire life."

She raised an eyebrow.

"Of course," I added quickly, remembering the oral pleasure we'd already shared, "they're always good …" she laughed, "… but only a few have been that good."

"Oh, you've not found the right woman."

I looked at her, her face set in an innocent expression. When I asked her what her selfish pleasure was, she'd jokingly said it was giving blowjobs.

Later that evening, she asked me if I remembered her saying she was proud of her oral technique. I did, at one of our dinner dates.

"Want me to show you what I can really do?" she asked, unbuttoning my trousers.

What followed aroused me now just thinking about it. She wouldn't let me touch her. She got us both naked, pushed me back on the sofa, and knelt between my legs. What she then did with her mouth, tongue and lips was almost unreal. Forget those few times I'd told her about; this was in a different league.

She toyed with me, hardly using her hands at all. At first, she worked quite firmly, and I thought I wasn't going to last two or three minutes. But she knew what she was doing. Exactly what she was doing. Once she got me worked up, she changed; light flicks, lingering kisses, licks, bites. One moment hardly touching me, others taking me as deep as she could. She brought me close, then slowed, then closer again. She was teasing me, edging me, amusement in her eyes, holding my gaze.

After fifteen minutes, I wondered how long this could go on. The sensations were incredible, spreading through my entire body. I was making noises I hardly recognised. I still don't know what she did, but suddenly I came, my cum exploding into her mouth before I could warn her. She didn't flinch, just stared into my eyes, and carried on. I had to reach out and slow her down as the feelings became too intense. As I came down, she gently licked and sucked my cock, maintaining eye contact all the time.

Eventually, she climbed up me and gave me a long lingering kiss. I could taste myself on her lips.

"Sorry," I said, "that caught me by surprise."

"I know. That's my special little trick. Works every time." Another long kiss. A wicked smile. "Gives me what I want."

I raised an eyebrow. She winked. Another long kiss.

"You were quite vocal," she said softly. "Was that good?"

"The best fifteen minutes of my life."

She chuckled. "Oh, I can make it last much longer than that."

I sighed. She was now sitting on my lap, our arms gently stroking one another.

"I'm not sure when I'll recover from this one."

"Oh, Marcus," she said trying to look innocent, "have I sucked you dry?"

Yes. Yes, she had. And now sitting on my own thinking about it, I wished she was here. But she wasn't. I'd have to go to bed and see if I could ignore my lust long enough to get to sleep. I had an idea I might need some strength for whatever she had planned for the weekend.

***

Friday finally arrived. I picked up a nice sea bass and bought a bottle of champagne. After all, this was a celebration. I had been wondering what she had in mind. Up until now, we'd talked about everything beforehand. We both knew what we were going to do. Now, I had no idea. It was a strange feeling. Exciting. But strange.

When she arrived, we hugged and kissed warmly, and she went and put her backpack in the bedroom. Well, that told me something; on several occasions, eager to satisfy our pent-up lust, we'd fallen on each other as soon as I'd closed the door. Once, not even making it past the hallway, me taking her while she gripped the bench I kept my shoes in.

We ended up in the kitchen while I started to cook. I poured her a glass of wine.

"It's all sorted, then?" I asked.

"Yes. I knew David would work something out if he could. I'm doing the new stuff two days a week, and my current role the rest of the time."

"Looking forward to it?"

"Oh, yeah. Always like new challenges. Besides, it allows me to use my knowledge in different areas."

She seemed pleased and excited. She was natural, alive, confident. But then, as a person, she was. That was what was so attractive.

Sea bass doesn't take long to cook, and within half an hour, we were sitting at the table, enjoying a relaxed meal. I'd opened the champagne by now, and we toasted her new role. She joked I'd gone a bit over the top with the bubbly, but I knew she liked it, so what the hell. I could afford it at the moment. I did reflect at one point that she never talked about money; I'd thought about it once or twice before. But the thought disappeared, and we meandered through the rest of the meal.

Afterwards, we took the champagne over to the coffee table and snuggled up on the sofa. There was a frisson in the air, but we knew we had all weekend, and, for once, neither of us seemed in a hurry. We talked about our weeks. It got around to our midweek meetings, and how good they were. But we both admitted having to deal with certain frustrations after we parted. We thought we might relax the rules a bit. After a while, she asked coyly if I fancied doing anything, and when I agreed, she got up and went through to the bedroom.

"Marcus?" she said a little later, still hidden in the hallway.

"Yes?"

"Close your eyes. And keep them closed."

"Okay."

"No peeking. Don't open them till I tell you."

"Okay." I wasn't going to cheat and spoil the moment.

"Are they closed?"

"Yes."

I heard her come in and walk towards me. She stopped in front of me, and I could hear some movement and shuffling.

"You can open your eyes now."

As I did, my heart leapt. I took in the view in front of me. She was on the floor, sitting on her heels, looking up at me, smiling, with a hint of shyness. As my eyes worked their way down her body, they drifted over a black and red bustier, leading to suspenders, stockings, a matching pair of knickers, and black heels. She had a black choker around her neck. I took a deep breath.

"Remind you of anything?" she asked.

"The picture."

"Well?"

"You're better."

She laughed at the compliment.

"Except I've left the knickers on. I thought you might like to take them off for me."

I just looked; stared really. She looked beautiful; innocent and wicked at the same time.

"Like what you see?"

"You know I do," I said, almost in a whisper. "But I'd like to change one thing."

"What's that?"

I reached forward, placed my hands behind her neck and undid the choker. I sat back a little weighing it in my hand.

"We both know what this can mean," I said. "And we both know you're never going to wear one full time, neither of us want that. But at some point in the future, you may want to wear one occasionally. For a few hours. Let's save it for then, so it means something. Fair?"

She looked thoughtful; looked at me, looked at the choker.

"I didn't think about it," she said softly. "I was copying the picture. But now you put it like that …" That beautiful passion appeared in her eyes. "Yes. Fair."

I laid the choker on the table and bent to kiss her. She returned my kiss and pulled away.

"I've got a present for you."

I looked at her, allowing my eyes to run over her body.

"Another one?" I replied.

Reaching behind her back, she brought out a bag. It was velvety, with a drawstring.

"I thought it was about time we started our toy collection."

She handed it to me. I took it and opened the top. Reaching in I drew out a flogger, a nice one. Suede, with a solid plaited handle and a thick bunch of fronds about twelve inches long. I put it in my hand and ran my fingers along it. I looked up; her eyes were sparkling.

"I think we're ready for the next step, don't you?" she asked.

"Yes, I do."

"So, where do you want me?"

"Well, I think I need to warm you up a bit before we move to this."

The next half an hour or so developed into a slow, sensual spanking session. First with her knickers on, then I slid them down her legs to expose that luscious bum. Spanking, squeezing, caressing. Both of us enjoying every movement.

"Can you roll off a minute?" I asked.

"Anything wrong?"

"No. I want to get naked too and feel your skin on mine."

"Let me help …"

Between us, we stripped my clothes off, and she leaned forward, taking my hard cock in her hands. Cupping my balls, she took the end in her mouth, and, holding my eyes, slowly inched forward. I resisted, and gently pushed her away. She pouted, but I sat back down and guided her over my knees again; she didn't complain.

Resuming the spanking, she began to respond to my hand as I increased the power and frequency of my strokes. She started to vocalise the sensations she was feeling. Little whimpers as I struck, little moans as I caressed. We knew each other better now and didn't need constant feedback. I knew from her sounds and movements how I was affecting her, how she was responding.

During my caresses, I allowed my fingers to stray between her thighs, to run lightly over her wetness. Every time I did, she raised her hips to meet my touch. Sometimes I pulled my fingers away so she couldn't reach them, and she dropped down, with a little groan of frustration. And I started the spanking again.

But sometimes I pressed them to her, gently rubbing them into those beautiful, soft folds. In those moments, it felt so good. My fingers building her up and up. We'd come to know the right blend of pain and pleasure to make us both hungry. To bring us both to the point where we were ready for the inevitable release.

I concentrated on spanking her again, giving her a firm, fast bout. She was wriggling under the onslaught, occasionally lifting a foot in response. I knew she would soon need the pleasure. The whimpering was gone, replaced by a grunt or a little cry with each stroke. I judged the moment and moved my fingers between her legs. She moved to get up; we had tended to finish our spanking sessions recently with an urgent, unbridled fuck. But I held her down and continued with my fingers. She didn't complain and gave in to them. Within a short time, her orgasm flowed through her, as I fingered her over the peak, and gently back down.

We said nothing for a few minutes; I gently caressed her. Her breathing slowly steadying. She looked around at me and smiled.

"Mmm," she murmured, "that was good."

"For starters."

She slid off my lap onto the floor, still breathing deeply. I dropped beside her, and we kissed; gently, slowly. She pulled away slightly, a flirtatious look on her flushed face.

"Didn't you want me? It felt as if you did," she giggled. My hard cock had been pressing into her tummy for ages.

"Oh yes," I replied, as she reached towards my groin. I guided her hand away. "But I've got other plans for you."

"Oooh. What?"

"Patience …"

I picked up the bottle, filled our glasses, and handed one to her. We sat there, sipping champagne. Occasionally exchanging a kiss, a look; running a hand over bare skin. When she went to the bathroom, I watched her walk away from me, taking in every curve of her body. When she was in this mood, she was totally confident. Walking back, she looked directly at me, fully aware of my gaze devouring her, and completely comfortable with it. Dropping beside me again, she smiled.

"Thank you for introducing me to quiet companionship."

"My pleasure."

"No." She picked up her glass and took a sip. "Ours."

"Ready for round two?" I asked.

She grinned and put her glass down again. Taking the flogger from the table, she ran it through her fingers for a few seconds, and then handed it to me, handle first.

"Where do you want me?"

We'd discovered a brilliant sex aid completely by accident. I had a small bean-bag cube which I used as a footrest. We soon found it was the perfect way for Sally to present herself. If she laid over it, she could rest her knees, shoulders and head on the floor, but her hips were well above it, leaving her bum … her pussy … It was proving very versatile. Now, I picked it up and placed it in the middle of the floor.

"Over this, I think."

She grinned, and seductively crossed the space between us on her hands and knees. Plumping the cube, she moved forward, wriggling her body to get herself comfortable.

"How's that?"

"Legs together."

"Like this?"

"Perfect," I replied. Because it was. I looked down and took in the sight. The bustier, suspenders, stockings, heels. Oh, she looked good. It meant I couldn't use the flogger on most of her body, but that could wait. Because it all framed the main target - her bum. I moved closer to enjoy it. It was still flushed pink from our earlier session, but I decided to reheat it a little. Her head was turned on one side towards me, and I squatted beside and kissed her cheek.

"Ready?" I whispered.

"Yes."

I turned and ran my hand over her cheeks. Without warning, I started to spank her. She was surprised, perhaps expecting me to use the flogger straight away. But she soon settled, making final adjustments to her position. I stroked her skin again; warm, pink. Ready.

I hadn't used a flogger for a while and knew I'd have to get back into practice. I picked it up, and settled it in my hand, swishing it about a bit. It was just right for us. Long enough to be effective, but not so long you needed real skill to avoid collateral damage. I knew Sally would be able to hear it going through the air. Holding it above her shoulders, I lowered it until the fronds met her skin; she flinched. I let them flow over her as I trailed them down her back, and all the way down her legs. Then up again, along her arms, and down her body once more. Finally, I let them rest on her bum.

I lifted it and started rotating the fronds so when they came into contact, they'd run from her hips to her thighs. I slowly lowered my hand and let them make that first light touch. I heard a slight intake of breath. Keeping the height, I moved the point of contact around. I was being gentle, the flogger kissing her skin two or three times a second. I lowered my hand a little so there was more contact between suede and skin. The moans increased slightly.

"Colour?"

"Ooh, green," she murmured.

After this first check, I wouldn't ask again. I trusted her by now to tell me if she wanted to stop; she trusted I would. I carried on, increasing the strength of the rotation, but occasionally altering the length of suede striking her skin. I watched her body reacting. Little twitches, little movements, occasional stretches. Her arms and hands stretched and moved sensuously on the carpet. Yes, she was enjoying this.

I stopped; saw her body relax slightly. I started twirling the flogger the other way. Up her body this time. I started at her stocking tops, and worked up her thighs, reaching her cheeks and increasing the power a little. Once or twice she uttered a louder noise. I had made sure her legs were together. There were plenty of future possibilities with a flogger and those tender areas between her thighs. I hadn't intended to go there tonight, but obviously, one or two strands had slipped through. But she didn't stop me. I moved up slightly so she wouldn't have to.

After a few minutes, she was moving her body gently, almost raising her hips to increase the contact area. I lowered my arm so she felt more of the suede on her skin. Her cheeks were colouring up nicely. Various sounds told me she was enjoying this. Even with her legs closed, I could see the moisture between her thighs. I was enjoying it too; my aching cock told me that.

I slowed down and stopped. As I knelt by her side, she looked up at me, flushed.

"Don't stop!"

I kissed her lightly.

"That was the starter. Now for the main course."

I moved back, and let the fronds touch her skin again. I got into a comfortable position and raised the flogger, holding the fronds in my other hand. And waited. Keeping her in suspense. Then I released my fingers and the suede hit her left cheek. She gasped. I drew my arm back and repeated the stroke two or three times. After the initial contact, her gasps reduced, but were still there. I changed the angle and landed on her other cheek. Back to the left, then over to the right. Then across both. Harder now, not twirling any more, but firm, measured strokes.

The sound of the suede hitting her skin was crisp, delicious. She was responding now; noisier, more movement, a loud sigh or two, followed by a gasp as I brought the fronds down for an occasional harder stroke. I kept up a regular rhythm, her bum turning red now. Pale red. But definitely red; no longer pink. And the colour wasn't even anymore. It was mottled, darker where the firmer strokes had hit. God, this was good. I took a risk.

"Open your legs if you want to."

They instantly parted. Her pussy spread open, glistening, moisture all down her thighs, oozing onto the material of the cube.

I slowed down, needing to aim carefully with her legs open. I allowed the occasional stroke to land on her upper thighs. One or two strands found a softer target, and she yelped. But she didn't stop me. She was almost writhing now. Grinding her hips. Pushing her hands along the carpet, her feet kicking up from time to time.

Finally, my balls couldn't take it anymore. I wanted her. I needed her. I had to have her.

I threw the flogger down and knelt between her legs. Grabbing her hips, I pulled her up off the cube. She let out a sharp breath but instantly got up on her hands, her head hanging between her shoulders. I put my hand between her legs, and roughly felt her pussy; soaking wet. She groaned, and pushed herself back towards me, searching for my cock. I guided the head to her entrance and firmly drove it in. She let out a cry.

"FUCK YES!"

We were both too far gone for control. I fucked her. Pure and simple. Hard and fast. I could feel her building to orgasm, her head came back. She started to tense, breathing hard.

"FUCK … FUCK … FUCK …"

Suddenly she froze and let out the biggest groan I'd heard from her. I felt her muscles grip and spasm around my cock. Her body jerked and shook. I slowed a little to let her recover.

"NO!" she gasped. "GO!"

I did; I picked up speed. Still moaning, she came again; smaller, less intense. This time though, she sank onto the cube, unable to support herself. But I was now lost in my own lust, moments from coming myself. I followed her, and when she landed, I resumed my pace, driving my cock into her. Her breath was coming in fast gasps. She was whimpering, her legs shaking.

I came. Oh, such a feeling. As always at that moment, my body took control of my rhythm. My hips bucked as I used her muscles to squeeze every drop of cum out of me. She groaned at every stroke. It was all I could do not to collapse on top of her. I bent and kissed her shoulder.

"Okay?" I managed to ask.

"Mmm," she mumbled.

I kissed her shoulder again.

"Am I too heavy?"

"No, stay right there."

I dropped myself gently on top of her, putting one arm out on the ground in front of her. She grabbed it, holding it tight.

Shortly after, my spent cock slipped out of her. She let out a giggle as it did so, and I kissed her shoulder. I lifted my weight and rolled onto the floor beside her. We could now see each other clearly; her face was flushed pink, very pink. She was looking at me, unreadable. I felt my breathing stop. Had I taken it too far? Gradually, as she took a deep breath in and out, her face broke into the most glorious smile.

"Boy, were we ready for the next level."

I breathed again.

"You can be a horny little minx, can't you?"

"When I want to be. With the right person. Problem?"

"Oh, no."

She joined me on the floor, resting her body against me, one leg between mine as we returned to earth. I could feel the results of our passion slowly seeping from her pussy onto my thigh.

No words. No feedback. That could wait.

She came back from the bathroom beautifully naked, enjoying her nakedness.

"I took it all off. Hope you don't mind?"

I shook my head and smiled.

"Did you take a look?" I asked.

"Yes."

"And?" I asked nervously.

"Well," she giggled, "it looks like it feels."

She joined me back on the floor, and I handed her a glass of now warm champagne. I grabbed the cube.

"When I bought this, I never imagined how useful it would be."

She looked at it, picked it up and turned it around. Then looked at me.

"It'll need a wash."

***

When I came back through the bedroom door in the morning, she was standing in front of the dressing table. She'd tilted the mirror and was looking over her shoulder trying to see the results of the previous evening.

"Look!" she said.

I went over and surveyed the reflection of her bum. Still a pale pink glow, but that was normal now the morning after a good spanking. But this time, there were several darker marks as well. Quite small, spread randomly over her cheeks. She looked back at me and pouted.

"You did that to me."

I was still looking in the mirror.

"I did, didn't I?" I looked back at her. "Well?"

She held the pout for a few seconds, then her face cracked.

"I've lost my virginity!" I raised my eyebrows and she giggled. "You know what I mean. I've got marks. Real marks." She put her arms around my neck. "What do you think?"

I looked in the mirror again. I had always been a little ambivalent about the aftermath of impact play. Part of me wanted the results to disappear as soon as the fun was over. For the giver, the session had ended. But the recipient had a lasting reminder, at least for a while.

"Marcus?" she asked softly. I looked at her.

"Are you happy with it?" I replied.

"Quite proud, actually."

"Good. Then so am I."

She gave me a quizzical look but said nothing. We went back to bed and cuddled up. We were in no hurry and lay there for some time.

"What were you thinking when you looked at the marks?" she asked finally.

I told her; tried to explain that although I was turned on by spanking and flogging, and even more by the thought of what else we might use, part of me was worried about what it said about me.

"Oh, Marcus," she said gently. "You haven't kidnapped me. I'm not here against my will. I'm here because these things turn me on. Because they turn you on. I want you to do these things to me; need you to do them. Remember how we felt last night? What it did for us? How you took me?"

She was slightly agitated now, the way she got when she thought I was over analysing things. Propped up on her arm looking at me, she was flushing slightly. Not just her face either. I allowed my eyes to take in the colour growing on her breasts and her nipples which were beginning to swell. I'd already discovered they responded to things other than pleasure. Images from the previous night flashed into my head. I was grinning before I realised it.

"Yeah."

"Well, I want to do that again. And again. And all the things we've talked about. Where we're going, my bum's going to look a lot worse than this …" she paused, looking thoughtful for a few seconds, "… or should

I say a lot better? Whatever. Yes, I am quite proud of myself for taking these marks. Of finally admitting I want them, and of finding someone to give them to me. If I can be proud to receive them, then I want you to be proud of giving them. I don't ever want you to feel guilty for giving me what I crave. Deal?"

I looked at her staring down, that fire in her eyes once again. Defying me to argue, but also imploring me to believe her.

"Okay," I replied. "But promise me you'll tell me if I go too far, if I hurt you. I don't want you to keep it to yourself because you think it'll fuel my … guilt."

"Oh, I'll tell you. I promise you'll know if you hurt me. But I don't think you will." She dropped down and kissed me. "So … Deal?"

"Deal," I replied.

"Good. I feel a bit flushed."

"Yeah, you are a bit." I looked at her breasts, nipples now erect.

"Still find it cute?"

"Yes."

"Just how cute?"

I showed her.

She was stroking my groin afterwards, running her fingers around the base of my cock, and over my balls. Drained as they were, I still loved her doing it, and she seemed to enjoy it too.

"I love the feel," she said.

"I don't mind it either."

"No, not that. Well, yes, that too. But I mean the smoothness. I've never had a shaved man before. When I uncovered you on that first night, it was quite a surprise. But it's nice. Have you always shaved?"

"No, only the last few years."

"Why did you do it?"

"Don't know really. Just wanted to try it, so I did. I liked it and carried on."

She went quiet for a while, her gentle fingers still roaming.

"Would you prefer me bare?" she asked.

"No preference. Whatever feels good for you; it's your hair. Have you shaved it off before?"

I liked the way she looked. Tightly trimmed around her pussy, but with a nice short bush above.

"No. Thought about it. But you'd like it?"

"I'd like whatever makes you feel good. Remember the talk about underwear? If you wear something that makes you feel good, it's going to work for me. But if you wear something just for me that you feel ridiculous in …"

"Yes."

"Similar thing. If you feel good as you are, then I'm going to feel good too."

"But you wouldn't mind me changing it?"

"No, not at all. After all, whatever you do with it, it's only hair. In a few weeks, you can change it. But whatever you do, do it for you, not for me. Or anyone else for that matter."

Chapter 10 – Sally

"Marcus, this is Lucy. Lucy, Marcus."

I was nervous. Always had been when Lucy had met my boyfriends for the first time. It was silly really. I didn't need her approval, just as she didn't need mine. But we'd proved shrewd judges over the years and had nearly always been right. We respected each other's judgement; didn't always accept it. But respected it.

Lucy and I did things differently. I wanted to like someone when I first met them. Keep an open mind and wait a while. She was the opposite, over-protective perhaps? She wasn't hostile. But she tended to start from a position of disliking my man on sight, until 'he proved himself worthy', as she'd once put it. Only half-jokingly.

"Hi, Lucy," Marcus said. "Come in." They shook hands as we stood in the hallway, Lucy and I glad to be out of the rain. "Why don't I leave you two to dry off?"

He went back into the living room. We put our bags down, kicked off our shoes, and hung our coats up. It had been raining most of the time we'd been in town. Light summer drizzle. The sort that gets you wetter than a downpour. We'd managed to dodge from shop to shop but still felt like drowned rats.

"All right if I grab some towels?" I asked as we went through the living room, giving Marcus a hug and a kiss on the way. "We need to sort our hair out. Can you make some coffee?"

I took Lucy through to the bathroom and started rough-drying my hair. She was luckier than me as hers was short, but she still looked a bit dishevelled. We dried and brushed until the moment we both looked in the mirror, laughed and gave up. It would have to do.

"Better?" Marcus asked as we came out.

"Yes. Still a bit damp around the edges, but it'll dry."

"It's been lovely for three weeks," Lucy said, "and we pick today to go shopping."

"Had a good day?"

"Yes," I replied. "Really good, apart from the rain. Lots of browsing, a bit of buying, a long boozy lunch, and a gossip."

Lucy laughed. "Makes us sound like footballer's wives."

I'd been spending every weekend with Marcus recently, and Lucy had complained she never saw me anymore. I knew it was light-hearted. We didn't live in each other's pockets, and we tended to see less of each other when either of us was with someone. But I'd decided this weekend would be the right time to introduce her to Marcus.

I'd had a bad week; well, two or three bad weeks in a way. I'd had my dreaded smear test. I hated them. I'm sure all women do, except perhaps true masochists. And this time, there had been one or two abnormalities. So, this week, I'd had to go in for them to delve a bit further. Lucy had come with me. It turned out there was nothing to worry about, just re-check in twelve months.

But I was told not to have sex for a few days, and the way I felt afterwards made me accept that advice readily. I'd anticipated it and had already written this weekend off as far as that was concerned. I decided to arrange the day with Lucy and suggested to Marcus she come back with me so he could meet her. She'd been mentioning it for a few weeks now. He seemed fine with it too.

"Oh, thanks," I said, as Lucy and I sat down and picked up the mugs. "Did you get anything done today?"

"Yeah. Managed to finish a story off. It hadn't been working, but it did today."

"A short story?" Lucy asked.

"Yes. I'm writing a few at the moment."

"Sally told me. What do you write about?"

"I'll write about anything if somebody pays me."

"What do you like writing about?"

"Well, something a bit different. The short stories can be about anything, although I don't do 'boy meets girl' or the 'earl and the milkmaid'. The novels tend to be historical. Something where I can use my imagination, but within a real context, I suppose."

It wasn't a bad start. On one or two of these occasions, Lucy had sat virtually silent for ages, clearly taking an instant dislike to my partner. At least they were talking. I watched Marcus; I could see he was nervous too. Although he appeared quite laid back, he could be shy like me. Well, we were both introverts. That was why I'd suggested Lucy came around to his place, rather than us all going out. It allowed us to relax on home turf, as it were.

"He writes some surreal stuff too."

They both looked at me.

"Surreal?"

"Yeah, sort of stream of consciousness stuff. You know, imagination poured out on paper."

"Oh, that," Marcus said, rolling his eyes. "Nobody wants to read that, let alone buy it."

"Why do you do it then?" Lucy asked.

"Because I enjoy it, I guess. It seems to come out. Sally tells me you're artistic; you must do stuff for yourself. You don't know why, it just appears."

"True. Most of my stuff nobody wants."

"What do you do?"

"I suppose I'd call them abstract figures. I started out doing portraits, but I was never happy with them. Truth be told, I wasn't particularly good. So, I started playing around with them, and they became looser. I like them, but they're not everyone's taste."

"Good," Marcus said. "God save us from a world of uniformity."

I was relaxing. It seemed to be going well, and I wasn't having to drive the conversation. I'd had a feeling they'd get on. Knowing them both, I knew they had quite a lot in common; liberal outlook, enjoyed using their intelligence, with a creative side.

The conversation meandered around. If Marcus realised he was being subjected to Lucy's interrogation techniques, he didn't seem to mind. After a while, I sensed she stopped probing and was simply enjoying the discussion.

"What shall we do for dinner?" I asked. We'd agreed we'd get a takeaway. "Luce. Any preference?"

"I haven't had Chinese in ages; wouldn't mind that, but not fussy."

We rang in an order and carried on chatting until it arrived. We moved to the table and opened it all up.

"God," I said. "How many did we order for?"

"Well, I know what we're going to be eating tomorrow," Marcus said drily.

"I'll take a doggy bag," Lucy added.

As the meal progressed, I watched Marcus using a technique I was all too familiar with. The meeting had started with Lucy determined to get information out of him. Slowly he turned it around. Answered all her questions with candour, but started to ask simple little questions in return, and gradually the balance switched. Almost before she knew it, she was practically telling him her life story. I didn't know if he did it deliberately or even knew he was doing it, but it was good to watch.

We spent the rest of the evening chatting. Lucy and I reminiscing about how we'd met; our days as carefree students.

"Did you go to uni, Marcus?" Lucy asked.

"Yes, but dropped out at the end of the first year."

"Do you mind me asking why?"

"Looking back, I'm not sure I know myself. I think I was too immature; didn't have the discipline, I suppose. And chose the wrong subjects."

"Oh. What?"

"Philosophy and politics."

"Not history?"

"No, that's what I've never understood. I was a history nut even then, so how I chose those particular subjects, I've no idea."

"Regret not finishing?"

"No, not really. Who knows how differently life might have turned out? I've enjoyed what I have done. But I do sometimes regret I didn't go back as a mature student; life always intervened."

Before we knew it, it was nearly midnight. Lucy did take a doggy bag; well, a couple of doggy cartons, and took herself home.

***

"Thank you."

"For what?" Marcus replied.

We had gone to bed and were lying in our favourite position. On our sides, curled up; my back to him, bum nestling in his groin, his arms folded around me, our legs intertwined. Only tonight, my bum was encased in an old pair of knickers, unfortunately.

"For tonight."

"Didn't do anything."

"That's what I mean. Thank you for being you."

"I'm not very good at being anyone else."

"I know, and don't ever try."

"You were nervous?"

"Yes, always am when Lucy does her inquisition."

"She is a bit obvious."

"You were nervous too, weren't you?"

"Yes."

"Why?" There was quite a pause.

"Because … Well, I'd like to think this is the beginning of something, so I wanted your best friend and I to get off to a good start."

He couldn't see the expression that came over my face, but at that moment, his reply told me everything I needed to know.

***

"Have you still got our checklists?" I asked after lunch.

"Yes. Somewhere."

"Fancy revising them?"

"If you like. But are you sure you want to do it when we can't do anything?"

"I can always do something for you."

"No."

"Okay. But at least it means we can look through them objectively."

Marcus had been brilliant over the last few weeks; supportive, warm, empathetic. Perhaps it was his own experiences of illness and the fear of it. He'd offered to come to the hospital with me, but I'd already arranged to go with Lucy. This weekend, I'd be happy to give him pleasure, but he insisted on waiting until I was able to join in again. He still didn't seem to understand how much I enjoyed pleasing him, even though he often did it for me without thinking of himself.

After he found the checklists, we had fun working our way through. There were several to change to 'done'. Most of those were now regular activities. One or two weren't, particularly the food play. We got the giggles as we remembered that particular evening. Perhaps we hadn't thought it through properly, but we hadn't got far before we both started to laugh at the absurdity of the situation. In the end, we'd given up.

Twenty minutes of playing with food, followed by fifteen minutes in the shower trying to wash the sticky mess out of everywhere we could find it. Then ten minutes trying to clear the remnants from the bottom of the shower tray, before twenty minutes cleaning the carpet. No; we definitely hadn't thought that one through.

We carried on through the list, giving our scores for everything, seeing if they'd changed. When we got to 'daddy/girl', I froze as he said it, hoping he didn't notice.

"Want to call me 'daddy'?"

"Do you want me to?" I asked, cautiously.

"God, no." My breathing started again. "That's one fetish I don't get," he continued. "I've never understood the dynamic around the whole 'daddy, little girl' thing. Do you want to?"

"No," I replied as casually as possible.

"I can't get my head around being in the middle of sex, and you looking up and saying, 'fuck me, daddy'. Quickest way to a limp cock I can think of."

We made quite a few changes. Things went from 'possibly' to 'want to do'; from 'not interested' to 'might'. One or two things even went from 'Definitely not' to 'with the right partner'.

After we finished, we cuddled up and talked about some of the fantasies we'd described to each other since we'd become lovers. We even used our colour code for them; green, yellow, red. Red was for some of our more extreme fantasies; they might turn us on, but we never actually wanted to do them. I wondered if there were fantasies Marcus hadn't told me; I was conscious there were a few I hadn't yet disclosed.

As evening approached, I knew I'd have to leave soon.

"Marcus?" My head was on his lap. "Do you ever fantasise about other men?"

He didn't reply straight away, thinking.

"Uh ... no."

"Have you thought about it?"

"Oh, yes. I've tried to imagine it; what it would be like. What we would do."

"And can you? Imagine it, I mean?"

"Yes. But it's always an intellectual process. I can visualise it, but don't get any feeling from it."

"Does it repel you?

"No. I've never met a man I fancied."

"What would happen if you did?"

"I have absolutely no idea."

"So, you don't get off on it then?"

"No. Why? Do you fancy watching me with another man?"

"Nope. Not on my list."

"Funny, isn't it?" he asked.

"What is?"

"I bet most straight men would get off watching two girls. How many women would get off watching two men? I'm sure there are some, but I've never met one."

We fell silent for a while. I wondered if he would ask the question I needed him to ask. Finally, he did.

"What about you? Do you have fantasies about other women?"

I'd brought this subject up now because I had to, and resting on his lap, he couldn't see my face. I was having a bit of a shy moment.

"Sometimes," I replied softly. There was a pause.

"And?"

"And what?"

"Do they turn you on?"

"Yes."

"Always had them?"

"No. Only the last couple of years."

"What are you going to do about it?"

The question surprised me. I turned my head to look up at him.

"What do you mean?"

He stroked my hair.

"Don't you want to do something about it?"

I had thought a lot about that too. I laid my head back on his lap.

"That's not going to happen, is it?"

"Why not?

I was beginning to wish I hadn't started this.

"Well, I've got you now," I said. "Can't go out looking for some girl at the same time, can I?"

"Why not?"

Now I was starting to panic; this was getting out of control. I looked back up at him.

"Of course I can't. They're just fantasies, Marcus."

He bent and kissed my forehead.

"Okay, Sal."

***

"He's too good to be true."

"What?" I replied. "How?"

"Well, the way you talk, you'd think he was perfect."

Lucy grinned. I knew she was teasing me. A bit, anyway.

"No. He's not perfect. In fact, he's too ready to admit his faults sometimes. But he's damned near perfect for me. You've met him now …" I sat upright, trying to adopt a vaguely military bearing, and continued in a dubious mid-European accent, "… give me your report, please."

"He's nice," she smiled. "Quite tricky though."

"Tricky?"

"Yeah. When I thought about it afterwards, he got far more out of me than I realised."

"You mean he interrogated the interrogator?"

"Something like that."

"He did that to me when we first met."

"So … he's tricky."

"But you approve?"

"I don't need to approve, Sal."

"But do you?"

She rested her chin on her steepled hands, looking at me.

"Is the sex good?"

I felt myself flush a little; Lucy knew what to look for.

"Ah, I see it is."

I grinned.

"Oh, yes. Bloody good."

"And when you're not in bed?"

"That's great too. He's a quiet thinker, with a wicked sense of humour. Just about perfect for me."

"Well, I suppose he'll do. Now, tell me all about those faults of his."

***

By Wednesday, I was ready and able again and boy, was I willing. We still met up midweek but had relaxed our rule somewhat. We spent much of the evening chilling out, doing normal things. But it usually ended now with us relieving each other's tensions in one way or another. Making love, rather than 'playing'. That evening was no exception. Marcus was worried about me still hurting, but it didn't take me long to persuade him it was business as usual. At the weekend, we resumed our explorations.

We had been slowly building our toy collection. We regularly chose two new additions; one for pain, one for pleasure. We then spent a few sessions trying them out, seeing if they worked for us. A few didn't, but most did.

A few weeks later, sometime after a particularly good time with a butt plug and a leather strap, we had gone to bed.

"What shall we explore next?" I asked him. As usual, he was lying behind me, his body following the contours of mine. In the pause that followed, I thought he had fallen asleep already. It would have been unusual; we enjoyed this cuddle time, and it often prompted some of our most intimate discussions.

"Do you trust me?" he asked softly.

"Yes. You know I do." I was intrigued. No reply. "Marcus? What are you thinking?"

He slowly pushed me forward onto my front, rolling himself over me. His cock nestling between my cheeks, not so limp now. His breath on my ear, then a whisper.

"I want to tie you up …"

A little thrill ran through me.

"… to this bed."

I had to strain to hear him.

"Completely naked …"

I could feel his cock swelling.

"… spread-eagled."

An image came into my mind.

"Maybe blindfolded …"

A chuckle deep in my throat. It wasn't just his cock responding.

"… and then do wicked things to you."

Suddenly, he stuck his tongue right into my ear. I jumped, and he laughed softly.

"Will there be pain?" I asked.

"Not necessarily."

"Oh …" I complained.

"Well, it'd be your first time fully tied up, so I thought I might put a few gentler things together."

His cock was now stiff between my cheeks; I wanted it. I started to slowly move my bum up and down its length, but he rolled us onto our sides again.

"You know …" he said, beginning to move a hand lightly down my tummy, causing it to flinch. "… tantalise and tease."

His fingers reached my little bush.

"Make you beg for it …"

They went lower.

"… see how wild I can get you."

They brushed my …

"And perhaps then stop."

He moved his hand away and I let out a huff of frustration. Rolling over, I threw the duvet off the bed. Pushing him onto his back, I threw my leg over him and straddled his hips. As he looked up at me, a gentle smile on his face, I lowered myself onto him, and rode him, reminding him how wild I could be.

***

"Comfortable?" he asked.

"Yes, thank you."

Sally

Earlier in the afternoon, while we were watching rugby on TV, Marcus had asked if I fancied putting his wicked little plan into action that evening. Oh boy, did I! The minute I agreed, he'd surprised me by guiding me over the table, pulling my jeans and knickers to my knees and telling me not to move. When he came back a minute or two later, I felt his hand on my bum. He stroked my cheeks and bent to kiss them in turn. Well, I like rugby, but …

Then he gently spread them, and I felt his fingers on my perineum, lightly stroking. But instead of moving in the direction I wanted him to go, he moved towards my ass and ran one finger around it. I felt my ring of muscle twitch. The finger pressed on it, cold with lube. He massaged it gently. I caught my breath as I felt his finger penetrate it. He worked it in and twisted it around a little.

"Relaxed?" he asked.

"Yes," I replied. I enjoyed him playing with my ass now; we both enjoyed it and wanted to go much further. But up until now, we'd only done it during play when I was already horny. This was the first time he'd gone straight for it.

He gently slid his finger out, and I felt the point of a plug pushing into me. He twisted it, slowly pushing it in. My ass opened, and then contracted again, as it closed around the neck of the plug.

"Comfy?"

"Yeah," I replied. "Carry on."

"Okay, you can cover up now."

I turned and looked at him. He knew what I'd wanted. He was grinning. I knew I wasn't going to get it. I pulled my clothes back up.

"How does it feel?"

I rolled my hips.

"Rather good."

"Let's see how you get on. Take it out if it gets uncomfortable."

Hours later, he'd slowly stripped me in the living room and led me through to the bedroom. I heard the music first; soft, gentle, unobtrusive. Then I noticed the smell and saw a couple of candles glowing; he must have lit them some time ago, as their scent filled the room. Then I saw the restraints at each corner of the bed.

Now, I was lying on my back on that bed, naked. Wrists tied to each side of the headboard; ankles tied wide apart to the bottom corners. Spread-eagled. Vulnerable. Plug still in my ass. I hadn't needed to remove it; I'd quite enjoyed it. It hadn't hurt, just constantly reminded me it was there, and it had slowly worked on me. I wasn't sure if it was the physical effect or the promise of things to come; didn't matter really.

He slowly stripped himself, looking down at me. Kneeling by the side of the bed, he bent over and planted a delicate kiss on my lips. I tried to respond but couldn't move far enough and he pulled away. I let my head drop back, and he picked up a chiffon scarf and draped it over my eyes. I could see light and shapes, but no detail. Now all I could do was wait. Marcus had told me only a little about what to expect; no toys we hadn't already used, no impact play – except possibly a playful smack or two for the surprise element, and no talking. I had the colours if I needed them, that was enough.

I realised why the music was on. Although it was quiet, it meant I couldn't hear his movements or work out exactly where he was. I felt my body rippling gently, wondering where the first touch would be.

Nothing. Apart from the music.

I couldn't see him, couldn't hear him. I wasn't sure what I was expecting, I knew he was letting my anticipation build. I knew how patient he could be if he wanted. Time seemed to stand still. My body was tense, waiting for something to happen, wanting something to happen.

Nothing. Apart from the music.

Gradually, my body softened. I tried to clear my mind, to relax. After a while, I felt a sense of calm. My need changed. Wearing the plug, being stripped by him, being tied up by him, had all worked to turn me on. I had been wet, horny, driven. Now, that had gone. Well, I was still wet, but I felt different. Warm, safe, comfortable, cared for.

I cried out and seemed to jump three feet in the air. I didn't; I couldn't, but it felt like it. My body reacting to a shower of light touches all over it, from my breasts to my shins. I couldn't work out what it was, couldn't even guess. They stopped almost as soon as they started, and my body dropped again. After a while, a second shower. I didn't jump this time, just lay there, and let their touch invade me. Giving me goosebumps, almost needing to scratch them, knowing I couldn't.

Then nothing. Apart from the music.

A cool sensation appeared between my legs, right between my legs. My pussy was glowing, it had been getting worked up for hours. Now, every few seconds, I felt a cool feeling flow over it. It felt incredible. This continued for a while and I gave up trying to work it out. Suddenly, there was a much colder flash, followed by another and another. And then I gasped as an intense cold seemed to grow around my whole pussy. Engulfing it. The cold penetrating my clit, my lips, and moving into the entrance. Pain? Pleasure? I wasn't sure; the sensation was too strong.

And then it dropped away. I felt my own warmth flow back, and allowed my bum to relax, dropping my hips back towards the bed. How was he doing this? That was already two sensations I couldn't quite figure; I had an idea or two, but …

Then I felt his touch. His touch was magic; had been since we'd first met. He could do things with his fingers that made me melt, made me squeal, made me … his. And it didn't need to be the obvious places either. Now, I felt his fingers on my tummy. He lowered his fingers around my belly button, the touch light, almost imperceptible, but I knew they were there. As he slowly moved them around, little muscles reacted as they came into contact. His fingers moved all over my body. Never losing contact, always touching.

I felt his breath on my skin, then a kiss. Then another. He began to kiss my belly, planting light kisses, then sucking on my skin, pulling it into his mouth. Then light kisses again. Moving around. Working up to my breasts, my shoulders, my neck. I heard his breath; could smell him. Again, working his way around my body, gently kissing. He returned to my breasts, and this time went to my stiff nipples. It felt good as he licked and kissed around them, gently taking them in his mouth, teasing them with his teeth. He pulled away, and gently tugged one with his fingers, massaging it, making it even harder. I felt his breath on my mouth as he kissed me fleetingly. I raised my head for more, but he was gone again.

Suddenly a pain went through the nipple in his hand; a clamp squeezing tight. I took a deep breath in and let it out slowly. He let my breast relax and waited for the initial pain to subside; I knew what was coming next. He twirled my other nipple between his fingers, and I felt the same feeling as he let the clamp gently tighten on that. Pain. Then relax. I felt his lips on mine again briefly; then they were gone.

What next? I briefly tried to understand what I was feeling. Not lust, not a desperate need. Just a feeling of release. Of being in someone else's care. Of having complete trust in them. Was this what it meant to submit?

I felt the bed flex, as he climbed on. He was between my legs, his hands on my shins, slowly moving up. I shuddered as I felt his kiss on my thighs, his breath on my skin. Moving up, almost … Then on my abdomen, moving down. Each time stopping before kissing me where I wanted him to. God, I thought, patience can be overrated.

Then I felt his hands resting either side of my pussy, gently pulling, opening me up. I could feel myself unfolding, my lips swollen, my clit erect. Then it happened. I felt his tongue touch my perineum. My hips jerked as the sensation made its way up my body. But this time, he moved along it in the direction I needed. I knew I was wet; I'd felt my juices running for ages. He slowly licked them, moving up. Up one side of my pussy, avoiding my lips. I tried to shift my body to meet his mouth, but he was too fast; most of the time. He kissed and licked in an arc around my clit and went down the other side. Oh, it was good.

I groaned as I felt his mouth settle over one puffy lip, and gently pull it. Playing with me; licking it, kissing it, teasing it. I was building up now. He moved to the other side, repeating the process. My body was flexing, wanting to go further. I felt his mouth land over my clit, taking it and the hood between his lips, sucking gently. The feeling was all-consuming. He stayed there, covering me with his mouth, manipulating me with his tongue. I wanted him to finish me.

No. He released the pressure, and I felt his mouth move down until it reached my entrance. His tongue started to lick at my wetness, rough against my engorged, sensitive folds. I was moaning now, but it felt strange. Normally I could move around when he did this, allow my body to stretch and move as it wanted to. Not here. Not now. I was tied tight. I could move a little, but not much. He was working me now, fingers gently playing with the lips, mouth moving between pussy and clit. I felt a finger entering me and gently exploring what it found. I was in heaven; still not desperate, a different feeling. I couldn't identify it, but it was working. I was close to coming.

He gently pulled away, and I flopped back with an annoyed grunt. Then I heard a noise. The wand. Oh, God. The wand.

Sally

It touched my thigh first, quite low. The vibration sinking into my skin and muscle. He ran it up and down my thigh, then the other. The noise changed slightly, and I felt him slide it gently underneath me, touching my perineum as he pushed it gently on. I raised my bum, but that brought my cheeks together, preventing him from sliding it further.

"Relax," he said. I did.

This time, I let him slide it up under my bum, the round head working its way between my cheeks, the vibrations travelling through my groin. Suddenly it came into contact with the butt plug, and I moaned aloud as it carried the vibrations deep inside me. He pressed the wand up, pushing it tighter to the plug, and turned the vibration up. I almost came, I was so near now. He knew it. He turned the wand down, and let it rest under my bum. He went back to kissing and licking me, bringing me up again.

But never taking me far enough. Three, four, five times, he brought me to the brink of orgasm. And stopped. I tried everything. I tried to push my pussy towards him; I tried pushing my bum down on the wand. Nothing worked. I'd have to wait until he wanted me to come. Until he allowed me to come.

I felt him move off the bed. Bastard! Couldn't he see my need? Of course he could. That's why he hadn't satisfied it. I sensed him at my side. He moved the scarf from my mouth where part of it had fallen as I had thrashed about and bent down and kissed me. I felt the bed give again as he got on, and I realised he was climbing astride me, knees nestling into my armpits.

Just as I realised what that meant and that I wanted it, I felt the tip of his cock brush my lips. I opened my mouth eagerly, but he was in control here. He ran it along from left to right, and back again. I could taste it but couldn't see it. I could see his shadow through the folds of material moving about above me, looming over me. I felt his cock come to rest on my lips, and I opened my mouth. I gently pushed my tongue forward to lick it, coming up against his frenulum. He gave a little gasp.

Adjusting the angle, he tilted it and allowed me to take the head into my mouth, closing my lips behind the glans. I flicked my tongue around, tasting his pre-cum. Moving my head up, I tried to pull him towards me, so I could take more of him, but he pulled away gently. I dropped my head.

"No," he whispered. "You wouldn't be able to talk to me. Just relax… enjoy."

I knew he was right; I could hardly call out a colour if I had his cock deep in my mouth in this position. But an idea appeared in my head, and I filed it away for the future. He guided his cock over my mouth and let me lick it and suck the head. His audible responses turned me on even more. The ache in my pussy reasserted itself. After a couple of minutes, he pulled away, and I felt him climb off. His lips touched mine again, and his tongue traced around them, tasting himself on me. He moved to my ear.

"Now," he whispered. "I'm going to let you come. I'm going to make you come until you beg me to stop."

I let out a whimper. He climbed off the side of the bed. Moments later, I felt him arrive between my legs. I was breathing hard. I needed to come; was he finally going to let me?

I gasped as I felt his mouth completely cover my pussy, sucking greedily. Drawing everything in, his tongue pushing into me. I was already near when I heard the noise again. The wand. He pulled his mouth away, and this time there was no teasing. I felt the vibrations rush through my groin, as he placed it into the entrance, pushing it and moving it around. I felt his lips on my clit, sucking it hard. I felt myself give in to my need. Those flashes again, those colours. My body tensed as the feeling came over me. I arched my back, and the climax came, rolling over me. Touching every inch of my being.

But something was different. Instead of dropping from the peak, I was still there. He was carrying on. Still pressing the wand into me, still using his mouth. He reached up and flicked the nipple clamps, sending pain through my breasts. He wouldn't let me come down. I felt the sensations again; different now, not as intense, but still rushing through me. Almost immediately, I felt myself building up, heading for the peak again.

I cried out as I came. He slowed, allowed me a few seconds, then transferred the wand to my ass, pressing it up against the plug. My hips jumped off the bed, as the vibrations shot through me, his fingers entering me and roughly fucking me. It didn't take long before he had me squirming, pressing my bum down on the wand to get every sensation. Enjoying his fingers boring into my sex. I came again almost without knowing it.

I was losing it now; my breath was ragged, and I felt a bit lightheaded. How much more could I take? Now the wand was on my clit, pressing against it, running around it, almost painful. And here it was again, that feeling. My body froze as another orgasm soared through me. But this time, it was too much.

"Yellow," I whimpered.

He stopped. Laid a hand on my thigh, gently stroking. I lost track of time for a while. My mind blank, oblivious to everything but my own body. Trying to make sense of it. Coming down.

"Sally?" A whisper by my head …

"Mmm."

"Are you okay?"

"Mmm."

"I'm going to take the scarf off."

I felt the material slide across my face and squinted as my eyes registered the increased light. He was sitting on the edge of the bed, looking at me. A gentle smile, with a hint of concern.

"Shall I release you?"

I'd almost forgotten I was still tied up.

"No hurry."

Bending down, he kissed my forehead, then my cheek, then my lips. His hand went to my tummy and rested there.

"Just relax, take your time. That was quite something."

For a few minutes, I lay there, him stroking my belly.

"Shall I take these off?" he asked. I'd forgotten the nipple clamps as well. "I should have taken them off when you were away with the fairies."

He gently lifted a clamp, and slowly pinched it, releasing the pressure. Then removed the other one. Each time, the pain hit again, as the blood returned. He kissed me hard to take my mind off it. It wasn't very successful, but the pain quickly subsided to soreness.

"Away with the fairies?" I asked.

"Yes, you were away a while."

"How long?"

"About ten minutes after you called yellow."

I was amazed, it had seemed like a moment or two.

"I'm sorry."

"What for?"

"For having to say it."

He bent down and kissed me.

"Don't be," he grinned. "I wanted you to. All part of my wicked little plan. I wanted to see how far I could take you."

"Far enough?"

"For now."

We looked at each other. A sudden urge struck me.

"Marcus, you need to untie me."

An anxious look crossed his face.

"Are you okay?"

"Yes, but I desperately need to pee!"

When I came back, I found answers to one or two questions. The bed was covered in little coloured bits of paper. I picked up a few.

"Confetti?" I said.

"Yes."

"I couldn't work out what it was. And the cold?"

"Ice cubes in my mouth."

"Ah."

"How did it feel?"

"Amazing. And intense."

"It was pretty intense in my mouth as well. After a while, I couldn't feel what I was doing with my lips and tongue."

"Felt good to me!"

I joined him on the bed, and we cuddled together.

"Was that good for you, then?" he asked.

"Oh, yes. We're doing that again. And I want to do it to you as well. Fancy it?"

"Yes. Definitely up for it."

I was now stroking his groin, keeping him aroused. I knew what I wanted next.

"Weren't you tempted to fuck me? I was yours for the taking; couldn't move."

"Oh, yes. Really tempted. Perhaps if you'd been tied up with your bum in the air, I might have."

"Right, that's the position for next time."

"But this time, I wanted to concentrate on you. I wanted to tease you, then push you as far as you could go."

Still stroking his hard cock, I kissed him.

Sally

"Two can play at that game. Why don't I remind you how far this horny little minx can push you?"

Chapter 11 – Marcus

"I thought it was time to prove we don't live on takeaways," I said to Lucy, putting the dishes on the table. This was the third time she had come around for the evening, and on the previous occasions, we'd had Chinese and then pizza. I'd decided to cook this time.

"I don't mind Marcus. Whatever it is, it saves me having to cook."

"Not a fan, then?"

"Oh, I quite like it, but it gets a bit tedious cooking for one."

"Yes, I know the feeling."

"You're a good cook, Luce," Sally put in, offering us some bread.

"When the mood takes me. Every time I split up with someone, I get the urge to spend more time trying new recipes; make new stuff up. But the novelty soon wears off."

"I think you end up with more time on your hands, so you try and fill it. Don't want to sit around moping."

"Could be."

After our first meeting, Lucy and I had stopped interrogating one another, and the conversation flowed easily this time.

"How's the job going, Sal?" Lucy asked.

"Good. A bit more difficult than I'd expected, but it's still good."

"Difficult?"

"Oh, not the actual stuff they need me for. It's the infighting and decision making."

"Bad?"

"It's you academics, you're all the same. Don't know your asses from your elbows but insist you're experts in both."

Lucy laughed.

"We can be a bit pedantic."

"Pedantic? This week I had two of them arguing for days over whether a set text should be the hardback or paperback version of the same book; they're identical."

"What did they decide?"

"They haven't yet, as far as I know. I thought I'd have some fun, so asked 'what about the e-book?' and waited to see if they exploded."

"Did they?"

"Nah. Thinking back, I probably delayed the decision even more."

"Patience, Sal. That's the key. Do you remember when I got that first lecturing job at Leeds? I was so excited; it was everything I wanted. Then I went through the course material I was supposed to work with. It was awful; boring and so out of date. I asked to change it. Talk about heads and brick walls. It took me two years. Since then, I've learnt to be a bit more subtle."

"Yeah, I'm not always very patient, am I?"

"Not one of your virtues, is it Sal?"

"I'm trying …" we exchanged a secret look, both remembering her urgency the previous night, "… he's got the patience of Job, Luce. I'm hoping some of it might rub off on me."

I cleared the dishes and brought back some strawberries and raspberries with a tub of fromage frais.

"Are you still doing the life classes?" Sally asked Lucy.

"Yeah, I'm enjoying it. I've quite surprised myself."

"Why are you doing it?" I asked.

"Not sure really. Just fancied brushing up my skills. It's run by one of my colleagues, and he lets me sit in."

"Not just to ogle a naked woman, then?" Sal joked.

"Have you ever been to a life class?" Lucy replied. "Believe me, the models aren't chosen for their beauty. It's mostly for their extra folds of fat, or their interesting skin complaints. Half of them are men anyway. There's not much for me to get excited about. Besides, we're artists, we don't get excited."

We both gave her a withering look; she laughed.

"No, seriously. People really are there to concentrate and learn. It's probably the least fun you can have in the same room as a naked person. There's nothing at all erotic about it. Trust me."

"Methinks she doth protest too much!" I said.

She looked at me, a sly smile on her face.

"Besides, there's only been one girl who was interesting."

Sally looked at me; we had both picked up on the way Lucy had framed that sentence.

"And?" Sally asked.

"And what?" Lucy replied slowly, a grin on her face.

"Was interesting, or is interesting?"

"Don't know yet. But I'm thinking of finding out."

***

"It's your birthday soon," Sally said. "Anything you'd like to do?"

"No idea. Don't normally do anything for my birthday."

"Why not?"

"Never liked parties, didn't have a large circle of friends, and I get embarrassed being the centre of attention. Having a crowd stand around me while I open cards and presents is my idea of hell. I want the floor to swallow me up.

"And then that awkwardness when you open something, look at it, and want to ask why? Why did you buy me this? Did you think I'd like this? Did you think about this at all? But you have to force a look of delight and tell them how wonderful it was; before putting it on eBay. Or chucking it in the bin."

"Ooh, you old grouch!"

"Possibly. I love giving presents, though. You need to know a person to do it right. Spend time thinking about them; what they like, who they are, what their tastes are. I've been given things I imagine had come from a sweep around a pound shop."

"Hasn't anyone got it right?"

"Oh, yes. I've been lucky, too. One or two of my partners have been givers as well, and we had fun, especially at Christmas, when we shared dozens of presents. Not expensive, but things we'd thought about. Things we enjoyed watching each other open."

"What do you do on your birthday?"

I thought for a moment.

"I get a few cards and one or two texts."

"Is that it?"

"Well, I buy some good chocolates, some favourite food, and normally buy myself a present."

"A present?"

"Yes. Something I really want; it tends to be when I get myself some new tech."

"Ah …"

"You know, replace my iPhone or iPad, that sort of thing."

"At least you know you'll like it."

"Exactly."

"But are you happy with that? Would you like to do something?"

Eventually, I had to confess I wasn't, and I would. Oh, no parties. No crowds of people. But a friend or two, a good meal and a relaxing evening. Something to distinguish that one day from every other.

"And perhaps a surprise or two?" Sally added.

"Yes. That'd be nice."

"I could always wear a ribbon and a bow. Not sure where I'd stick it."

I grabbed her and showed her where I thought it might look good.

Chapter 12 – Sally

"What? How did you manage that?"

Lucy grinned. "She modelled for the class again, so I asked her if she ever did it privately. One to one."

"And now, she comes around to yours and poses just for you."

"Yup."

"Naked."

"Yup."

"Do you get anything done? Any actual drawing, I mean."

"Yes. Of course. What else would we do?"

"Ah, so you haven't got anywhere yet?"

She looked wistful.

"Not yet, no."

"Chances?"

"Well, I made sure she knew. Since then, she has been asking the odd question, quite detailed sometimes."

"Is she curious, then?"

"Possibly. I haven't asked her directly. And I am getting a lot of practice sketching her. So at least I'm getting something out of it."

"What, like frustrated?"

"A bit," she said, grinning.

"Just ask her, Luce."

"Yes, I might; she's only here for another six months, so nothing to lose really. Have you worked out what you're doing for Marcus's birthday yet?"

"I've got a few ideas."

"Apart from the ribbons and bow!"

I'd told her about the conversation I'd had with him about birthdays.

"Yes. It's on a Saturday, so I'm thinking about a few things. Spreading it over the weekend. Fancy joining us for dinner on the Friday?"

"I thought you'd want him to yourself."

"Oh, there'll be plenty of time for that. I thought about inviting Mary as well."

"I haven't seen her for a while. How is she?"

"Much better. Seems it was probably a post-viral thing, and there's a good chance she'll recover. She's already starting to get out and about more, and she does like Marcus."

"That would be good. I'm in if you're inviting. Do you want me to pick Mary up?"

***

The plans were coming along nicely. I'd told him nothing. I had booked the Monday morning off, so I could stay over Sunday night as well. That gave us three evenings; one was filled, so now I had to think of the other two. I also spent time buying things for him; some of them were for us, but I didn't think he'd mind. I wanted to give him a really special birthday.

While I was doing all this, I thought about Marcus and me. We'd been lovers for a few months now. We'd gone into it with our eyes open. We were helping each other explore and getting a hell of a lot out of it. But we knew at the beginning it wasn't a normal relationship. I suppose you would call us friends with benefits. Neither of us liked the expression, and I began to realise I hated it. It didn't sum up my feelings at all now.

We spent most weekends together, and not just in bed. We enjoyed each other's company, each other's sense of humour; enjoyed … quiet companionship. I smiled every time I thought of that phrase. It summed up our relationship. Well, most of it, until it burst into a blaze of passion or sensuality. I couldn't think of anything missing.

So, what was our relationship? What were my feelings for Marcus? How did this compare with my previous lovers? One thought kept coming back. Trust. I didn't trust people easily, hadn't for years. Every time I did, things seemed to conspire against me. The past came back to ruin things.

But some of the things Marcus and I did needed absolute trust and we had had to evaluate each other more quickly. And I trusted him completely, had never doubted him. And he seemed to trust me. That felt good. But I realised this was getting a bit more complicated than I'd expected.

***

"Don't worry, Marcus. They're under strict instructions. I've told them on no account are they to stick a party hat on your head and sing 'Happy Birthday'. Besides, this isn't McDonalds."

I'd brought us back to 'our' restaurant, where we'd first discovered mutual interests. We still came back occasionally. Even when it was full, it didn't feel overwhelming, and it was a bit special to us. We'd dressed up for the occasion. I'd worn the red dress that always reminded me of that first session with him. I'd thought carefully what I'd wear under it as well.

"Are you not a fan of birthdays, Marcus?" Mary asked.

"Well, I don't mind birthdays, Mary. But I'm not very good at some of the fuss that goes with them."

"Fuss?"

"Yeah. I don't like being the centre of attention. I get … embarrassed, I suppose. Then I don't enjoy it."

"Well, each to their own. I've always liked attention." She smiled.

I knew this side of her; she was right, she had always been the life and soul of the party. Marcus only got to know her after she was ill, when she'd been exhausted all the time. But she was getting some of that spark back now. It was so good to see.

After our starters arrived, the conversation flowed. Marcus knew us well enough to feel comfortable now. We knew him well enough to know he didn't join in all the time. His periods of silence weren't rudeness or boredom. He listened; only spoke when he had something to say, not because he felt he should. It was something I really liked about him.

"Found your dream girl yet, Lucy?" Mary asked with her tongue firmly in her cheek.

"Funny you should say that Mary …" She paused. "No." Mary laughed. "But I have met someone who might keep me entertained for a while."

She caught my questioning glance and winked. She'd obviously made some progress there.

"Well, have fun when you can, dear. I always say it's better to regret what you did than regret what you didn't do."

"That's a fine philosophy, Mary," Marcus said.

He was having a glass of wine tonight. He was careful with alcohol, it sometimes caused him problems. Mary had found this too, but not been as accepting as him. She liked a drink.

The evening went well, we were all relaxed. The food was good as usual, and we wished Marcus a happy birthday – quietly. I told him both Lucy and Mary had given me presents for him and he could open them at home tomorrow. I saw even this embarrassed him slightly, but his gratitude to them was genuine enough.

"Wait until you've opened them," Mary joked. "We did check them with Sally first, so it's her fault if you don't like them."

"Thanks!" I said.

"You're welcome, darling."

By the end of the meal, Mary was beginning to tire a little and asked if she should call a taxi, or if Lucy was ready to take her home. Lucy was happy to oblige. But I could see Mary was pleased to have lasted the evening. They both wished Marcus happy birthday for tomorrow, gave him a hug and a kiss, and we were left alone. We popped to the toilets and came back. I rested on the bench beside him, leaning into him.

"Do you remember when I first wore this dress?"

"I'll never forget it."

"Do you still like it?"

"Yes, you look wonderful."

"Well, how about we go home, and I'll show you what I'm wearing underneath."

I paid for the taxi, and we headed for the door. I was feeling good. Very good now. Starting to anticipate the next hour or so. I'd had to control myself during the meal, because after thinking for ages what to wear under my dress this evening, I'd finally decided. Nothing. Nothing at all. But I'd known if I got worked up, it could have got … messy. As we went inside, I felt moisture between my legs, but it didn't matter now. I knew, after what I'd said, he'd be thinking about my underwear; he loved lingerie. I did too, it made me feel good. But most of all, I enjoyed the reaction it prompted in him.

As I turned around from closing the door, he waited for me in the hallway. I walked over to him and put my arms around his neck. He took my head in his hands and kissed me. He slowly ran his hands down my neck, then my back, making me shiver. He reached my bum, and gently squeezed my cheeks, separating them through the material of my dress. I felt his hand reach the hem, but before he could lift it, I gently pulled away.

"Patience, Marcus. Patience."

I took his hand and led him into the living room. By the sofa, I stopped and stood in front of him. Kissing him, I slid his jacket off his shoulders and let it drop. Still kissing him, I undid his tie and threw it on the floor. His shirt followed. I dropped to my knees, and undid his trousers, slowly lowering them to the floor; he stepped out of them, and I took off his socks. Looking up at him, I put a finger in each side of his briefs, and slowly lowered those. As he sprang free, I whipped them down his legs and off.

Without taking my eyes from his, I laid one hand along the bottom of his stiff cock, and the other under his balls. I slowly took the end in my mouth, and kept going, taking as much in as I could. He shuddered. I pulled away again and repeated the process a few times. He appeared to be enjoying it. I stopped, and still holding his sex, I stood up.

"On the sofa. Make yourself comfortable."

I kissed him, and he sat down. I put some music on and returned to stand directly in front of him. I'd never been an exhibitionist, but since I'd been with Marcus, I was becoming more comfortable about teasing and entertaining him. Not good at it, but more willing, and he loved it.

"Do you remember what happened when I first wore this dress?"

I tried to move softly to the music, running my hands up and down my dress. I hoped it looked sexy rather than demented.

"Yes."

"So do I. You put me over your knee, lifted my dress and spanked me. The first time. Then you peeled my knickers off and continued on my bare ass. Do you remember?"

"Yes." He was keeping his cock entertained, as he watched me.

"And then you used your fingers on me. You fingered me until I came."

I was quite in the mood now, feeling good. I went with it. Just moving gently, trying to sound seductive.

"Do you remember what happened next?"

"I seem to remember you were disappointed!"

"And why was I disappointed?"

"Because you wanted me to spank your ass, then bend you over and fuck you. That was your fantasy."

I could feel the moisture creeping down my thighs, my sex swelling.

"Would you like to fulfil that fantasy for me now? Take me over your knee, spank me until my cheeks are red, then bend me over and use me. Use me until you're spent."

"Yes," he said simply.

"Dress on or off?"

"You were going to show me what was underneath it."

"Off, then."

I reached and grabbed the hem, slowly lifting it, pulling it up and over my head, letting it drop behind me. I stood there naked.

He ran his eyes over my body, and I turned around slowly, so he could take it all in. I knew he'd noticed the change I'd made.

"Have you been like that all evening?"

"Yup. I wanted to tell you; to tease you by telling you. But I knew if I did, I might get in a bit of a mess."

He looked between my legs. I parted them slightly, exposing my newly shaven mound.

"Do you like it?" I asked.

"Looks good. But I'll need a test drive or two. Just to make sure."

He held out his arm, and I moved towards him. I took his hand, and he pulled me firmly, almost on to him. I ended up kneeling over the sofa, astride one of his legs. He brought his head close to mine.

"I'm looking forward to tracing my tongue over that smooth skin."

I was gently rubbing myself against his thigh. I sighed as we kissed.

"But not now," he whispered.

"No," I whispered back. "Now, you're going to spank me until I scream, then fuck me until I squeal."

He looked at me, lust in his eyes.

"Say please …"

I giggled.

"Please."

"Good girl. Over my knee."

I shifted position and laid over his lap, his cock pressing up into my belly. I felt his hand touch my bum and start to rub it. As the first stroke landed on my right cheek, I closed my eyes and gave in to the moment.

***

I opened my eyes. Sunlight silhouetted the curtains. I looked over to Marcus; he was lying on his back. I listened. Was he still asleep? He normally woke before me, but I hoped I'd beaten him to it this morning. I watched and listened. Yes, definitely still asleep. I tested it by wriggling about a bit, but he didn't stir. It had been a warm night, so I hoped he wouldn't wake as I slowly pulled the duvet off him.

He made a couple of sounds, but it was soon on the floor. I looked down at him. He didn't like his body at times. He certainly didn't have a six-pack – too many surgery scars. But I didn't care; I knew how sensitive he was to my touch, and I loved watching his response to it, as he did with me.

I looked between his legs. It had always amused me how much men varied when not aroused. Some almost as big as when they were erect, others small and compact. I'd learned years ago you couldn't tell anything from this; Marcus was proof. His cock was big, but looking at him, flaccid, you wouldn't have guessed. As I gazed at him, I wondered …

Kneeling by his hips, and leaning down, I gently pulled his sac, so his balls came free from between his legs. He moved slightly. I lowered my mouth over his limp cock, moving down and pushing his balls gently together. Holding my tongue to one side, I managed to get them in my mouth as well. Just. I closed my lips around the base as best I could, and started sucking my cheeks in. Well, I'd done it. But I couldn't do anything with it. There was no wriggle room.

I slowly released it, but I'd already had some effect. I could see it was starting to grow. I started working on his balls, licking and sucking, taking them into my mouth one at a time. More sound from Marcus now. I moved to his cock; still growing. Slowly pulling the foreskin back, I began to lick the glans with my tongue. It had a different feel before it was engorged with blood. Placing my lips over the head I began to gently suck, sometimes sliding them further down his shaft, still massaging his balls. I was enjoying the feeling of him swelling in my mouth.

109

Sally

He woke up with a slight start. After a few seconds, he looked down quizzically. Then chuckled as he saw me kneeling by his side, my lips over his cock. I smiled up at him. Removing my mouth, I continued to massage his balls with one hand and moved towards him. I kissed him.

"Good morning. Happy birthday."

"Good morning," he said, stretching a little. "Thank you."

He reached out to touch me.

"Ah, ah, ah. No touching. Just lie there and enjoy."

Kissing him again, I moved back down his body and gave him his first present of the day.

"That was a hell of a way to start the day," Marcus said as I put the tray by the bed.

"Now breakfast. First course. Champagne and strawberries."

"Perhaps birthdays aren't so bad after all …"

He propped himself up, I lay by his side and we drank champagne. I fed him strawberries. Gave him a couple of small presents to open. We didn't speak. Just a gentle kiss occasionally; a 'thank you' from him. Looking at the bottle, I asked if he wanted more champagne.

"No, I don't think so. Not at this time of the day."

"I didn't think this through," she said, looking thoughtful. "It won't keep. Seems a shame to waste it."

"It does, doesn't it?"

He suddenly jumped off the bed, and I shrieked with surprise as he grabbed my arm and pulled me off it too. I saw that look on his face; he'd had an idea. He picked up the bottle, and led me out of the bedroom, into the bathroom.

"Get in the shower," he said.

"What?"

"In the shower, go on …"

I got in and turned to face him. He was raising the bottle above my head, and it dawned on me what he was going to do.

"Marcus!" I cried and gave another shriek as he upended it, and the cold champagne rained down on me, taking my breath away. Drenching my hair and cascading down my body. It felt weird; fizzing slightly as it ran over my skin. After the initial shock, I started to laugh. When he'd emptied it, he put the bottle down, and looked at me, a broad smile on his face. I could feel my hair hanging wet and limp; I could feel the droplets all over my body. My nipples had reacted instantly to the cold liquid. He slowly let his eyes rove over my nakedness.

"Champagne suits you."

"Marcus," I replied, trying not to giggle. "I'm all wet now."

"Well," he said, stepping into the shower. "I'd better dry you off then."

Starting on my lips, he began to kiss and lick me. Moving down my neck and shoulders, turning me around to do my back, then turning me again to work on my breasts and nipples. Gradually going lower and lower. I didn't remember the champagne ever reaching one or two of the crevices or folds he explored, but by the time he got there, they were wet enough. And he spent some time getting acquainted with my newly shaved pussy while I leaned against the cold tiles. I think he liked it. I certainly did.

Chapter 13 – Marcus

After we'd showered, and I'd convinced Sally her hair didn't smell like a wine bar, I got dressed, and went out to open the flat up, while she dried her hair. When I went into the living room, I saw a pile of presents on the coffee table, a big pile. Mostly small, but one or two bigger ones. One was so big it was on the floor, propped up against the edge. I regretted telling her about bygone Christmases and hoped she hadn't taken it as a hint. I hadn't meant it that way.

I heard her call from the bedroom.

"Marcus? Can I borrow you a minute?"

I went through and found her lying naked on the bed on her front. She was facing me, head resting in her hands, feet waving in the air. It was a favourite view of mine, as I could follow the curve of her body, generally not getting much further than the gentle rise of her bum. But that curve was broken today by a little beribboned box resting in the small of her back.

"Want to open the next one?"

"I'm beginning to think you've gone a bit mad."

"No, just wanted you to have fun. Open it."

I kissed her, placed my hand on the back of her neck, and ran my fingers down her back until it reached the present. I picked it up and sat beside her. She looked up at me as I took off the bow, and fought my way in. A little butt plug; stainless steel, with an impressed 'M' in the end.

"I saw that and thought of you," she said. "Want to put it in for me? I want to wear it all day."

I went behind her, picking up some lube on the way. She spread her legs, and within a few seconds, it was in.

"Comfy?"

"Yes. Do you like having your initial there?"

I gave her bum a playful slap.

"Horny little minx. Thank you."

"You're welcome. I know some of your presents are really for us …"

"I don't mind at all."

"Didn't think you would. Want me to put anything on? I've got this evening planned, but between now and then?"

I looked down her body and laughed.

"If you've got plans for this evening, I suspect I might need to save some energy. So, no, let's just chill out."

"You can open them all at once, or I can drip feed them to you through the day. Oh, and I've got one special present for you later, as well."

"Okay, drip-feed then. That sounds fun. But I still think you've overdone it."

Over breakfast, she gave me three more presents to open. A subscription to a writer's forum, a very intricate metal puzzle, and a first edition Patrick O'Brian, one of my favourite authors. Then the present from Mary. It was quite heavy. Opening it I saw a cast figure of a dog. I had one already, a cherished present from my past. A memory of a much-missed hound. This one was similar and equally beautiful.

"She remembered you noticing hers, so found something similar."

"It's beautiful, Sally. I'll ring her later."

"Want to open Lucy's?"

"Yes, why not?"

"It's the big one on the floor."

We went over to the coffee table, and Sally sat on the sofa while I got to grips with the wrapping paper. It was a framed drawing of a nude. Simple, very subtle. A delicate combination of minimal lines, and a little shading.

"Oh, it's beautiful. One of hers?"

"Yes."

"Is this Zoe?"

"Yeah, I think so. She didn't want to give it to you, though."

"Protective of her muse?"

"No, nothing like that. She doesn't think they're good enough. But when she showed me some of the stuff she'd been doing, this was one of them. I thought of you, can't think why."

"Nor me, disgusting!"

"When she talked to me about what to give you, I suggested this. I think she's still expecting you to send it back."

"Well, she can't have it."

Over the next few hours, she gently pampered me. Made me a favourite for lunch. The presents were gradually opened. She got everything spot on; the silly ones were genuinely silly, including a set of chocolate spoons. The thoughtful ones were just that. Considering we'd not known each other long, I was surprised as I gradually realised how well she knew me already. I did wonder at one point how I was going to match this on her birthday in a couple of months.

By the middle of the afternoon, the pile was much reduced. A larger box, and a few small ones. She made some tea and brought in some eclairs. Still treating me. After we'd eaten two each, she gave me the larger present.

When I opened it, I was speechless. I looked at her. She placed her finger under my chin and closed my mouth, which had dropped open.

"Well, you needed to replace yours, didn't you?" she asked.

"Yes, but …"

"And you said you've always wanted one."

"Yes, but …"

"Happy birthday Marcus," she said, kissing me.

"But …"

I had been an Apple fan for years; I had the iPhone, the iPad, the watch. Even the TV box. But I did most of my writing on a Windows laptop; cheap, functional, and old. Now, resting on my lap, was a MacBook Pro. She was right, I had always wanted one. But never considered it; I could never justify the cost. And now, someone I'd only known six months had bought me one.

"Sally. Thank you. I don't know what to say."

She leaned forward and kissed me.

"You've said 'thank you'," she said softly. "You don't need to say any more."

"I know you said special, but that's more than special."

She gave me a flirty look.

"Oh, that's not the special one."

"Sally …"

"Have I embarrassed you?"

"Close."

"Sorry," she smiled. "Didn't mean to."

"I know. Thank you."

"Are you enjoying your birthday?"

"God, yes. It's been wonderful."

"It's not over yet."

She took the MacBook and placed it on the table before climbing astride me, arms on my shoulders, leaning over me.

"Still got to give you your special present." She was talking softly, flirting with me, her eyes bright and enticing. "Want to know what it is?"

"I think you're going to tell me."

"Yeah, I think I will."

She was kissing me lightly in between each phrase.

"I'm going to give you my cherry." I raised an eyebrow and she slapped my arm playfully. "No, not that one. Not sure I can even remember losing that. But I do have one left." I knew what she meant. "And I want to give it to you. Tonight."

She was still moving around my face, planting delicate little kisses. She'd also started gently moving her hips and thighs on my lap.

"I want to give you my ass," she whispered into my ear. "Do you want it?"

"Yes. I do."

"I can tell," she giggled, pushing her groin onto mine. "I want you to stretch it. I want to feel you inside it. I want you to fuck it. I want you to come in it. Do you want to?"

"Yes."

"Good boy!"

That broke the tension. She pulled away and smiled at me.

"I thought we might have a bath, get dressed up a bit, then I'll cook dinner. After that, I thought we'd enjoy each other; no pressure, no playing. I want to be relaxed. Sound good?"

I kissed her.

"Yes. Sounds perfect."
"Does, doesn't it?"

Later, we had a bath together; warm, soft. Soaping and rubbing one another. Letting our hands wander. Nothing that went too far, we were saving that for later. But lovely, nonetheless.

Afterwards, she asked me to put a larger plug in – 'to get things started' – and I put on a suit and tie. She occasionally liked us both to dress up; more fun to take it all off. She sat naked at the dressing table watching me.

"Off you go. I don't want you to see me till I'm ready."

When she eventually came through, I just stared at her. She was wearing a blue dress I knew she felt good in. She'd spent time on her hair and makeup. Subtle, as always. Blue heels, just-white sheer stockings. I immediately tried to guess what was under the dress. And a blue bow in her hair.

"Sally, you look stunning."

She did a slow twirl.

"Like it?"

"Good enough to eat."

She smiled.

"Maybe later."

She came over and kissed me. I touched her hair.

"I did try wrapping myself in ribbon, but it looked silly. You'll have to make do with the bow."

I sat on a stool in the kitchen as she cooked dinner. We shared a word, a look, a kiss. She continued to indulge me; ham and asparagus, followed by lamb. We took our time over dinner. Enjoying the occasion. Every so often, she'd flirt; an expression, a look, a phrase. We both knew she was teasing me, so it didn't work us up too much, but it was getting us in the mood.

When we finished, we moved to the sofa, and she gave me the last two presents. A box of my favourite chocolates, and one of the few Prince DVDs I didn't have. I had been a fan almost from the beginning, and Sally loved him too. She put it on, and we watched it while dinner settled. Curled around me, we let ourselves touch and kiss each other slowly, taking breaks to feed each other chocolates. I had the advantage here, as her dress made her more accessible than I was.

After stroking her stockinged legs, I eventually reached the top, and laid my hand on her bare thigh, hardly moving it. Just pulsing my fingers on her skin. It felt so good, and her little movements to allow access showed me it was good for her too. When the film ended, she put some music on and turned back to me.

"I think it's about time I showed you what I'm wearing under this dress, don't you?"

Standing in front of me, she pushed the dress off each shoulder, watching me. She slid it down in a slow, sensuous movement until it dropped to the floor. She picked it up and threw it out of the way.

"Well? Right choice?"

She knew the answer. It was probably our favourite set at the moment. Almost colourless, but with defined edges and subtle decoration. Bra, briefs, wide suspender belt. And sheer, almost completely transparent. Definitely there but hiding nothing. With the matching stockings, and her heels still on. I thought she looked fabulous in it. I knew she felt fabulous in it too and could already see her arousal.

"Beautiful."

She turned around slowly, allowing me to enjoy everything she was offering, bending forward slightly, so I could see the plug still in her rear end. She turned back to face me and held out her hand; I stood up. She took the next few minutes slowly undressing me, rubbing her body against mine as she did so. Teasing me by going to kiss me, then drawing away as I went to meet her lips.

When I was naked, she stood in front of me and pressed herself into me, finally allowing me to wrap my hands around her and caress anything I could reach. We kissed now, and I could see so much depth in her eyes. So much passion.

"So," she whispered, still rubbing her body against mine. "I thought maybe I'd seduce you. Satisfy you. Then perhaps take a break. Then if you still want to eat me …" I smiled. "… that might get us ready for your special present. How does that sound?"

I kissed her, my hands clutching her bum.

"Perfect," I replied.

She had become more confident in taking control in these situations. Really enjoyed it sometimes. Tonight was one of those times and I was happy to let her. She dropped to her knees, and slowly used her mouth on me for a few minutes. Rising, she gently pushed me onto the floor on my back, spreading my legs. She stood between them, and peeled off her bra, dropping it to the floor beside us.

In time to the track playing, she squeezed her breasts and pinched her nipples. Then she turned around, and bent forward, right down to touch the floor, stretching her briefs tight over her bum. God, that was a view. Putting a finger in each side of the waist, she slowly peeled them off, down her legs, and stepped out of them.

Kneeling between my legs, she started licking me, her eyes wide. In no hurry, she teased and toyed with me, using every little trick she knew to give me pleasure. Using her lips, her tongue, and her whole mouth, she soon had me sighing and whimpering. Watching me; her eyes burning into me, erotic and sultry. After a while, she lifted her head.

"Would you like a different view?"

I smiled, and she got up. Dropping to her knees by my head, she bent and kissed me gently. Then she lifted her leg, and straddled me, bending again to reach my cock. As I looked up, I took in the sight. Her bum was above my chest, cheeks spread apart, plug securely in place. Her thighs were covered in shimmering moisture, coming from her sex which was pink and swollen. I felt her lips encase me again and do their beautiful work.

I knew what her rule would be for this position tonight. I could look and enjoy. I could touch her legs, her thighs, her bum. But if I tried to touch between her legs, she would stop, and lift it all out of reach. So I rested my hands on her calves, stroking with open palms. Gradually working up her thighs, finally resting them on her bum. I gently began pulling her cheeks apart and pushing them together, watching the plug move as her ass flexed. Her pussy stretched and contracted as I did so. I could hear little moans now and then, and I felt her mouth working harder now.

A little shiver ran through her, and she knelt back up. Getting off me, she turned around and bent down to kiss me again. She moved down and straddled my hips. Looking into my eyes, she guided my cock into her pussy and lowered herself all the way down. Leaning back, and putting her hands on the floor behind her, she began to rock herself back and forth on me. I loved watching her do this. After a while she sat up and started stroking her breasts, slowly moving her hands between her legs. I loved watching her do this even more.

Still rocking on me, she started to play with herself. I could see she was near. She moved faster, grinding harder, and using both hands to stroke her lips and clit. As she reached the apex, her eyes closed, and she let out a few loud groans. I felt her muscles spasm gently around my cock. She stopped, breathing deeply, her eyes still closed. Her hands dropped onto my tummy, and she looked down at me. Smiling, she bent forward and kissed me.

"Now it's your turn."

Still kissing me, she started to raise her hips up and down, slowly at first but rapidly speeding up. I knew I didn't have a chance. With that fire in her eyes, she looked down.

"Now come for me … Come on … Come for me …"

I did. As I did, she paused at the bottom of every downstroke, holding my cock as far into her as possible, then rising, trying to squeeze every last drop out of me, before dropping hard. After doing this a few times, she bent and kissed me again, then laid on my chest, head by mine. I put my arms around her, and we got our breath back. When we had, she raised her head again and smiled.

"Like a break before round two?"

I heard her go through to the bedroom after leaving the bathroom.

"Might need these," she smiled, coming back in, laying on the table some lube and a dildo.

She kicked her shoes off and cuddled up to me on the sofa. We had plenty of time. No words; just touches, kisses. Bliss.

"Well," I said. "I fancy something to eat."

"Anything in particular?"

"Yes. You."

She kissed me, exploring my mouth with her tongue. I knew it would be a while before I was ready again, but that gave me plenty of time to enjoy her and make her feel relaxed.

"Where do you want me?"

"Wherever you're comfortable. This is about you, not me."

She stood up, and I looked at her, naked now, except for the suspender belt and stockings. Still looking fabulous. She sat on the sofa beside me and laid back. I opened her legs and knelt between them. Leaning up over her, I gave her a kiss, then started moving down her body, still kissing as I went. When I reached her sex, I moved past it and concentrated on her thighs. I pulled her forward slightly, so I could reach more of her. I placed my hands either side of her pussy, and slowly pulled it apart, watching the lips move, and the folds open up. All covered in glistening moisture.

Gently licking her thighs, I moved suddenly to cover her with my mouth, and she gave a little surprised shiver, before settling back again. I sucked her hard into my mouth and let it relax a few times, before releasing my grip, and starting to lick her sweetness with my tongue. I enjoyed the taste of her, and even though I could detect traces of myself from our earlier coupling, tonight was no different.

I spent some time toying with her; using my tongue, lips, and fingers to explore every millimetre. I was soon getting the response I loved. Her reactions to oral sex varied considerably. Sometimes it drove her wild, but at others, as now, when she had already taken the edge off her lust, it was much softer. Now, she laid back and went with it; not needing, not desperate. Just taking, her body moving as if in slow motion. I had improved my technique too and was better able to read her responses. To know what she wanted. Sometimes I gave it to her, sometimes I denied her. It was fun.

But tonight, I didn't deny her. Working slowly, I brought her to a couple of orgasms, so delicate you might almost have missed them. But we felt them. I pulled her forward a little more so I could reach under her to the plug. She looked down and stroked my hair. Slowly lifting her legs, she locked her arms behind her folded knees.

"How's that?" she asked.

"Much better. Beautiful."

It was. Completely open, completely exposed. Uninhibited. And fucking gorgeous.

I started tracing around her with my fingers; running them around her lips, allowing them to slide down her perineum and around the plug. All now well moistened. I looked up at her; eyes closed, her mouth slightly open in a faint smile, her tongue slowly playing along her teeth. Lowering my mouth to her, I started to play again and to manipulate the plug in her ass. Slowly pressing and rocking it.

Her body responded, little moans coming from above me. As she built, I started to ease the plug out, bit by bit, allowing it to slide back in when her response told me to. Gradually, I could ease it out to its thickest point, still using my mouth to tease her. Another little ripple ran through her body, and I left the plug in place.

I settled back on my heels, stroking her thighs. Her face was now gently flushed; that colour I still found cute, and very attractive. She opened her eyes.

"Turn over," I said softly. She smiled, a hint of shyness crossing her face, and dropped her legs to the floor. Leaning forward, she kissed me, slid to her knees, and turned to bend forward over the sofa. I was responding now, enjoying what I'd done, but also enjoying what I was seeing. I laid my swelling cock between her cheeks and lay over her, pressing myself into her body. She sighed as she felt me against her.

I kissed her cheek, and pushing her hair to one side, kissed her neck a few times. Rising, I put my hand between her legs, stroking her, and she automatically opened them slightly, pushing her bum up towards me. I gripped the plug and started moving it again, firmer now, stretching her. I slowly pulled it out, and bent down, running my tongue around her ass, bringing another round of little moans to join those from my fingers between her legs.

I picked the things up off the table and put them on the sofa beside us. Kneeling in behind her, I guided my cock into the entrance to her pussy, and slowly slid it in. She groaned as she felt me penetrate her. I dribbled some lube onto her ass and started to massage it in. Gradually pushing, my finger went inside, and I worked it around. Another moan. I slowly introduced a second finger, spreading her wider. A little gasp. All the while, making sure she remembered my cock was in her.

Removing my fingers, I spread lube on the dildo and pressed the end to her. Again, she pushed up to meet it. I pressed it down, twisting and turning it, and suddenly the end popped through the initial barrier; another gasp, and it slipped further in. I began to rock my cock backwards and forwards, in rhythm with the dildo. I listened to Sally; definitely pleasure. After a minute or two, I let the dildo slip out, an intake of breath as it did so. Her tight hole was slightly open now, ready.

I covered my cock with lube and dribbled some more on her ass.

"Do you want me?" I whispered.

"Yes," she hissed, almost before I'd finished the question.

I shuffled a little closer and placed the head against her hole, slowly rubbing it around the surface. Making tiny movements, I began to apply pressure. Little gasps, as I went a little further each time. I saw her hands grip the back edge of the cushions. The tip was through now, her muscles relaxing to take more of my glans. With a stronger push, the head finally breached the barrier, and her ring of muscle contracted back around my shaft. A cry as it did so, followed by a few short, sharp breaths. I paused, to let her relax again. A sudden deep throaty chuckle gave me permission to continue.

I began to rock backwards and forwards, moving in slightly, then pulling the head back against her muscles from the inside, stretching them again. More sounds from her throat. Slowly, I invaded her further, bit by bit. Each stroke going in further than the last. Occasional grunts. Finally, I found myself fully immersed, and she realised it as she felt my balls against her skin. Another deep chuckle. I leaned carefully over her and kissed her neck.

"Okay?" I whispered.

"Yes."

"How does it feel?"

"Full."

My turn to chuckle. I raised myself up again and began to move my cock around inside her. A little in and out, but more round and round. Allowing the head to brush around inside, to stimulate the sensitive nerves all around it. She was breathing heavily now, slightly unevenly. I reached down, and gently flicked her clit. Instant reaction. I continued, and very quickly an orgasm rolled through her. I stopped; let her relax again. Then I pushed a hand under her waist, and dropped back on my heels, taking her with me, my cock still in her ass. She let out a cry as her weight fell on me, driving me deeper. I placed my arms around her tummy, exploring it and her breasts and nipples.

"Try moving," I said softly, "ride it."

She started moving her hips. Rocking backwards and forwards, side to side, round and round. Little gasps and moans as she did so. I moved my hands down in front of her, reaching between her legs. It felt strange, knowing she was impaled on me, but her pussy was open; available. I made the most of it. Stroking, pressing, teasing. She responded, and another little shudder went through her.

I slowly pushed two fingers into her, and she groaned, moving more urgently on my cock. She'd found the right motion now. I slowly introduced two fingers from my other hand. She groaned louder. Gently rubbing my four fingers into the tissue inside her, I used a thumb to tweak her clit. That did it. She cried out and ground herself onto me. Her body trembling. Her head tilted back, and she let out a long, low sound I'd never heard before, and slumped forward; arms flopping on to the cushions, head dropping between her shoulders. Limp; breathing unsteady and heavy. I withdrew my fingers, and held her tight, hugging her to me.

I felt her coming back; an arm came off the sofa and laid over one of mine on her tummy.

"Are you okay?"

"Oh, fuck!"

I kissed her neck. She shivered.

"Do you want me to come out?"

"No. Give me a minute."

I did. Her breathing slowly calmed. I held her. Close.

"Wow!" she finally said. "Wow! Wow! Wow! What was that?"

"Was it good?"

"Oh, boy. Yes."

I kissed her neck; no shivers this time, just a head movement to allow me to continue.

"Your turn now," she said.

"Sure?"

"Yes. This is supposed to be your present, after all."

"Right."

In one movement, I rose, pushing us both forward. She let out a little shriek as she landed over the sofa, feeling my stiffness deeper inside her. I gently pulled out until the head of my cock hit the inside of her ring. I dribbled some more lube over us. I knew I wasn't going to last long, so I started moving in and out, feeling her tightness move up and down my shaft as I did so. Sally was uttering little gasps and moans on every stroke. I looked down; what a sight. Her gorgeous bum spread wide. My cock travelling in and out of her ass. That did it for me. I felt the moment approach, and my cum flooded into her. It was quite an orgasm, causing me to jerk more than usual.

As I subsided, I stroked her back and bum, then bent carefully over her.

"Are you okay?"

"Yeah."

"Want me to come out?"

"No, stay there."

She liked to feel my weight on her after I'd come, particularly in this position. She couldn't explain why, but she always wanted me to stay put. We lay like that for a while, our breathing recovering, gradually synchronising. My cock rapidly shrinking inside her.

"Marcus."

"Yes."

"Happy birthday."

"Thank you. That really was special."

"Wasn't it?"

"I'm going to ease out now."

I knelt up and, gently withdrawing, I allowed her muscles to expel what was left of the invader. She let out a little gasp as they did so. I looked down. She was definitely open now.

"How does it look?" she asked.

"Ruined!" I replied. "How does it feel?"

"Used. Tingling. Open. Is it?"

I reached forward and took her hand. Drawing it gently back, I placed her fingers between her cheeks and guided them to her hole. She ran one around it.

"Put it in," I said softly.

Brief hesitation. Then she allowed her finger through. As I watched, she explored the rim and a little way inside. It was strangely thrilling to watch. She withdrew it, and the hole tightened, already nearly back to normal. I noticed how wet she was; all down her legs, stockings damp. I helped her slip onto the floor beside me, and we held each other for some time.

While we recovered, we checked on each other, as always, but we'd talk about it later. Not now. I went to clean up, but she wanted to as well, so we ended up having a shower together, washing each other, close and relaxed. After tidying away, and some cuddle time, we went to bed, and fell asleep in each other's arms.

***

I was quite relieved when Sally told me she hadn't planned anything for Sunday. Just a quiet, restful day. We lazed in bed, talking about the night before. Reality versus expectation. Reality won. It was part of the repertoire now. We had lunch and went for a walk. Happy with each other. She cooked again in the evening, and we settled down to watch a film. When it finished, she snuggled up.

"Fancy some fun?" she asked, a wicked look on her face.

"What did you have in mind?"

"I fancy being cheeky. Tease you. Dare you. Frustrate you. Wind you up. See how long it is before you punish me. Have your wicked way with me. Nothing heavy, just a bit of fun."

She was looking at me with a gorgeous smile on her face, eyes bright and wide. Innocent and intensely erotic at the same time. How could I resist? Two hours disappeared. Turned out she was good at it; being cheeky, being provocative. Then shrieking and giggling as she succumbed to the inevitable results. Just a bit of fun. But satisfying in every way.

By the end, she had a pink bum and little bite marks in several tender places. Just something to remind her of what happens to cheeky girls. We'd finally ended up with her lying on the sofa naked, her legs resting on my shoulders. Me steadily penetrating her, watching her play with herself – and me - at the same time, finishing in near-simultaneous orgasm.

When she came back from the loo, she straddled me, and we held each other.

"Tell me," I said, "that fantasy of yours."

"Which one?"

"Two men."

"Mmm."

"After last night, has that become three men?" She looked at me, then looked over my head, as if into the distance. No reply. "Well?"

"Quiet Marcus, let me think about it." I gave her bum a slap; she jumped. "I'll need to think more about that, a lot more," she giggled. "It might. Still red mind; still fantasy only."

"Yes, I know. I was thinking we can simulate the two men thing with a strap-on or dildo cushion. But I can't for the life of me work out how I'm going to fill all three holes at once."

She burst out laughing.

"Oh, Marcus. I do love you!"

Before she finished the sentence, I felt her body freeze. Her face flushed, and a look of horror spread across her face, as she took a sharp intake of breath.

"Oh, Christ. I'm sorry," she said, closing her eyes and looking away. "I didn't mean …"

She went to move off me, but I stopped her, holding her tight.

"Sally."

A tear.

"Sally. Look at me."

Another tear.

"Look at me."

She turned back towards me.

"Didn't mean it? Or didn't mean to say it?" I asked softly.

She closed her eyes, not wanting to meet mine.

"Sally, look at me."

She opened them.

"Well?"

"Oh, Marcus, I'm so sorry. It's been such a great weekend, and I've spoiled it. I'm sorry."

"Sally, stop apologising. You haven't spoiled anything. Did you mean it?"

She looked through damp eyes.

"Yes," she said, almost inaudibly. Nodding. "Yes."

I moved a finger up to wipe away her tears.

"Well," I said softly. "That's a pretty special present too."

Pulling her towards me, I kissed her gently and wrapped my arms around her. She rested her head on my shoulder, and I felt her crying softly as I held her.

Well, another birthday surprise I hadn't been expecting.

Chapter 14 – Sally

"What a question!"

"Sorry, Luce. I just wondered. But I don't know if you—"

"What? Play with each other's butts?"

"Yeah. Sorry. Never really thought about it before."

"Sal, I'm gay, not a freak. I probably do everything you do. Just not with a man."

"So, have you?"

"Yes. Depends on my partner. Why do you ask?"

I looked at her; it had taken a drink or two over the meal before I felt comfortable asking her. We were sitting on the terrace, enjoying the warm evening sun.

"Because I think I might have had one."

"You think?"

"Well. It was my first time. Our first time."

"Oh. Marcus is still corrupting you then?"

"We're corrupting each other."

"So how did it go?

"Uh. Good. Very good. But … different."

"Oh yeah, it is …"

I listened as Lucy told me a bit about how an anal orgasm felt for her. It was about as explicit as I could remember us being, but she seemed happy to talk about it, and I ended up telling her about my experience. By the end, one thing was certain. I knew I'd had one.

"What else have you two been getting up to?" she asked, a sly grin on her face.

"Oh, just having fun, you know."

She picked up her glass and took a swig.

"You'll be telling me you love him next."

My hesitation was all she needed.

"Sally Fletcher! You do." She giggled, leaning forward. "Have you told him?"

I hesitated again; hadn't intended to tell her.

"Uh, yes."

"And I suppose he declared his eternal love for you, and then took your ass!"

"No. It wasn't like that."

"But does he love you?" I wondered what to tell her. She watched me closely. "I gather not. Oh, Sal."

I told her. I told her everything that happened after I'd blurted it out. She listened, concerned at first, then a bit surprised.

"He's cool with it?"

"Yeah."

"And you?"

"I wasn't cool at the time. Really thought I'd messed everything up. Took him ages to get through to me what he was saying. I didn't want to listen at first."

"And now?"

"I'm cool with it too."

"Well, at least he was honest."

"Yes, I almost told him I loved him more for that but managed to keep it to myself."

Lucy chuckled.

"You know what Sal? Patience. I think you might have found something with Marcus."

"Me too. Even if it doesn't work out, it's a hell of a ride."

She topped up my glass, and we sat looking out over the rooftops.

"Have you told him anything?" she asked.

I let out a heavy sigh.

"No, not yet Luce. Let's see what happens. I may not even need to."

"Would you even then? You've not told the others."

"I know, but I think Marcus might be different."

"You two are still okay?"

"Yeah. Gets better all the time. I just won't tell him I love him again. Not for a while, anyway."

"The three most dangerous words in the world." I looked over at her. "I. Love. You. Cause as much pain as pleasure, I reckon."

We looked at one another for a few seconds, lost in our thoughts. Then I picked through what Lucy had said and burst out laughing.

"Well, as long as the pleasure keeps pace with the pain, I'm happy."

***

Closing the laptop, I took my glasses off and rubbed my eyes. It was nearly midnight, but I'd finished. It had taken much more effort than I'd expected, but it had been interesting. I wasn't taking on much research work at the moment. My two jobs occupied me full time during the week, and weekends were … well, fully occupied too.

But an acquaintance had asked me to look into a few sources for her. They proved to be in poor condition, and reading them had been difficult, let alone making sense of the meaning. I'd scanned them as well, carrying the copies around with me. I'd even looked at them a few times when I'd been with Marcus. As usual, he was supportive. I think he would have quite liked a life in academia. He looked at the copies, and although he couldn't read a lot of it, he was often able to suggest what a particularly faint letter or word might be; a fresh pair of eyes. It did help.

He had been helping me a bit recently. Mainly reading stuff I wrote, almost acting as an editor. As a writer, he knew the value of a fresh perspective. He had a keen eye, a common-sense approach, and could be a bit pedantic. But it meant he questioned everything. He knew he wasn't an expert about the subjects, but he helped me make sure what I said was logical and readable. He refused my offer of payment, but he proved willing to accept other rewards.

I sometimes thought back to what Lucy had asked; 'still okay?'. Yes, we were, much to my relief. Still spending every weekend together; me going straight to work on Monday from his now, not going home on Sunday evening. It meant we had more time. No rush. Passion, yes. Lust, yes. But we could take our time and spread it further. Spend more time on other things too. We went out a bit more, and although Marcus had the odd bad day, I thought he seemed to have more energy. If he felt low, we enjoyed each other's company, doing nothing. He'd rest, I'd read. Quiet companionship.

***

Lucy finally brought Zoe around for dinner. I knew she was having fun; she'd told me. But she was nervous because Zoe wasn't her usual type. She was sporty; very sporty. Sports science degree from Sydney, then a spell at the Roosters, a Rugby League team in Sydney. She was taking a year out to travel and visit friends here and planning to go home in the spring.

She seemed nice enough, open and straightforward. Lively. We spent a lot of the evening talking about sport. The usual rivalry between England and Australia, but everyone was taking it light-heartedly. Marcus had a passion for cricket, and Zoe was a fan as well, so they hit it off. I was getting more interested, as I watched it occasionally now, and had begun to understand how people got excited about a game lasting five days but ending in a draw. Lucy wasn't though. Sport was outside her comfort zone, so we chatted while Ashes matches were dissected across the table.

When we settled after dinner, Lucy noticed her nude hanging on the wall.

"I didn't think you'd hang it, Marcus."

"It's beautiful. You're really good."

Zoe laughed.

"I keep telling her that," she said, turning to Lucy. "But she doesn't believe me."

"I think I am getting better, but they're still not right to me."

"Just keep going, Luce," I said. "Particularly while you've got a willing model."

Zoe laughed again, looking at Lucy.

"Oh, I'm always willing."

After they left, we cleared up and went to bed. I asked Marcus what he had thought of Zoe.

"Well, she's quite … bubbly."

"Nice, though."

"Yes, fine."

"Attractive?"

"Mmm."

In the darkness, he couldn't see the smile on my face.

"Nice body?"

"Didn't really notice."

"Liar!"

He laughed and kissed my shoulder.

"Yeah. Nice enough. Not as nice as this one though."

***

His phone rang. I looked at the clock. Three-thirty. He turned the light on and answered the call. One or two brief words, as I turned towards him. I saw his face.

"Mum's been taken ill," he said. "I need to go."

Chapter 15 – Marcus

The funeral went well. As well as any funeral can. A handful of relatives, a few old friends, and three staff from the home. I had persuaded Sally not to go. She had wanted to, to support me. But she had never met Mum, nor any of my distant family, so to me, it made sense for her to stay away. She hadn't been happy about it, though.

I hate funerals. Not that anyone likes them. I always want them to end as soon as possible, but afterwards, think what insignificant events they are to mark the end of a life.

I wondered how her death would affect me. I thought back all those years to the death of my father, also a victim of dementia. That had affected me, even though he hadn't known me towards the end either. In some ways, that had helped. I found it allowed me to grieve before he died. The person you knew, the person who brought you up, had already disappeared, leaving a husk that looked like your parent, but contained nothing of their spirit.

When I got home, I was surprised to find Sally there. I wasn't sure I wanted company. But when I got through the door, she came up to me and held me in a soft embrace. That felt good; comforting, warm. She fixed us something to eat – I probably wouldn't have bothered – and allowed me to consume it in silence. Eventually, she asked how things had gone, and I gave her a brief account of the day. She listened; didn't ask me how I felt, she knew I'd tell her if I wanted to. And I didn't. Not yet. I didn't know myself.

I was grateful there wasn't a lot of practical stuff to do. We'd done most of that when Mum had gone into the home, so now it was a question of tying up loose ends. I had time to think. No tears. I hadn't shed a single one since she'd died. I wasn't holding them back; I could be very emotional. They just weren't there. I thought I understood why, but it still felt strange. Surely, I should be upset? Was I as cold as her? Would they come later?

One night after we went to bed, Sally finally asked me how I was feeling. In the safety of the darkness, I felt able to talk.

"I'm not sure really. A bit numb. I'm not feeling anything. When Dad died, it hit me quite hard. I started getting bouts of anxiety, and a bit depressed. That's when I went to counselling."

"Did that help?"

"Yes. Though it took a long time; over a year, I think."

Neither of us said anything for a few minutes. Sally not wanting to push; me unsure I wanted to open up. Eventually, I did.

"A year dissecting thoughts, feelings, emotions. Many of them long forgotten. Eventually, I'd come to conclusions which had helped, but been difficult to accept."

"Difficult?"

"Yes. The problem wasn't anything to do with Dad. It was Mum."

"Oh?"

"I didn't like her. Oh, I loved her as a son I suppose but didn't like her. She's — well, she was — the antithesis of everything I am. Everything she said or did tended to wind me up. It wasn't deliberate on her part. She was self-centred, self-obsessed, and selfish. Everything revolved around her. She only asked how you were so she could list her own aches and pains.

"You couldn't have a conversation with her because she didn't listen to you, just lined up her next unrelated outburst. Then she complained I never told her anything. And cold, the coldest person I think I've ever met. No warmth, and that hit me hard during counselling.

"Thinking back, I can't remember hugs or love as a child. If I ever went to hug her as an adult, she froze, as if terrified of human contact. It made me feel sorry for Dad; I suspect married life was a grave disappointment to him, perhaps to both of them."

Silence fell again, neither of us wanting to break it.

"Now Mum's gone, and I don't feel anything. Pete — he was my counsellor — told me years ago her death would affect me more than Dad's. But at the moment, there's nothing. I've no feelings for her at all. Isn't that wrong? Shouldn't I be upset?"

Sally didn't reply for a while.

"I can relate to it," she said softly. "I … I didn't have much in the way of feelings for my father. Perhaps you could see Pete again? When you're ready?"

"I can't. Silly bugger went and died."

"Ah …"

"Very inconvenient."

"Very." She stifled a laugh, which made me smile.

The conversation stopped, and we lay there. Sally moulded herself to my body and we held each other close. Thoughts of Mum — and Dad — floated around in my head. Eventually, tears did come, lots of them. But they weren't for my mother; I think they were for me, for my own confusion. Only later did I remember that Sally cried as well.

Over the next few weeks, I didn't do much work. Sorting out the estate was relatively easy, but it still took energy. Every task was a reminder of the issues I was trying to resolve and prompted a lot of reflection. I was now alone. No parents. Only child. Cousins I only saw at funerals. That was it. My illness had greatly reduced my social circle, which had never been big anyway.

Mary had said to me once how isolating she found the fatigue, and she was right. Chronic illness is isolating. People slowly melt away. Not out of malice or neglect, but because you're no fun anymore. You let them down so many times, they stop inviting you, stop visiting.

Alone. How did that feel? I'd always been happy with my own company. In the past, I'd never been short of things to do on my own. I'd gone on holidays on my own. Enjoyed them. Except every so often when you saw a beautiful view, a wonderful castle or a stunning sunset, there was no one to share it with. That had caused the occasional moment of melancholy. Was I happy that that could be my life now? It had been since my last relationship had ended. I'd got used to it again. Accepted it.

Then Sally had appeared. Reminded me what I was missing. Time with her was good. It was doing me good too. She seemed to give me energy, give me confidence. What had she said? 'Concentrate on what we can do, not what we can't'. And that was what we were doing. Having fun, enjoying being together. She never seemed to mind if I wasn't up to something we'd planned, simply leaving it to another time.

My mind went back to my birthday, and the look on her face when she'd blurted out her feelings. She'd been horrified. I'd been amused; as much by her reaction as what she'd said. I talked to her late into the evening trying to explain my reaction and my feelings. I couldn't tell her I loved her; not yet. I wouldn't say it without meaning it. And what did it mean? What is love? It's a clichéd question, but none the less important for that. And I didn't know. Not anymore.

I'd told her about the times I'd been in love. What it had meant to me. Three times it had evaporated. Did that mean I hadn't been in love at all? Or that love can be fleeting? Was I afraid of commitment? No. I'd made a commitment on each of those occasions; willingly. But it hadn't been enough. I'd still ended up hurting; no doubt my partners had too. I wasn't sure I wanted that hurt again, or to inflict it on someone else. These weren't excuses; just truths, as they seemed to me.

I think she understood me eventually. Since that weekend, we had continued much as before, but perhaps with a deeper understanding of each other. Now we both knew where we were. And at least accepted it. We both got a lot out of our relationship, invested in it; but I wondered how long Sally would be happy. Had she meant what she'd said? Did she really love me? I found it difficult to understand. My self-confidence was low, and when I looked in the mirror, I saw a man with little to offer. What could she see in me that I couldn't? And how long would she wait for me to recognise it?

***

My heart and mind were racing as I drove.

[SAL TAKEN TO ROYAL HOSPITAL AM ON WAY]

That's all Lucy's text had said. I'd jumped in the car and set off. I eventually found a parking space and walked as quickly as I could. When I arrived, I asked to see her. I was thrown briefly when the receptionist asked who I was to Miss Fletcher, before calling myself her boyfriend. I'd never used the word before about us; there had never been any need.

I was shown around to a cubicle and caught sight of her. Lying in a gown, propped up, all the usual paraphernalia surrounding her. I was heartened by the fact most of it was not connected to her. Lucy was sat on a chair on one side of the bed. Sally looked flushed, and a bit frightened; I could understand that. She looked up, straight at me.

"Marcus," she said, through obvious pain. "You didn't need to come."

"I think I'll be the judge of that," I replied, kissing her on the forehead. "What have you been up to?"

She explained she'd had some pain in her abdomen for a couple of days, but it had suddenly got a lot worse at work and she'd been sick a couple of times. One of her colleagues had called a First Aider, and they'd insisted on bringing her to hospital.

"I'm sure it's nothing," she said, without conviction.

"How do you feel?"

"It hurts. Really hurts. They've given me some painkillers, but it still hurts."

"What are they doing?"

"They've taken some blood and stuff and had a good feel around, inside and out. I think I'm waiting for a scan now."

A nurse came to check her blood pressure and temperature and told us she'd be going for an ultrasound soon. I grabbed a chair, and we sat, not saying much. Sally was in obvious pain but had stopped throwing up. After an hour, a porter came and wheeled her away. Lucy went and got us coffee, and we sat in the now empty cubicle, largely lost in our own thoughts for a while.

"She loves you," Lucy finally said softly.

I took a deep breath.

"I know. Just not sure why." I was briefly surprised she knew.

"Oh, Marcus. Love isn't something to explain. It's something we feel. Ask yourself how you feel. Don't analyse it, just go with it. These last few months, she's been happier than I can remember in a long time. Don't know why, but it seems to have something to do with you."

We sat silent again for a while. My mind was filtering now, running rapidly through the last few months. Through getting to know each other. Through the discussion after she told me her feelings. Through Mum's death, and everything that had highlighted. Through my panic during the journey here today.

"Do you love her?" she asked simply, taking me by surprise. I was brought back to the present.

"Are you always that blunt?"

"When I think someone is being an idiot," she chided me.

"Is that Sally being an idiot for loving me, or me being the idiot for not telling her I love her?"

"Do you love her?" she asked again.

"Yes," I finally whispered.

"Then tell her, you idiot!"

Sally came back and they wheeled her into the cubicle. We stepped out as they did the vital checks again and gave her some more painkillers. As the nurse left, we went back in.

"Well?" I asked.

"Bloody appendix."

"Oh," I said and grinned before I could stop myself.

"It's not funny," she snapped, but with a smile forming on her face as well. "It bloody hurts."

"I know. But hopefully, it's easily sorted."

I held her hand, and she confessed her earlier fears; how she'd imagined all sorts of things. I knew that feeling. Shortly after, a doctor came around and told her they'd be keeping her in and removing her appendix the next day. Provided it went well, she might even go home the day after. Lucy went off to get a bag of things Sally would need, and I was again briefly reminded I'd never been to her home; didn't even know her exact address.

I went to grab a bite to eat, and while I was pondering which option in the vending machine might be vaguely edible, Lucy came back through the waiting area.

"She's not been ill since I've known her. How does she deal with it?" I asked.

"Not sure really, she's only had minor things before. Then she tends to shut herself away. I have been around to check on her, but I wasn't always welcome."

"Well, she's going to need looking after when she leaves here, at least for a few days."

"I can pop in and make sure she's eating and stuff."

"It makes far more sense if she comes and stays with me."

"Good luck persuading her to do that!"

"She's not going to get a choice."

We went back in, and the nurse was with Sally. We put the bag under the bed and asked the nurse when she might be moved to a ward.

"Oh, I wouldn't wait around for that; it could be hours. Possibly not until the morning. You go home and get some rest. We'll look after her."

Lucy said she'd leave and ring up tomorrow to check on her. After she'd gone, I sat and held Sally's hand.

"You go as well, Marcus. No point in you hanging around tonight."

"I will, but we need to sort out your recovery."

"Oh, I'll be fine at home. Knowing her, Lucy will pop in every day and fuss over me."

"No."

"What do you mean, no?"

"I mean no. You're not going home. You're staying with me until you're fit again."

"Oh, Marcus, I can't ask you to do that."

"You're not asking, I'm telling you. That's what's going to happen. And besides, Lucy agrees with me, so you're outvoted."

"But I'm not very good at being ill. It could be hell for you."

"I'm not leaving you on your own, that's final."

"Why not?"

I looked into her eyes; those eyes that were always so expressive. Humorous, passionate, cheeky, sultry, intelligent. They changed all the time. But now infused with the exhaustion of pain.

"Because I love you," I said softly.

I couldn't describe the look that came over her face then. But those eyes opened wide, and managed to brighten, if only briefly.

"Marcus?"

"I love you. But I'm not sure I've realised in time." She looked at me confused. "Remember you told me how you felt? Do you still feel that way?"

"Of course. More now than I did then."

"I'm sorry," I said.

"What for?"

"For being an idiot. For trying to analyse something rather than just feel it." I offered up a silent 'thank you' to Lucy. "And it feels so good."

"Doesn't it?" she said, smiling.

I leaned in and kissed her, still holding her hand. She raised her other arm to place it around my shoulder but flinched as it caused her pain. I lowered it back to the bed.

"I thought I might lose you …"

"I'm not going anywhere, Marcus."

"But you are staying with me when you come out, and I'm not letting you go until you're recovered."

A nurse appeared, wanting to go through the admission details.

"Can Marcus stay?" Sally asked.

"Of course," he replied, and started to explain the process, and what was going to happen. He filled out a couple of forms.

"We have your next of kin as Mary Fletcher." That it was Mary didn't surprise me, but the surname did.

"Yes."

"Is she the first point of contact?"

Sally looked at me with a questioning look. I smiled and nodded.

"No," she replied. "That would now be Marcus, Marcus Foxton."

The nurse took my details.

"And Marcus is …?" he asked Sally.

She looked at me again, love flickering through her drained face.

"… my partner."

Chapter 16 – Sally

I was exhausted by the time we got to Marcus's flat. The operation had not been too bad; in fact, I remembered little about it. Just the slight panic as the anaesthetic had flooded over me, then vague memories of the recovery room. By the time Marcus appeared in the afternoon, I was sitting up in bed; tired, sore, and feeling a bit sorry for myself. Seeing him, my spirits rose.

I hadn't slept the night before. I was in pain, they moved me to a ward at four in the morning, and I had never spent a night in hospital, not as a patient, anyway. I laid there, thinking about what had happened, what Marcus had said. It seemed ironic we were finally aware of each other's love at a time when we couldn't express it physically, but it didn't matter. That could wait.

He took me home the next day, having sat with me while the nurse went through the list of advice and instructions. I knew I was going to be made to stick to them. No point arguing; but, in truth, I was too tired to argue. I hadn't slept the second night, either. I couldn't turn onto my side and wasn't good at sleeping on my back. When we got home, he led me to the spare bedroom, and I pouted at him.

"Lie on the bed," he said. I slowly climbed on and laid back.

"Now turn over."

I rolled over carefully, trying to hide the pain.

"See," I said. "Fine."

"No, Sal. You rolled. Try turning over on one spot."

He was right. I could roll over, but not turn; it was too painful. It used too many tummy muscles. And I needed the whole bed to roll, so I was consigned to the spare room. Lucy had been over and left loads of my stuff for me. I didn't want to spend more time in bed, so changed into a pair of comfortable PJs, and we had some lunch while he laid down the rules.

"You can do whatever you want," he said. "Unless I say you can't. Ask me for anything you feel like. Get used to it. Shout or scream at me but get used to it."

I gave in; for now. He made sure I was comfortable but didn't fuss. He made sure I rested and made sure I got up and walked about. And kept me fed and watered. Lucy came over every day to see me and fetch anything I needed. I told her Marcus had told me he loved me.

"Of course he does," was all she said.

Mary visited me and brought me some flowers and so many cream cakes we had trouble finishing them. David popped in after work one day, with cards from the team, as well as some flowers and chocolates, and when Marcus finally let me near my phone, there were lots of 'get well' messages.

I was getting some good sleep now - even managing to turn more easily - as well as a nap in the afternoon, and by the fourth day after surgery, I was feeling much better. Still sore, but no longer exhausted. In the afternoon, we were sitting having tea and crumpets.

"Lucy didn't seem surprised that you loved me," I ventured. Although we told each other several times a day, we hadn't talked about it.

"Didn't she?"

"No. Want to tell me why?"

He looked at me, smiled sheepishly, then told me. About his doubts again, but also about the energy he got from our relationship; the joy I gave him. I got a bit embarrassed by his compliments but knew him well enough to know it wasn't false flattery. He told me about his thoughts while he was driving to the hospital. That during the journey, he'd feared the worst. Then he told me about the conversation with Lucy.

"Never shy, was our Lucy," I said.

"No. But it worked. I realised I was the idiot. An idiot not to grab what I most want. You."

Lucy popped in again in the evening.

"Ah, the matchmaker," I said.

She smiled and looked at Marcus, who looked a bit embarrassed.

"Well, he just needed a prod. I hear men often do."

That night after we'd gone to bed, I'd had enough. I crept along the hallway, went into his bedroom, and quietly climbed in beside him. He reached out his hand, and I clasped it.

"Love you."

"I know."

***

The following week, I felt much better. The wounds were still sore. One morning I lifted my top to show him; I'd looked at them and wondered if those four little red puffy bumps would ever heal. He lifted his shirt to expose his own scars and cried out 'snap!'. But his were extensive. I'd looked at them many times, occasionally tracing them across his tummy. Now I looked at them closely; they were very visible, but that was because of their size. At any given point, they were virtually the same colour as the skin around.

"Yours will fade eventually," he said. "They're tiny, so you won't even notice them."

"How long?"

"Oh, a long time to fade completely. Certainly, months."

"Oh, great. Thanks."

I could move more easily now and stopped Marcus from doing everything for me. He still insisted on me wearing PJs in bed 'in case I accidentally knock your tummy'. We were cuddling up now, so his hand could have hit the scars, but I think he was keeping any desire under control.

I suppose inevitably, my own had vanished since I'd fallen ill but was replaced by more emotional feelings, from the changed status of our relationship. I drew a lot of strength from the love he offered. To my relief, it returned as the tiredness cleared, but we couldn't do anything about it. Among all the instructions about recovery, there was a brief mention that sex was usually best avoided for at least two weeks, and then only gently.

By the second weekend, I'd convinced Marcus I was fit enough to return to work the following week. I also stopped wearing my PJs, and we could finally cuddle naked again. It felt so good, but inevitably aroused both of us. Marcus didn't want to do anything, but I convinced him gentle stimulation would be fine.

Big mistake. He tried his fingers, and his mouth, and was incredibly delicate, but every time I started to build, it pulled my tummy muscles and hurt. Eventually, we got a fit of the giggles, which was even more painful. Marcus eventually adopted a 'told you so' look and held me. I could feel his arousal and my own was still there. I tried my own touch. I don't know why, but that was better. He soon worked out what I was doing and held me close and kissed my neck and shoulders. I asked him to watch me while I watched him; it was something we had done when we were learning about each other, and it was strangely erotic now.

Lucy took me and a load of my stuff home on Sunday evening. I was ready to go back to work and get back to normal. But I couldn't drive yet, so she ferried me to work every day, and home every evening. She hung around and fussed over me; got me something to eat. She was worse than Marcus.

"Do you want me to take you over to Marcus's?" she asked on Wednesday.

"No, I think I still need to rest a bit. I'm more tired than I expected."

"You could invite him here you know."

"I know."

"Have you told him anything yet?"

"No."

"Are you going to? It must be strange for him."

"Why?

"He's not stupid, Sal. He must be wondering why you never talk about your family. Why he's never been here."

"Yes. I know. I can't face it. It raises too many questions I don't have answers to."

"Now who's being the idiot. Just tell him."

The next weekend, I drove to Marcus's and stayed. We couldn't resist any longer, and we made love for the first time since the op. He was cautious and let me take control. My orgasm, when it came, did produce a few pains, but it was worth it. Well worth it. The softness seemed to enhance our emotions, and the love we felt was palpable that evening.

***

Over the next few weeks, we slowly returned to our old passions. It seemed even better, more intense. Marcus was careful, letting me lead, and he went back to asking for feedback for a while. Only a while; after the fifth week, I stopped him, and told him to get on with it. I'd use the colours if I needed them. I didn't. Our relationship had changed. We were like a pair of teenagers at times. As if we were in love for the first time. Except we could combine that eagerness with our experience.

It was a mind-blowing cocktail and we made the most of it. At the end of November, we spent the better part of a weekend going through most of our repertoire, something we hadn't done before. The next day, we were both exhausted. I was sore; mostly on my rear, but my scars ached a bit too. I was proud of one and no longer worried about the other.

"You still haven't told me what you want for your birthday," Marcus said one weekend. "It's only a couple of weeks away."

"Oh, just you."

"You can have me anytime. Frequently do."

"That's sorted then."

"Anything you want to do?"

"No, nothing special."

Oh, but there was. I knew exactly what I wanted to do for my birthday. And it was very special.

***

My birthday fell on a Sunday, and Marcus suggested I take the Monday off, so I didn't have to leave early in the morning. He also told me to keep the whole weekend free. I was quite happy with both ideas. I knew Lucy was taking me out on Friday night, making sure at some point I ended up safely at Marcus's flat. Beyond that, I knew nothing.

I spent Wednesday evening with Marcus as I always did. Our 'quiet' evening. We had dinner, watched a film, then made love; slowly, deliciously. For some time afterwards, we lay on the floor, our bodies entwined, my head on his chest. I knew what I wanted to say but couldn't think of the right way to say it.

"What are you planning for the weekend?" I finally asked him.

"Wait and see."

"Will we have some time free?"

"I'm sure we will. Why? Is there something you want to do?"

I moved on top of him, straddling his hips, my hands on the floor, either side of his head. He stroked my hair, pushing it back so he could see my face.

"Yes. I know what I want to do. I've known for weeks."

"Well, you could have shared it", he said. "I've only got two or three days to arrange it."

"Nothing to arrange."

"Want to share it now?"

I looked deep into his eyes. Saw the man I loved looking back at me.

"Yes. I want to submit. I want to submit to you, Marcus. Submit completely. Utterly. Give myself to you. Body … mind … soul. I'm ready. Are you?"

I could see him thinking. I knew him now. He was analysing again, but this time, I was quite pleased. I wanted an honest answer. If this was going to be anything like I wanted it to be, we both had to be ready.

"Yes," he said quietly.

***

Lucy turned up with Zoe on Friday evening. It was bitterly cold. They took me out for a meal, and we went on to the Forum. It was a great evening, and we gossiped, ate, drank, and danced. I did think occasionally about what the weekend held. Marcus and I had discussed what we were going to do, what the rules would be, how long the session would last. It had turned us on again. I had been thinking about it ever since.

But tonight, I was relaxed and enjoying a night out with my old friend and her new lover. I had to agree with Lucy that Zoe was fit; very fit. I had already noticed. By the end of the evening, we were all fairly inebriated. Lucy and Zoe weren't shy about showing their affection. I didn't mind; I'd spent plenty of time with Lucy and various girlfriends over the years, and she was always a bit frisky when she'd had a few drinks. Finally, I thought I'd better let them get home.

We wandered out and found a cab. They dropped me off at Marcus's flat first and went off into the freezing night. It was past one in the morning; late for me these days. After I closed the door as gently as I could,

Sally

I stood in the hallway. I realised I was very drunk; giggly and horny. Watching Lucy and Zoe had been a strange experience, I had found it difficult to take my eyes off them. It had turned me on. Marcus might be asleep, but he wasn't going to be for much longer.

I went to the bathroom and managed to strip off unsteadily while I was in there. Going into the bedroom, I saw he had left the sidelight on for me. I could see his shape under the duvet, his head on the pillow facing away from me. I turned the duvet down and got onto the bed, rather clumsily, for he stirred, and turned over to face me.

"Hello," he said sleepily. "Had a good evening?"

"Yes," I giggled. Marcus had never seen me this drunk. "I'm a bit tipsy."

"A bit?" He smiled, amused at this giggling naked woman advancing on him on all fours, and pulling the duvet off the bed.

"Yes. I've had a really good evening. I've had something to eat. I've had something to drink - quite a lot to drink, actually. And I've had a bit of a dance."

I'd reached him by now; I'd exposed his nakedness and saw his cock was already well advanced. I reached out for it.

"And you know what I need now?" I was still giggly, and his face showed his amusement at my condition. "I need a good fucking."

I was a bit delicate in the morning. I wasn't used to drinking so much anymore. Marcus got up and brought me some orange juice and green tea. He lay beside me quietly, allowing me to come to slowly. After a while, I draped myself over his side, feeling his gentle touch caressing my body. I fell asleep again in his arms.

I had a pleasant dream; sex. Gentle sex, not like the night before when Marcus had done what I'd asked. He'd been powerful, goaded on by my urging him to take me harder, faster, rougher. Now my dream was gentle again, soft; someone between my legs, lapping me up. Suddenly conscious and looking down, I realised it wasn't a dream, it was Marcus.

After breakfast, I felt more human again, and I recounted the evening.

"… and then I got home. The rest you know. I feel bad about waking you now."

"You didn't. Not then anyway. The whole street probably heard you shutting the front door."

"Oh. Sorry. But you looked asleep when I came to bed."

"Yes. I thought you might want to crash out."

"I didn't, did I?"

"No. You were quite … demanding."

"Sorry."

"God, don't be," he grinned. "It was fantastic."

"Wasn't it?"

He took me to a gallery for lunch, and a wander around an exhibition we both wanted to view. Afterwards, we went home, as we were apparently going out in the evening as well. We had a peaceful couple of hours, both having a nap. In the evening, we dressed up and he took me to a new venue that was having a jazz evening.

Lucy and Mary were there waiting for us. None of us were avid jazz fans, but the performers were good. A mix of styles, never too obtrusive, but good. The food was excellent, we could easily talk without being drowned out, and I was staying largely clear of the alcohol. Lucy noticed.

"Headache this morning, Sal?"

"I'm getting old."

"I know the feeling. I was knackered this morning, too."

"Not sure that was purely the alcohol."

"Not entirely."

"Are you having fun with Zoe, Lucy?" asked Mary.

"Yes, thanks. It certainly passes the time."

"Good. I like to see you all happy." She smiled at me.

"We need to find someone for you now, Mary," Marcus said.

"Funny you should say that," she replied. "I do have a suitor."

"Ooh," Lucy said. "Tell us more."

"A chap from my bridge club. Quite nice really. I might give him a try."

"What …" Marcus said, "… see how fit he is?"

"Oh, now I'm feeling better," she shot back with a glint in her eye, "I doubt he'll keep up with me, but I can still hope."

During a break in the performance, I had to go to the loo. As we were in a booth, Marcus had to step out to let me pass, and Lucy and Mary decided they'd come with me. When we were a few steps away, Marcus called to me, and I went back while they went on. When I got to him, he handed me a little bag with a couple of hard objects in it and pulled close to my ear.

"You'll know what to do," he whispered, "and leave your knickers off." I looked at him with a questioning smile. He had a wicked look on his face. "Just do it. I'll be checking."

I hurried to catch up with Mary and Lucy.

Minutes later, I returned wearing no knickers, and with a plug in my butt. Boy, things had got a lot more … interesting. This time, Marcus didn't get up; he moved to the end of the bench and turned, allowing me to go past. I don't know how he did it, but as I moved in, I felt his hand reach up between my legs, fingers touching my sex, and nudging the plug. It was all I could do not to gasp, but his hand disappeared as quickly as it had arrived, and when I sat down, neither Lucy nor Mary seemed to have noticed.

"Okay?" he asked casually, looking at me.

"Yes, fine thanks," I managed to say in a level voice.

The next performance started, and having finished our meal, we relaxed and took it in. I was enjoying it and allowed myself another drink, but every movement reminded me of my predicament. I tried to take my mind off it by making small talk. It didn't work. But I finally found if I leaned on Marcus, my hand resting on him, my head on his shoulder, I could lift a cheek off the seat, which took the pressure off the plug, allowing me to relax a little. He put his arm around me, and we listened to the singer. She was good, and none of us said much.

I felt his hand slowly moving down the back of my dress. He'd worked out what I was doing. He reached my bum, and his fingers crept down the valley between my cheeks, pressing the material into it. Finding the plug, he slowly tweaked it. He waited for the first little gasp in his ear, then returned his hand to its original position. And while he was doing all this, he was talking to Mary about the singer.

When the performance ended, we all agreed to have one last drink. There was a resident band on later, but we'd had enough by then. I was glad; much longer, and I'd turn into a quivering wreck. I knew I was already getting in a mess; I could feel it. Fortunately, I'd not worn too short a dress. They all wished me a happy birthday one last time, and I accepted as gracefully as I could. Lucy offered to share a cab with Mary, and we all said goodnight. When we came outside, it was snowing lightly. We walked to the car arm in arm; Marcus hadn't drunk tonight.

"You bastard," I whispered to him. "You beautiful bastard."

He stopped, and pulled me into a doorway, kissing me sensually.

"When I want to be," he smiled. He looked around and kissed me again. He loosened my coat and I felt his hand reach under the front of my dress. I drew in a sharp breath, though whether it was his touch on my leg or the cold air now invading my warmth I didn't know. His hand reached my stocking top and slid up my thigh, a memory flashing into my mind. He knew.

"Remind me," he said. "What happened last time?"

"You stopped."

"So I did." His hand stopped short of my sex. Again. He turned and walked slowly towards the car and I wrapped my coat around me and hurried to catch up. As we got in, I gave him my best pout.

"What did you do that night?" he asked.

"Take me home, and I'll show you. I might even let you join in."

I was awoken by a kiss in the morning. Opening my eyes, I saw Marcus crouched by the bed.

"Good morning. Happy birthday."

"Good morning," I said, stretching. "Thank you."

As he stood up, I started to giggle. He was naked, apart from a black bow tie and white cuffs; he was holding a notepad and pen.

"What would madam like for breakfast?" he said in a plummy voice.

"Oh, Marcus! You," I said, reaching out to grab him. He stepped back.

"I'm sorry madam, I'm not on the menu. At least, not until I'm off duty."

I was trying not to laugh.

"What would you recommend?"

"I thought perhaps some fruit, coffee, and a bacon sandwich, madam."

"Ooh, sounds perfect, thank you."

"Very well, madam, I'll prepare it. In the meantime, a strange old man asked me to give you these."

He picked up three or four presents, handed them to me, and left the room. I turned down the duvet, rearranged the pillows, and sat up. I was happy. I'd had a good evening, which got better when I'd got home, and, well … it was my birthday. I picked up the first present and opened it. A silver torc-style bracelet with art nouveau decoration; I remembered us looking at it somewhere but couldn't remember where. I put it on as Marcus returned with a bowl of fruit pieces and some coffee.

"This is beautiful, thank you."

"I'll let the strange old man know, madam. Your bacon sandwich will be ready in a few moments."

I opened a second present. A ring to match the bracelet. I put that on as well. The third present was a matching necklace and that went on too. I could smell bacon now, and Marcus came in with a stacked plate.

"Well, how do I look?" I asked.

"Beautiful. But … something missing …"

"What?"

He threw something in the air, and I saw petals floating down all over me and the bed. I laughed as they fell.

"I know it's a cliché, but I couldn't think of anything better."

"It's perfect. I love these," I said, touching the necklace. "Thank you."

He sat on the bed at my side, and we ate our bacon butties while they were still warm. He gave me another present. A bottle of edible massage oil.

"How about I give you a nice warm bath," he said, "then we try it out. And as it's edible …"

Over the next hour or so he pampered me, gently bathing me, giving me a sensual massage, and then slowly licking me all over, finally taking me over the peak. When he'd finished, I felt wonderful. He was lying between my legs, looking up at me. As he sat up, I saw his rigid cock.

"You now," I said.

"No," he replied. "That'll wait."

"Whose birthday is it?"

"Yours."

"And don't I get what I want today?"

That wicked grin flashed across his face. I shrieked as he grabbed my ankle, and pulled me down the bed on my back, petals flying everywhere. I ended up with my bum virtually hanging over the edge, my legs wide open. He knelt between them and gave me exactly what I wanted.

After we'd made an attempt to tidy up the bed, we had a shower and got dressed. It was still snowing outside, so we spent the day indoors. There were more presents. Some thoughtful; memberships for a museum and a coffee and tea club. Some eclectic; a couple of quirky books and a rainstick. Some beautiful underwear too. He told me he wasn't trying to compete with his birthday, as that might get silly next year. But I loved what he did.

I was still thinking about the coming evening; had been since we agreed. During the day, I couldn't get it out of my mind. He knew, he was too damn perceptive sometimes; was probably thinking about it too. We briefly discussed it again, agreeing the rules, the timespan; both eager to take this next step.

A leisurely afternoon followed. We had dinner early to leave plenty of time for the main event. He'd initially baulked at doing it on my actual birthday, in case it didn't work, but I'd been insistent. He cooked me scallops followed by pigeon breasts; served it with champagne. We left dessert for now, cleared the table, and nestled up on the sofa.

My mind was now solely occupied with what was to come. I wanted it, really wanted it but didn't know what to expect. Oh, I knew what might happen, he had enough options to choose from by now. But would it be any different to our usual sessions? Would I feel different?

A few times now, I'd had glimpses of a deeper satisfaction; not a physical one, but a mental one. Glimpses of a deeper calm when I gave in to my feelings and let my mind go where it wanted. Was this how it would be when I gave control to someone else; to him?

After an hour or so, I couldn't wait any longer.

"Are you ready?" I asked him.

"Yes."

Showering slowly, I considered my mood. Butterflies, masses of butterflies. Not really horny though. The excitement was more mental than physical, although I knew that would change. Or would it? He could be patient, very patient. What if he stripped me, and made me stand in a corner for three hours? He wouldn't, would he?

I knew what I was going to wear; one of his presents. A black waspie with suspenders, rich lace with delicate red strands; matching bra and briefs, black stockings, and heels. And the choker he'd once asked me to take off in anticipation of this event. I'd leave that for him to put on. I brushed my hair, applied a little makeup and scent.

When I looked in the mirror, a smile appeared on my face. I looked as good as I felt. Well, I thought I did. I saw I was a little flushed; it didn't happen so much now. We were comfortable together, and it only really came out in the heat of passion. He told me he still found it cute. I was ready. As I walked down the hallway, I paused. I took a couple of deep breaths and smiled to myself; time to take the next step.

When I entered the living room, he had dimmed the lights a little, and put some music on low. I took a few paces, did a slow twirl, and stood still. I knew he liked to look at me; I liked him to look.

"Oh, Sally. You are beautiful. You do know that, don't you?"

"I was happy with what I saw in the mirror, yes."

"You should be. I am one lucky guy."

"Not luck, Marcus. You deserve me. You taught me to love myself. And I deserve you."

I walked over to him and held out the choker.

"Put it on the table and come and sit down."

When I'd done so, he turned so we were facing each other.

"Happy with the rules?" he asked.

"Yes."

He reached behind a cushion, and pulled out another present, handing it to me. I started to unwrap it, finding a square flat box. Inside, a collar. Soft black velvet about a centimetre wide, with a fastening at the back. At the front, there was a silver knot, hanging from it were several fine slinky silver chains, six or seven centimetres long. I suddenly realised it was a tiny flogger.

"Thank you," I said. "It's beautiful."

"That's my gift to you," he replied. "That is your submission. You own it. If after tonight this becomes a part of our lives, I can't tell you to wear it. Only you can gift it to me." He was looking deep into my eyes, his voice soft, but strong. "But when you do, when you put the collar on, or give it to me to put on you, you're mine. Until I take it off, or you call safe, you're mine. Yes?"

"Yes, Marcus. Yes."

I leaned forward and kissed him gently. Straightening up again, I ran my fingers along the collar and held it out towards him. He reached out and took it from my hand.

"Stand up."

He led me to the centre of the room and stood directly in front of me; close. I could feel my heart beating. He moved behind me, and I felt the collar brush me, as he draped it around my neck. He found the best place for it and fastened it. I could feel the silver chains moving against my skin.

"Is that comfortable, Sally?"

"Yes, thank you ... sir."

A shiver ran through me as I said the word for the first time. 'Sir'. I'd never used it before, not in this context. Now I stood in front of a man who I was happy to call 'sir'.

"Good," he said, still soft. "Now you're mine. You will do what I say, how I say, when I say. Until I say stop. You will only speak when spoken to. Do you understand?"

"Yes, sir."

He kissed me.

"Good girl."

Another shiver. He went and sat down. I stayed exactly where I was. I could feel his gaze following every curve of my body. I enjoyed it now, knowing how he felt about me. And with that confidence came a happiness, a freedom to show myself off. For him.

"Down here."

I went down on the floor at his side and leaned against his leg. He started slowly stroking my hair, allowing it to slip between his fingers. His fingers found the back of my neck and stroked the skin. I was so sensitive there. A couple of times, I had to stop myself saying something that came into my head. No, I had to wait. What for? At first, I was on tenterhooks, expecting anything and everything to happen at once. I don't know how long he continued doing this, but gradually the tension drained away. I closed my eyes, and let my body enjoy his touch. I concentrated on it, and the soft music in the background.

"Sally."

"Yes, sir?"

"Go and get the profiteroles."

I brought them in and placed them on the table.

"Now stand in front of the fireplace." I complied. "Place your hands on the mantelpiece either side of you." I stretched them out. "Move your feet further away and stick that bum out." I did. Silence. I knew he was enjoying the view; I pushed my bum further out.

"Good girl," he said, failing to suppress a laugh.

"Thank you, sir."

After some time, he came up behind me. His hands touched my shoulders and slowly flowed down my sides, past my hips, and down my legs to my feet. I took a deep breath as he did so. He came all the way back up and undid the clasp on my bra. Pulling one arm through at a time, he stripped it off me. Still from behind, I felt his hands move from my back, under my arms, and slowly enclose my breasts. As his fingers sought my nipples, I was suddenly aware of how hard they were. He played with them gently and I whimpered at the touch.

Hands moving again, he reached my knickers. Putting a finger in each side, he slowly peeled them over my bum. As they came down, I felt them separate from my sex and realised how wet I was. I didn't feel that horny, not filled with lust. But something was working. He slid them down my legs and lifted each foot to remove them. I heard him move away and sit down.

"Spread your legs, Sally"

"Yes, sir."

"Wider."

I was now vulnerable. If I let go with my hands, I'd fall forwards. He let me stand there for some time.

"These are good. Do you fancy one, Sally?"

"Yes please, sir."

He brought the plate and put it on the mantelpiece. Picking one up, he put it to my mouth, but as I was about to take it, he pulled it away.

"There's a price."

I looked at him. He was enjoying this.

"One profiterole costs six strokes of my choice." He ran his hand over my naked bum, making me shiver. "Not now; later. Still want one?"

"Yes, sir."

"Defiance, Sally?"

"No, sir. Just a price I'm willing to pay."

He smiled and placed the profiterole in my mouth. It did taste good. His hand was still feeling my bum, occasionally slipping down to my thighs. I was beginning to swell now.

"Another one?"

"Yes please, sir."

He fed me another one, and his fingers ran right across the top of my thighs, brushing past my sex. I quivered. Then gasped as his fingers gently separated my lips and moved backwards and forwards a few times. My hips rose to meet his pressure. He watched me as he withdrew them, and put one to his mouth, sucking it. He gave me the other finger, and I licked it greedily.

He leaned close.

"Dirty little devil, aren't you?" he whispered.

"Yes, sir."

He sat down, and I was alone again. My arms were beginning to ache, taking a lot of my weight. I willed myself to ignore it and was surprised when I realised I could. I concentrated on my position, on the feelings in my body, on my arousal. On the music playing. On how he was watching me. I pushed everything else out of my mind. Nothing else seemed to matter. I was his. At this moment, he was all that mattered, even time became meaningless. I smiled as another piece of the jigsaw slotted into place.

"Sally, you may stand."

"Thank you, sir."

"Now on all fours, bum to me, shoulders on the floor."

That was harder than it looks; I'd been practising.

"Are you horny, Sally?"

"Yes, sir," I admitted.

"Good. Play with yourself."

I reached back between my legs and started to stroke myself. I knew he liked to watch me, so I enjoyed doing it. Right now, I needed to, though it wasn't so easy in this position. But again, I gave in to my feelings, letting my need guide my fingers. I was soon building.

"Use the other hand on your ass."

I wondered how I was going to do that, but shifted my weight onto one shoulder, and was able to reach. Taking my own juices, I rubbed them around my hole and started to stroke and probe. I could feel my breathing getting heavier.

"Push that finger in."

I pushed gently, and my ass accepted my finger, stretching around it. But it added instantly to my level of pleasure. I was near now. Nearly there. My body started to stiffen.

"Right, Sally. Stop."

I heard, but it took a second or two to sink in. I managed to stop, but only just. Just at the moment when the need was greatest but unsatisfied. A literal anti-climax. He let my breathing subside.

"Good girl."

"Thank you, sir," I managed to say through gritted teeth. He got up and left the room, but my head was facing the other way, so I only heard him return. My breathing was back to normal now, and I felt the sense of calm again. Then I felt coldness hit as he dropped lube on my bum and spread it around. He slowly inserted his thumb into my ass, and I felt his fingers enter my pussy. Firmly squeezing and sliding them, he proceeded to stimulate me, quickly building me up again. And again, stopping as I got perilously close. I let out a cry of frustration.

"Patience, Sally. Patience."

"Yes, sir." I gasped. "Sorry, sir."

He withdrew his fingers, and I felt him ease a plug into my bum, one of the bigger ones.

"Sit up."

I pushed myself up and sat on my heels.

"Would you like another profiterole?"

"Yes please, sir."

"Help yourself."

I went to get one.

"I think that's eighteen so far …"

"Can I have another one, sir?"

"If you wish. But that will be twenty-four."

"Yes, sir."

I took another one and went back to him as he stood up.

"Take my shirt off."

I did, slowly. Followed by the rest of his clothes. His cock was rigid. Ready. I was interested in my reaction. Aroused, yes. But not desperate. I needed to come but was calm enough to wait. My whole being was in the now. Not the past, not the future.

"Suck it."

I dropped to my knees in front of him and took it in my hands.

"Hands on my thighs."

Complying, I still managed to catch his cock between my lips and attack it with my tongue. He took the enjoyment for a while, then put his hands either side of my head. Pushing slowly forward, he slid it between my lips until the tip hit the roof of my mouth, then out again. I closed my eyes and concentrated on breathing through my nose; concentrated on the moment.

I felt the contact between the head and my mouth, the shaft sliding between my lips, running over my tongue, which eagerly pushed up to press against it. It felt so good. Those feelings filled my mind; I was conscious of nothing else. He increased the speed slightly, holding my head still. I moved my hands to his buttocks and gripped them tight.

I realised I was building to an orgasm; I couldn't believe it. I loved giving him a blowjob, it turned me on. But it had never brought me to orgasm before. I opened my eyes and looked up, straight into his eyes. Instantly regretting it, because somehow, he knew, and slowed to a stop. He gently removed himself, and I took a few deep gasps of air.

"Nearly caught me out there, Sally."

"Yes, sir. Nearly caught me out too, sir."

"Well, we'll have to work on that one sometime. For now, though, I think you do need a reward."

"Thank you, sir."

He laid on the floor, his cock standing proud.

"Climb on, facing away."

I eagerly straddled him. Guiding the head into my pussy, I lowered myself onto him with indecent haste and shuddered as I felt his length fill me. I felt his hands on my hips, stroking across my bum.

"You may claim your reward."

"Thank you, sir." I wasn't sure; would he stop me again? Then I realised that doubt was adding to my arousal. I started gently sliding up and down his cock, loving the feel of it deep inside me, tissue stimulating tissue. Then I heard that noise. I hadn't seen the wand, but as it touched my perineum, I cried out. Sensations seemed to shoot everywhere.

"Keep going, otherwise I might change my mind."

I couldn't say anything. I had to concentrate. My mind took over; took over the rhythm of my body moving up and down his shaft. Took over as I dealt with the vibrations; sometimes between my pussy and ass, invading through the butt plug when he touched it with the wand. I wasn't my normal self; I was in another place. I was aware of everything going on but wasn't in control of it. I was making all the movement, but at his command. He was controlling me, controlling my actions, controlling my spirit. Controlling my…

I screamed as a massive orgasm overtook me. My body started jerking and my head threw itself back against my shoulder blades. My whole lower body overflowed with sensation, almost too much to cope with. I gave in to it. I desperately locked my arms to stop myself falling forward. My heart was racing, and I began to feel lightheaded. My head fell forward in front of me. I stopped moving. Just sat, speared on his cock. I heard a voice through the haze.

"Keep going, Sally."

I obeyed. I didn't think not to. Hips rising up and down. My head spinning. It was automatic. Another climax surged through me as I felt him pull the plug out of my ass, stretching it painfully wide. In the middle of my orgasm, I heard a loud groan and felt his cock spasm, his cum spurting into me. I cried out as it hit me and slowed to stroke the whole of his length with my pussy, determined to squeeze out every last drop. The wand stopped.

My whole body sagged, as I sank onto him, and almost froze in time. Going from frantic movement to delicious stillness in a few seconds. I felt his hand stroking my bum and lower back. Unable to stop myself, I let my arms relax, and my body sank between his legs, still impaled on him. I closed my eyes, and my mind went blank. Perhaps I passed out. I don't know.

"Sally?"

"Yes … yes, sir?"

"Turn around."

I raised myself onto my arms and slowly moved my legs. They were shaking. I swivelled on his hips, his limp cock slipping out as I did so. I looked down at him, and he beckoned me. I put my hands either side of his head and lowered myself down. He kissed me when I was within reach. He had a broad smile on his face.

"Good girl, Sally."

I managed to smile back.

"Thank you, sir."

He reached behind my neck, and undid the collar, showing it to me, as he dropped it on the floor beside us.

"Oh, don't take it off," I said. "I'm in such a wonderful place, I don't want to leave."

"Are you okay?"

"Way beyond okay. Can we carry on?"

"We're well over the three hours."

Where had the time gone?

"What time is it?" I asked.

"Nearly midnight."

"Wow. When can we do it again?"

"You want to?

"Oh, yes. It felt like I was somewhere else. Felt like I was … something else. I was part of you. An extension of your mind. Unable to resist."

I flopped down on him, and he wrapped his arms around me, gently caressing me. The spasms had now gone, replaced by a feeling of tremendous warmth from head to toe. And complete peace. Peace like I'd never known before. I could have stayed like this forever.

"Shall we go to bed?" he asked.

"Yes," I said simply.

"Happy birthday," he whispered.

As we left the living room, he picked up the collar and handed it to me.

"This is yours. Keep it safe."

In the bedroom, he undid my waspie and rolled my stockings off. We collapsed into bed, and he curled himself around me and held me close. I was asleep before I could even begin to think about what had happened.

***

On Tuesday, I was reminded of the weekend every time I sat down. On Monday evening, Marcus had extracted payment for the profiteroles I'd eaten, although I didn't remember eating quite as many as I paid for. But boy, I'd enjoyed clearing the debt. It had been a snuggle day, and we had talked about the submission. I was still struggling to find the right words, but it was quickly clear it had worked for both of us, better than we had dared hope. It was a part of us now. But we agreed it would not be a routine thing. Just occasionally, when it would mean more. At work, I had a smile on my face all day, and when people asked me if I'd had a good birthday, I could honestly tell them it had been my best ever.

But there was a problem. As my – our – happiness had increased, so my shadow had grown stronger. When I got back to my own home in the evening, my mood dropped. It was there that night, mocking me. It always did when life went well. Kept reminding me there was a price to pay for hiding the truth. Could I tell Marcus? Had I finally found someone I trusted enough to be open with? Could I now confront the past?

Chapter 17 – Marcus

I love Christmas shopping, especially when I have someone special to buy for. I spent a few hours wandering around the Christmas market, getting some ideas, picking up a few quirky things, and one or two things for myself. By early afternoon, I was tiring, and it was getting hectic as the coachloads of people continued to arrive. I went home and closed the door on the world.

The flat had a permanent trace of Sally's scent now; it always made me feel good to come home and sense it. And there were always a few of her things here; books, a robe, spare clothes, some toiletries in the bathroom. As I put my feet up with a cup of tea, I wondered what the future held. We still hadn't finalised what was happening at Christmas, but I was thinking beyond that. As usual, I found myself thinking more about potential problems than solutions. So I stopped and took a nap.

We didn't meet up that week, as Sally had to attend a seminar, but she arrived on Friday evening as usual. She seemed tired, but dinner and a glass of wine soon relaxed her.

"I think Christmas is sorted," she told me. "Mary is going to spend the day with Ken and his son and daughter-in-law."

"Blimey, she's a quick worker."

"I know. I was surprised, but she said she had checked with them that Ken hadn't forced the invitation, and she wanted me to be free to be with you. I wouldn't have left her on her own."

"Of course not. Is Lucy going to be with Zoe?"

"No. That's even odder. She's going to her sister's for the day."

"Didn't know she had a sister."

"Yes. They're not close, though. The invitation came out of the blue. I think she's only accepted to find out why she's been invited."

"Has she not got any other family?"

"Yes. But don't ask her about them."

"Oh, okay."

"So, it's just the two of us. I'm cooking."

"You don't have to."

"Marcus, when was the last time you didn't have to cook Christmas lunch?"

"Uh, about thirty years ago."

"Exactly. This year I'm taking care of it."

I looked at her. I don't think she realised quite what that would mean to me.

"Thank you."

After dinner, we settled down. Sally was quiet, a bit clingier than usual, but she said she was fine, and we ended up in bed rather earlier than usual. She went into town with Lucy on Saturday to do some Christmas shopping, and I cooked dinner for them both in the evening. Lucy was footloose; Zoe had gone off to visit some relatives in Scotland and wouldn't come back until the New Year.

"I don't mind too much," she said. "We're good, but she tires me out."

"You need to get out of bed occasionally, Luce," Sally said.

"It's not that, that's fine. It's the rest; she's on the go all the time. Never seems to stop. You know me, I like some thinking time, time to chill."

"What are you doing between Christmas and New year?"

"Nothing much."

"Fancy coming over for a day? Boxing Day?" I asked.

"I don't want to butt in; you'll want to be on your own, won't you?"

"Always happy to see friends," Sally said.

"Then yes, love to. Thanks."

After Lucy left, Sally returned to the quietness of the previous night. I checked it had nothing to do with our experience the previous weekend, but she assured me it didn't, and she was just a bit tired. Later she asked me if I was feeling 'forceful'. I told her I could be if she wanted me to be. She did. I was. She was very responsive, asking for more and more, but I caught occasional glimpses of unease on her face which worried me slightly, and I controlled my enthusiasm.

After we went to bed, we held each other before reverting to our usual cuddle position. After a while, I realised she was crying. Softly, but she was crying. I was mortified. I asked her if I had hurt her. No. Upset her. No, it was nothing about us. But she wouldn't talk to me about it; just asked me to hold her. Eventually, she fell asleep, but I didn't. I worried I had hurt her. We'd pushed quite hard that night, but no harder than we'd done before; she'd actually pushed me. But had I missed something?

The next morning, I felt the distance between us. She wasn't rude, didn't brush me off, but the warmth was a few degrees cooler. We had breakfast, saying little, and she seemed preoccupied. I tried to find out what the problem was, but she told me she was fine. We went for a walk, mostly in silence and had some lunch. When we got back, she curled up against me, and we said nothing for what seemed like an eternity. Then I felt her take a deep breath and sit up.

"Marcus, I've got something to tell you."

I looked at her.

"I need to take you somewhere. Will you drive?"

We grabbed our coats, and she picked up her bag. The journey was silent, apart from her directing me. We ended up in an area I didn't know; quite expensive houses. What my mother would have called 'posh'. She finally pointed me down a narrow alley and told me to pull up in a space for about three cars at the end of a garden to the rear of a large terrace. We got out, and I followed her into the garden and up the path. She got some keys out and fumbled at the back door, which led onto a back stair. Up in the hallway, she climbed the main staircase to the first floor and unlocked a door.

"Come in."

I followed her through the door; a long hallway led to the left, off which I saw two or three rooms, and she led me into what appeared to be the main living room. I took it in quickly; liked it at once, elegant, beautifully furnished. The walls were a deep, rich green. A high ceiling, and huge windows, framed by heavy curtains. Lots of books and interesting objects all around the room. I was confused and intrigued. I assumed this was her place, but knew it was way out of the reach of even the best-paid archivist. She turned and noticed my interest.

"Yes, this is my place. Sit down, Marcus."

She waited for me to sit on one of the sofas, then went to sit on the other one, facing me. She looked more serious than I could remember.

"When we met, we promised openness and honesty, and that's been so refreshing. I've had men lie to me, cheat on me. Even lied and cheated a few times myself. And now I've got to confess. I've lied to you too; I haven't been honest."

"Don't tell me, I'm going to meet your husband." I instantly wished I'd kept my mouth shut.

"Marcus! This is so difficult for me. Please let me say what I have to say."

"Sorry," I said softly. She fidgeted, clearly still unsure how to start. She was sitting on the front of the sofa, knees together, arms resting on them, fiddling with her hands. Like a naughty schoolchild, waiting to see the teacher.

"I told you my parents were dead, didn't I?" I nodded, determined to keep my mouth shut. "Well, that is true. They are. But I didn't tell you the whole story. Didn't tell you any of the story."

She took a deep breath and let out a big sigh.

"My mother died when I was eleven. Breast cancer. It was horrible. They thought they'd caught it. I didn't understand the whole thing at the time. She'd had a mastectomy, but it came back aggressively, and she was gone within six months. Charlie was seven."

I must have looked puzzled.

"Charlotte. My sister."

That was news to me.

"For Charlie and me, Mum was everything. Neither of us were close to our father. We didn't see him often. He was away most of the time, and even when he was there, he wasn't interested in us. Oh, he brought us presents and stuff; we had what we needed. We had a good life. Looking back, it was very comfortable. But never any love from him. Only from Mum. Then she was gone."

I heard the cracks appear in her voice.

"We didn't know what would happen next. Charlie was still too young to ask questions really, but I wondered how we'd manage. He was never there, so who would look after us? Then Mary arrived. We both knew Mary quite well; she was Mum's sister. We visited her occasionally, but even at eleven, I could see they weren't close. Mum wouldn't let us go and stay over at Mary's house.

"Now, she moved in to look after us. Once she was there, he carried on as before. Short visits of a few days, then gone again. Although we missed Mum, we soon came to love Mary. She was very different from her sister. Mum was kind and loving, but quite reserved. I think she was a bit of a puritan really, a bit snobbish even. Mary was so different; well, you've met her. You can see that."

She paused; I could see emotion and pain in her face.

"Anyway, we carried on. We were young, and you gradually accept things, don't you? Mary was wonderful; she looked after us, encouraged us, played with us. Read to us; I think that's where my love of books came from. Not from Mum, and certainly not from him. She guided me through puberty, explaining anything I asked about. I don't think I'd have got that from Mum."

I began to understand the bond between Sally and Mary.

"She was happy for us to stay at friends' houses. She took us out, showed us things, took us to museums, zoos, the theatre. These were all new to us. But when he returned, there was always tension. I sometimes heard them arguing; never fiercely but arguing about us. About how she was bringing us up. We were always glad when he left.

"Then when I was nearly fifteen, everything changed again. Wendy appeared. brassy bleached blonde, make up like a panda, short skirts, big jewellery. Voice like a little girl. She came with him whenever he visited. I took an instant dislike to her. She either ignored us or patronised us. God knows why, she was thick as shit. And she treated Mary like the hired help. Mary put up with it for our sakes, and fortunately, Wendy wasn't there often. Until she moved in. I was nearly sixteen by then, about to sit exams. Within a week, Mary had moved out."

I felt a little uncomfortable. I began to wonder why she was telling me all this. It seemed to be far more information than I needed to know. I stopped trying to take in all the detail; I knew I wouldn't remember it all. And it was obviously painful for her to tell me.

"From then on, Wendy looked after us. Sort of. She fed us, cleaned, did the washing. But she didn't do anything with us. Charlie was only eleven, the same age I'd been when Mum died. I looked after her. I did all the things Mary had done for me; helped her understand what was going on, you know. The saving grace was Mary hadn't gone far, and Wendy was more than happy if we went to stay with her. So, we did. Often. Mary supported me through my exams, persuaded me to go on to sixth form college. I'll never forget that. I've never been able to thank her enough."

The odd tear was appearing now. She paused and sniffed.

"But then I found a release. Boys."

I let out a soft chuckle. She looked at me sharply, then shrugged.

"That was my escape. Got a bit of a reputation. Most of it unfair, but you know what teenagers are like. Mary made sure I knew what I was doing; she didn't try and stop me, just made sure I was safe. She knows a lot of my secrets. Not all, thank God."

She smiled and looked out of the window for a while.

"Life at home wasn't good, although Charlie did begin to get on with Wendy better than me. She was old enough now to look after herself, and as long as the panda didn't have to do any work, she didn't bother us. I don't think she was happy. He ignored her as he had Mum. She spent a lot of time alone in the house. Drank more. I was living my own life. I'd decided to try to get into university. Wendy mocked; Mary helped. The day I went off to uni was the happiest since Mary had moved out. I didn't even think about how it affected Charlie. I've regretted that ever since."

She stopped, a few more tears now. Clumsily wiping her eyes with the back of her hand. I stayed silent while she recovered her thoughts.

"I loved life at uni. Learning, studying, became a bit of a nerd. Even took less interest in men. Had one or two but was pickier. Knew by then some were better than others. I met Lucy at the beginning of my second year, she was starting her first. We hit it off straight away. Have done ever since."

She paused again, wiped her eyes, sniffed.

"Then one day, someone brought me a message. Please call a hospital, there had been an accident. My father, Wendy and Charlie had been in a car crash. Only Charlie had reached the hospital alive; barely. Lucy had a car, and I asked her to drive me there. She did it without question. It took us hours and by the time I got there, Charlie was unconscious. I was holding her hand when she died during the night."

A long pause; tears flowing. A little composure returned.

"I don't know what I'd have done without Lucy. I didn't know what to do. She looked after me. I rang Mary, and she came up to meet us. Between us, we somehow made all the arrangements. The time between the accident and the funeral passed in a daze. Honestly, I only missed Charlie. I cried buckets, but they were all for Charlie."

Another pause as she stared out of the window.

"Sal—"

She held up her hand.

"No, it's not over yet. I thought it was. But it wasn't."

I began to wonder how it could get any worse.

"I went back to uni, even more determined to throw myself into my course. My friends knew what had happened and were brilliant. Lucy fussed; making sure I ate, making sure I still got out and about. A week or two later, I got another message from the solicitor; could I visit them to discuss the will.

"I knew there was one; Mary had asked them about his wishes before the funeral. But I hadn't thought about it at all. There was the house, but I had no idea about anything else. I sat in a bit of a daze as the solicitor went through the details. Everything came to me; that wasn't a surprise, I suppose. There wasn't anyone else left. I got the house and everything in it, money in bank accounts, so on and so forth.

"He concluded by adding 'and the proceeds of his investments'. I asked him what investments. He showed me a statement and I froze in shock. It was a fortune. I asked where the money had come from. He didn't know or wouldn't say. Told me they'd only had my father as a client for a year or so and had no details before that. I asked if he could find out."

She looked out of the window again. The silence was deafening. I was even trying to breathe quietly, to avoid distracting her.

"I went back and tried to make sense of it. Eventually, I talked to Mary. For the first time, I thought she was being a bit evasive, and told her so. She finally told me what she knew; that she'd always suspected Dad had been a bit dodgy. Some things Mum had told her hadn't rung true. She thought either he was lying to Mum, or Mum was lying to her. She didn't believe it was anything heavy. No armed bank robbery. But dodgy, nonetheless. But I believed her when she said she didn't know the details.

"The solicitor came back with nothing but did suggest he could ask for any information the brokers and banks had. It didn't tell us much. The money had been invested in a few large chunks, starting shortly after Mum and Dad married, and ending a few years before he died. Beyond that, nothing. When I questioned him, confessing my fears, he assured me wherever the money had come from, it was legally and legitimately mine.

"But I couldn't accept it; I never have. I left it with the people who looked after it for Dad, and it's been there ever since. I sold the house and stuff, which allowed me to buy a car, and eventually my first house. But I've never touched the money. I can't. It's … tainted."

She looked exhausted. Tears were always near. But this last part had produced a bitter tang to her voice.

"I don't know where he got it. Now it hangs over me, over everything I do. My shadow. I hate him for it. I can't think of Mum, or Charlie, without seeing it hover over them as well. It hangs in this place sometimes, mocking me at night. It's hung over me for fifteen years. I've tried to escape it by using my mother's name – Fletcher. I've tried to hide it. Mary knows, Lucy knows. I've never told anyone else. No boyfriends, no partners, no friends."

She was getting emotional now.

"But I have to tell you. We've been so good together. I wanted to make this work."

Looking down at the floor, her face was a mixture of anger, relief, and sadness.

"But I've lied to you Marcus. I've not been honest with you. I can't expect you to trust me now. I don't know how I would have handled it differently, but I knew I had to tell you. If you want to get up and leave, I can't complain. I'll understand."

She broke down, face in her hands. Shoulders and chest shaking as the sobbing took over. I took a few deep breaths. Trying to take in what she'd told me. I waited, allowing the emotion to spill out of her.

After a few minutes, she had settled a little, but hadn't moved; hadn't even looked up. I stood up, walked around the coffee table, and sat on it directly in front of her.

"Sally …"

No response. I took her hands away from her face and held them. But she still stared down.

"Sally. Look at me."

She raised her head. Her face was a picture of distress; hot, tear-stained, eyes red and puffy.

"Do you want me to go?" I asked.

"No."

"Do you love me?"

"Yes."

"And I love you. That's all that matters."

"But how can you say that? Everything we've done was based on honesty. I've lied to you."

"No, you haven't. You couldn't tell me the whole story. Until now. Do you think I don't understand why?"

"But how can you trust me again?"

"This hasn't affected my trust in you. Some of the things we do, you really have to trust me. And you do. I have to trust you too. I still do. This makes no difference. I'm not going anywhere."

A weak smile, mostly of relief, crept onto her face.

"But," I said firmly. The smile swiftly vanished. "You need to sort this out. Fifteen years is far too long. You need to find a way to deal with it."

"But how? I've tried so hard to forget it."

"That's not the answer. You need help to get over it. Sort out your feelings for your family, and deal with the money."

"That makes it sound so easy."

"The money is."

She looked up sharply.

"How?"

"I don't know how much it is …" she opened her mouth, but I held up my hand, "… and I don't want to know. But I'm guessing it's not just a few thousand." She shook her head. "So, you either accept it or get rid of it."

She looked astonished.

"Get rid of it?"

"Yes, give it away. Get rid of it. That's easy. The hard bit is going to be the way you feel about your father. Hatred is a vicious emotion. It hurts you more than the person you hate."

"So how—"

"Not now. This isn't the time to think about it. But you need to do something. Not for me, not for us, but for yourself. Stop it eating away at you. Fifteen years you've hidden this, that's not good. I'm surprised you're not madder than you are."

She smiled. I leaned over and kissed her.

"Right. Where's the bathroom?"

"Oh, it's down the hall. Second on the right."

"It's not for me. I'm going to take you there, and help you look less like a … panda!"

"Oh."

When she looked in the mirror, she gave a little shriek and put her hands over her face. She took her time to wash away the tears. I waited in the hall while she used the loo.

"What now?" she asked, coming out.

"Well, I reckon you need some coffee or something stronger; then you can show me around this palace of yours if you like."

She was calmer now. Made some coffee, and we drank it in the kitchen. The flat was typical of her; understated, but tasteful. She showed me around; living room, dining room, study. A kitchen, two bathrooms, and three bedrooms. It was warm, enveloping, but I wasn't convinced she was completely comfortable in it. On the way back, we picked up the coffee and went back to the living room. This time, sitting close on the same sofa.

"Do you like this place?" I asked.

"Yes. I know, the shadow. But I'm not sure it lives here. I think it lives wherever I am."

"Do you feel it when you're staying with me?"

"No, only when I'm alone."

I kept her talking for a while, letting her come back to normal.

"You meant therapy earlier on, didn't you?" she asked. "Counselling."

"Possibly. It helped me."

"Lucy's suggested it too; it's helped her in the past as well."

"It's not easy. No miracle cure. But it can help."

"But what—"

"Not now, Sal. You've had a tough day. Leave it for another time."

After we finished the coffee, she cuddled up to me and told me about some of the things in the flat. She got up several times to fetch things to show me.

"I suppose I'd better come back with you and collect my car," she finally said.

"No."

"What?"

"No. You're going to put what you need for tomorrow in a bag and come back and stay with me."

"Marcus …"

"You're not staying on your own tonight, Sally."

She kissed me.

"Thank you."

By the time we got home, she was brighter; relieved, I guess. I cooked dinner, and while we ate, she talked a little more about what she'd told me.

"Have you really never told previous boyfriends any of this?"

"Not about the money, no. I told one or two about how Mum or Dad died, but only briefly."

"Mind if I ask why?"

"I think initially because I didn't want gold-diggers. Then it became a habit. Even if I was with someone for a while, it didn't seem necessary. After all, I couldn't touch it, so it would have made no difference. And I never talked about Charlie."

I looked at her; sad, thoughtful. She smiled, but it was a forced smile.

"It's Charlie I've always missed. But every time I think of her, all this comes flooding over me. I try not to think of her at all."

"That must be hard."

"It is. Because I want to remember her; we were so close growing up. Even Mary doesn't mention her unless I do first."

We were quiet for a few minutes.

"Would you really not mind if I gave the money away?" she asked.

"It's not mine. And I didn't know you were a rich heiress when I fell in love with you."

"But it might be useful."

"Sally, at the moment you can't use it for yourself. It's useless. Leave it where it is until you've found a way to move forward. Then decide what to do."

"Well, leaving it a bit longer isn't going to hurt."

"Besides, I'm beginning to wonder if I'm in one of my own stories. You know; beautiful, rich, nymphomaniac heiress shacks up with struggling writer. I'm quite glad I didn't know about this earlier. We both might have doubted my motives."

"I've never doubted you, Marcus. Not before, not now."

Sally went off to have a bath and get ready for Monday. I settled the living room down and prepared for a quiet evening. She seemed to have recovered, but her emotions must have been in turmoil, so I wanted her to relax.

A while later, she returned. Refreshed, happy, bright eyes, hair done, makeup. In nothing but a pair of white hold-ups and heels, laying some toys on the table. I spent the rest of the evening trying to keep up. She was demanding; pain, pleasure, passion. Almost ferocious at times. I didn't mind at all. Everything she wanted, I was happy to give. Everything she offered, I took. We were both very relaxed by the time we laid our heads on the pillow.

Chapter 18 – Sally

Closing the door after arriving home on Monday evening, I stood still and looked down the hallway. Home. Yes, it was my home. And Marcus had finally been here. I threw my coat over a hook and walked into the kitchen. While I made some coffee, I thought over the events of the previous day.

Had I expected him to leave? To walk out? I'd tried to convince myself he would understand, that we loved each other enough to deal with it. But the shadow had been there, nagging at me, telling me it would all go wrong. That I'd lose him.

But for once, the shadow appeared to be wrong. Telling Marcus had been the most difficult thing I'd had to do for years. It wasn't just telling him; it was going through the whole story again myself. Dragging all those memories from the places I normally tried to hide them. But he loved me, I knew that. Felt it even more today.

His reaction was what I now realised I should have expected. Caring, supportive, loving. The feeling of relief had been overwhelming. I was so glad he wouldn't let me stay on my own that night. We both were by the time our passion exhausted itself. But tonight? I would be alone. How would I feel? I knew he was right; I needed help to deal with it.

***

The ten days leading up to Christmas were busy. I rushed around finishing my shopping, had Christmas parties to go to. Marcus accompanied me to one of the department events; the quieter dinner arranged for the library team and their partners. I was chuffed, and he seemed to enjoy it. I was pleased he got to meet more of my colleagues. We also arranged one for the book club, which was going from strength to strength, and now had over a dozen regular members.

We decorated Marcus's flat, putting up a tree.

"Do you like Christmas more than birthdays?" I asked as we garlanded the fireplace.

"Oh, yes. Love it. There's a feeling, an atmosphere. I've always loved it. Since Mum went into the home, I've had three Christmases on my own. To be honest, I was dreading them, but even they weren't too bad. They were probably better than when it was just Mum and me. This year's going to be much better, though."

"You haven't tasted my Christmas lunch yet."

"Don't really mind. It's not about the food, or any one thing, really. It's everything together. For once, everyone seems to want to put differences aside, and enjoy a few days."

"I'm not sure that applies to big families. Lots of arguments about who does what and who visits who."

"Good job neither of us have big families, then."

"True."

I was looking forward to the holidays. For the first time in many years, I'd booked the whole period off, and was staying with him for ten days. As he helped me ferry stuff from my car into the flat on the twenty-third for our first Christmas together, I was sure it wouldn't be our last.

The day itself was perfect; the way all new couples would want it to be. Making love before getting up. Breakfast on the floor under the tree, opening a present or two. A leisurely morning, with me banning him from the kitchen. When we sat down to eat, Marcus was a bit emotional. He paused and looked across at me.

"Thank you, Sally."

"What for?"

"For cooking today." I noticed a catch in his voice, and he must have seen my surprise. "I've cooked Christmas lunch for as long as I can remember. I didn't mind doing it, quite enjoyed it. But it is so good to have someone else do it, for a change. It means more than I can explain. Thank you."

I got up, went around to his side of the table, and kissed him gently.

"You're welcome. You know I love you, don't you?"

He let out a deep breath.

"Yes. I do."

After lunch, a few more presents. Our gifts to each other were a great success. After our previous discussions, we'd agreed not to buy anything expensive. Just lots of little things. In truth, quite a few of them were going to benefit both of us, but that was half the fun. We tried one or two of them out as the day wore on. Yes, a great success.

Lucy came over to spend Boxing Day with us. We chatted, played games, had more crackers and hats at lunch. At my request, Marcus prepared it that day, so I could check with her about her Christmas.

"How was yesterday. Really?" I asked her.

"Honestly, not too bad. Annie was friendly all day, so was Tim. They had a good time, the kids were fun, and they made me feel at home."

"Did you work out why they invited you?"

"No, and I didn't ask. I did get the impression Annie isn't as close to Mum and Dad as she was. She hardly mentioned them, and when she did, it was without much enthusiasm. Tim even made a couple of sarcastic comments about them, which is unlike him. But I didn't want to spoil the day, so nothing to tell really."

"Good, just wanted to check."

"I know. Thanks."

"I've something to tell."

"When's the baby due?"

She laughed as she saw what must have been a horrified look on my face.

"Oh, God," I said. "That's not going to happen. Not if Marcus or I have anything to do with it."

"I was joking. I know your views on children. So, what's the news?"

"I've told Marcus."

"Everything?"

"Yes. Well, everything I know."

"And?"

"He was fine with it; I should have known really. He even suggested giving the money away."

"Have you?"

"No. I thought it might come in handy if I can sort myself out."

"Sort yourself out?"

I paused. Lucy had suggested therapy several times over the years, but I had ignored her.

"Yes. Marcus has suggested … counselling."

She burst out laughing.

"And …"

"I'm going to give it a try."

She was grinning now.

"Oh, I see. Your best friend nags you for years to get some help. Do you? No. Then some random bloke comes along, suggests counselling, and off you go."

"Oh, Luce, it's not … Well, I suppose it does seem …"

"Don't worry. I'm not being serious." She gave me a hug. "I'm really proud of you for telling him. I can recommend Jenny if you want her details. She really helped me."

"Yes, please. If she helped you, she might be right for me."

We watched an old Bond film in the afternoon, picking holes in it all the way through. Lucy and I got steadily drunk; Marcus encouraged us. Probably remembering the last occasion I climbed into his bed in the same state. After we saw Lucy safely into a taxi, we didn't get as far as the bed.

The next few days were wonderful. Relaxed, easy. Quiet companionship. Mary came over for a day. She had had a good Christmas; Ken's family had been lovely, and it had been good seeing their children so excited. She started to recall Christmases with me as a child; suddenly looked horrified and tried to change the subject. I told her Marcus knew.

"Oh." She smiled, looking at me, then Marcus. "This is serious, then."

Marcus and I smiled at each other.

"Yes, it is. And I'm going to get some help."

She looked concerned for a moment, then softened.

"Good for you, darling. I'll be here if you need me."

After she left, I asked Marcus if he was happy to tell me about his counselling, he'd already been open about it. He told me how it felt for him, the emotions it could release. The unexpected revelations. The possibility it could completely change your outlook on life. He warned me it could be painful, distressing even. That it could make things worse before they got better. And it was a long-term commitment, not a three-week fix. Lucy had told me a similar story. But I was determined to start, and soon. He offered one final piece of advice.

"It doesn't matter much about the counsellor's qualifications. The only thing that matters is to find a person you can work with, build a rapport with. You'll probably know by the end of the first meeting. Any doubts, find someone else."

We stayed in for New Year, neither of us were party animals. It was a lovely winter's day, so we went for a long stroll in the afternoon. When we got back, we warmed ourselves with tea and croissants. 'Mary Poppins' was on TV, and we settled down to watch it. After a while, I noticed Marcus was quiet and intent on the film.

"Are you okay?" I asked, and he almost jumped.

"Sorry, yes."

"Do you like this?"

"Yes and no."

"Come on. Explain."

"Well, I have to admit, in many ways, it's not a very good film. A bit soppy, terrible accents; typical Disney version of a Britain which never existed."

"True."

"But it always gets to me."

"Do you know why?"

He thought for a moment.

"I suppose it's a vision of lost childhood. A reminder of what it's like to *be* a child, to see the world through a child's eyes. It's something we lose as we grow up, and I think that's a shame. It's one of those films that always brings tears to my eyes. Sorry."

"Marcus."

"Yes."

"Never apologise for who you are. That's who I love."

He was an emotional man, I knew that. Happy for me to see his emotions. I was interested to see what made him react, what made him cry.

It didn't tend to be soppy, sad stuff. It was more those things that touched his values; a powerful film ending, a particular music track, a superhuman achievement. I even noticed he was sometimes quite emotional after sex; particularly when it had been soft, loving, and intense, rather than purely physical and playful. I suppose crying is another way to release pent up emotions.

We decided to get dressed up for the evening. Have dinner, and then … well, I had an idea for later. He put on a suit and tie, and I put on one of the new sets of underwear he'd given me for Christmas, under a black dress. He watched while I dressed. Sometimes I let him, sometimes I playfully sent him away, telling him to wait and see. This time, I let him.

We cooked dinner together; something light, we had more food for later in the evening. We talked about the old year and how we'd met, what we'd done. About the new year; our hopes, our predictions. Both of us keeping it light, not introducing issues that could have got a bit heavy. We sat at the table long after we'd finished eating. Laughing, joking, flirting.

"Do you want to watch a film or something?" he asked. "New Year's Eve TV is awful."

"True. But I've got a better idea."

"What?"

I looked into his eyes. Unseen by him, I'd hidden my collar on my chair. I pulled it out now and laid it on the table between us.

"My New Year gift to you, if you'll accept it."

Chapter 19 – Marcus

I didn't need to think about it. We'd been flirting since we'd got dressed. Sally had been doing it outrageously at times. She was good at it, and she knew it. She knew what to say, which expressions to make to get me going.

"Yes," I said softly. Those eyes flashed for a moment.

"Good. I want to make a small change."

"What's that?"

"I want to agree a safe word."

"Okay."

"I don't think I'll need it, but I don't want to use the colours when I submit. I want it to be different. Let's have a safe word just for this."

I thought about that, it was a good idea.

"Agreed. What's it to be?"

"Brian," she said quickly.

"Brian?"

"Yes, Brian."

"Why?"

"I'll tell you sometime," she replied, a big grin on her face. "But it's perfect for me. Is it okay for you?"

"If you're happy you'll remember it under any circumstances, it's fine. But still the three taps if you can't speak."

"Yes. Brian it is then."

I had to wonder to myself who Brian was, and why she was so amused by him, but let it go.

"Shall we wait a bit?"

"No," she said, walking around the table and kneeling beside me. "Now."

I stroked her face.

"Rules?" I asked.

"Same as before?"

I kissed her and picked the collar up from the table. Laying it around her neck, I reached behind her and fastened the clasp.

"Comfortable, Sally?"

"Yes, sir. Thank you." Her bright eyes drilled into me; it was going to be a struggle to stay patient tonight. Part of me wanted to bend her over the table and take her. But I had a sneaking suspicion she'd have been more than happy with that. I looked at the clock; plenty of time.

"Good. Stand up." She got to her feet. "Take the dress off."

"Would you undo the zip for me, sir?" I slowly pulled it down to the end. "Thank you, sir."

She took a step forward and turned around to face me. Easing it off each shoulder, she wriggled the dress down until it passed her hips and dropped to the floor. I'd watched her put the underwear on, but seeing her standing in front of me upright, confident, hands behind her back, it still stirred me. We'd been working our way through what she'd had for Christmas; she'd even bought me a couple of things to wear.

"Go and run me a bath, Sally."

She looked slightly surprised.

"Yes, sir."

While she set about her task, I put some music on and thought about how the evening might pan out. As with the first time, too many options came into my head. I wasn't capable of carrying them all out. Not sure any man was. Keep it simple again, but something different.

"Your bath is ready, sir."

She led me through to the bedroom, and following my instructions, she slowly took my clothes off, until I was naked. I climbed into the bath, and she bathed me; slowly, sensually. She was enjoying it a bit too much, but I didn't stop her. I was enjoying it too, that much was obvious.

"Right," I said, standing up. "Now you're going to shave me."

"Sir?" she replied sharply, a look of horror on her face.

"You're going to shave my groin and bum."

She looked at me, clearly nervous now. I understood that. She shaved, but it's not the same as doing someone else. When I'd first shaved myself, I was nervous too, thinking of all the possible dangers. In truth, it was easy; I'd never caused myself any damage. Now I guided her through the process, starting with my bum, then moving around to my groin. Working up the scrotum, and finally my cock itself. In some ways, it was easier for her. Although it normally tried to hide from the blade, today it was happy to display itself. I saw the concentration on her face, her tongue flicking over her lips, as she ran the razor over me. Partly nervous, partly fascinated by what she was doing.

"Good girl. Now rinse me off."

She put the razor down and using the shower, rinsed me off; again, being rather more sensual than she needed to be. Again, I let her. The result seemed to be pleasing us both.

"You've done a good job." She smiled up at me; pure relief, I thought. "Strip."

She removed her bra and hipsters, standing naked by the bath. I stepped out.

"Now dry me off."

She picked a small towel off the radiator and started at my neck and shoulders, working down my back, then moving to the front, and drying my chest and legs. Kneeling in front of me now, she finished off by gently dabbing between my thighs. When she finished, she knelt up straight, face directly in line with my stiff cock. I decided I could afford to take a little pleasure now.

"Good girl. Now suck it."

She raised her hands, but remembered the last time, and moved her shoulders forward instead so her lips found the head and eased over it. She was looking up at me; God, I loved that. She concentrated on the head first, but without her hands to hold it still, she couldn't be quite as delicate as usual. Instead, she rocked gently to feed me in and out of her mouth, her tongue flitting around me inside. I let her do this for a while, knowing it turned her on almost as much as it did me. I'd never met a woman so keen on this particular act. I eventually pulled away from her.

"Move back."

"Yes, sir."

Her back was now against the wall, and as I moved towards her, she knew what I was going to do. She opened her mouth, and I slid my cock between her lips. Her hands came up to grasp my buttocks. I placed my palms against the wall and started to move my hips in and out. She couldn't escape, so I didn't need to hold her head this time.

Looking down, I watched myself disappearing into her. It sent a thrill through me. I also noticed her legs were open as far as my own would allow. I carried on slowly, small movements to start with. I could still feel her tongue flicking as I went in and out. Sally moaned gently each time I slid in. Since she'd almost come doing this during her first submission, we'd tried it on a couple of occasions. Although it was good for both of us, it hadn't happened again, and we wondered if it would only work when she wore her collar.

I changed my pace and depth every so often; it was certainly working for me. But I noticed her sounds were getting more ragged, and louder, although that was difficult to judge with her mouth full. Finally, I was sure she was building up. I had to last long enough to get her there, but that was getting increasingly difficult. I felt her hands pull me in towards her; in that sense, she had some control. But instead of trying to push me away, she was pulling me in.

I let her guide me; wanted to see what she needed. She pulled me in further than I thought she could take, and I heard her gag slightly. She relaxed her hands, and I eased back, but she pulled me in again. I watched as she guided me in and out, it was some sight. She was near now, so I followed her lead; I was too. Suddenly, I heard a groan deep in her throat, and felt her lips and tongue press hard around my shaft, almost pushing me over the edge. Her hands gripped my bum hard, and her legs twitched a couple of times against my ankles.

Taking control, I began to move in and out again. More groans from her, and I felt my own climax coming. The feeling was amazing, and I felt my legs shaking. Slowly but firmly, I slid in and out along almost the whole shaft, her lips wrapped tightly around it. Within a few strokes, I felt the release, and cried out, as I had one of the strongest orgasms I could remember.

Above my own groans, I could still hear a deep moan every time she felt a new rush of cum in her mouth. After I'd finished, I gently pulled my hips away, but her hands worked against me. I could see she was still intent on cleaning it all off. I let her, my legs still shaking.

When I'd given her time, I pulled out. And smiled to myself; I'd had a thought.

"Stand up."

I was still leaning against the wall, hands stretched out, so she didn't have much room, but eventually wriggled up in front of me. Her face was flushed. A contented look. Our faces were inches apart.

"Very good, Sally. Did you come?"

"Yes, sir. Thank you."

I took one hand off the wall and put it between her legs; she gasped as I did so. I'd had the bath, but she was the wettest. I played with her for a few seconds, eliciting some more moans, then put my hand back on the wall.

"I don't remember giving you permission."

We hadn't had that as part of our rules, but I thought I'd see what she'd say. Her face was a mixture of pout and defeat.

"No, sir. Sorry, sir."

"I think you might pay for that later." Her look changed to one of challenge. "But not now. Now you're going to give me a massage."

We went through to the bedroom. She put a couple of large towels over the bed, and I lay down. The next hour was bliss, she was very gentle. I sometimes reacted badly to full massage; it could make me feel rotten. But this was heaven. She used light touches, kisses, and various parts of her body to rub and stroke me. She took liberties, straddling my thigh and rubbing herself along it, then straddling my chest to massage my legs, her sex exposed and swollen a few inches from my face. I resisted, just. I waited, amused, to see how long she would carry on. Eventually, though, I felt my own arousal start to stir again. She saw it too and moved her hands towards it.

"Good girl, Sally. That will do for now."

"Yes, sir. "

She stopped and knelt on the bed beside me; still, looking at me. I knelt up by her side and gave her a kiss.

"Now. I want you to put on the blue stockings, suspenders, and briefs. When you come out, bring the flogger and the pegs. Time you paid for your error."

"Yes, sir."

I went back into the living room. Clamps hadn't worked for us; they were a bit too brutal. Perhaps we hadn't found the right ones, but these wooden clothes pegs had proved ideal. Sally could take them on many parts of her body; they hurt, but the pain was good for her. I thought I'd have some fun with them.

She came in looking gorgeous, put the things on the table and stood in front of me. A mixture of submission and desire.

I looked at her slowly; her nipples hard, her wetness already visible through her knickers. Her face was calm now, serene even. I guessed she might be in the place she'd tried to explain to me, but this was new to both of us, so I couldn't recognise all the signs yet.

"Now I'm going to punish you, Sally. Punish you for your disobedience."

"I deserve it, sir," she replied, adopting a cheeky grin.

I suppressed a smile. Her voice was calm. I could almost feel her submission, feel her need to obey. It was a powerful feeling, a strong stimulant.

"Go and bend over the table."

She walked over to the dining table, stood in front of it, and bent slowly forward, extending her arms in front of her down the length of the table. I stood up and picked up the flogger. As I approached, I took in the view; beautiful. That perfect bum, framed in blue. I placed the flat of my hand on her back, and lightly ran it up and down, moving down to trace it over her covered cheeks. She twitched and opened her legs a little wider. I removed my hand and stood still.

Normally in this position, I would pick up on her anticipation of the first strike; a tense cheek perhaps, or a held breath. But now, there was none of that, she seemed to be utterly calm. And when I brought my hand down quite hard, she grunted softly, but the reaction was muted, accepting. As I continued, her response was the same. The sounds were clearly positive, but different. After a while, I slowly peeled her knickers off; she raised her hips off the table and spread her legs further still. Her cheeks were beginning to get a pink tinge. I ran my fingers between her legs, and she moaned loudly and deeply as I did so. I used my hand to spank her bare flesh for a while; her response growing slightly, but still calm.

Picking up the flogger, I settled it in my hand and started to let the fronds flow over her body. She stretched and arched at their touch. I let them drag from her bum right up over her head, along her arms, and back again. Then taking up position, I started to lightly twirl it, allowing it to flick along her back. She moved gently with each touch.

I stopped and brought it down quite hard on her bum. She let out a soft cry, but I continued, bringing it down regularly, targeting a different spot each time. Watching her flesh tremble as the suede came into contact, then spring back. Her moans were louder now, not short in response to each stroke but rolling over them. I stood behind her and changed to a figure-of-eight pattern, crisscrossing her bum. The fronds coming down hard and fast and her moaning grew louder. I could see her flesh darkening under the onslaught. I stopped as suddenly as I had started.

Her body relaxed back onto the table. In the stillness, I suddenly became aware of my erection. I placed the back of my fingers on her bum and ran them up and down her back. I put the flogger down and squatted behind her. Spreading her cheeks with my hands, I started licking around her ass, eliciting gasps and muscle twitches. I pressed the tip of my tongue into her hole, and she pushed back to meet me.

Dropping down, I moved towards her sex; when I reached it, the moaning increased. I worked around it, lapping at the entrance, flicking up to her clit, and pulling at her swollen lips with mine. Her breathing was now heavy, an almost continuous moan coming from her. I replaced my mouth with my fingers, inserting two into her, pressing them down to find her sweet spot and massaging it. A louder groan.

"Are you learning, Sally?"

"Mmm. Yes … sir."

"Good girl."

I stood up and drove my cock into her; she cried out loud. Her hands reached out to grip the edges of the table. She blew out a few short sharp breaths. I held myself deep inside her.

"So next time?"

"I'll ask, sir." Her voice now breaking.

"Why don't we try it now?"

"Please can I come, sir?" she was gasping for air. "Please. Please, can I come?"

"Yes, Sally. You may."

On my last word, I grabbed her hips, and started to fuck her; hard, fast, and deep. With one hand, I grabbed a bunch of her hair and pulled it; enough to make her raise her head off the table. Within a couple of dozen strokes, she cried out loud, and her body gave in to her need. I felt her legs shake; her hips rolled. A variety of garbled sounds came from her mouth. Suddenly her body froze, and I slowed my movement, relaxing my grip on her hair. She stayed that way for a short while, then dropped onto the table, still shaking. I stopped, still inside her, and stroked her back. Giving her a respite. A brief respite. Then pulled out, another little groan as I did so.

"Stand up."

She struggled to move, slowly sliding back off the table and standing up. I saw she was supporting herself with one hand on the table, her legs buckling slightly. She turned around to face me; her face was flushed, her breathing still heavy. Her expression gorgeous.

"Well, I think we need to reinforce the lesson. Fetch the pegs."

"Yes, sir," she managed and walked a little unsteadily to the coffee table. She brought back the bag and handed it to me. I got her to stand in front of me and proceeded to attach some of the pegs. Some in a circle around each aureole, completing the pattern with one on each nipple. Little cries, as each one bit. She had not yet got over her orgasm, still breathing heavily. But each moment of pain seemed to heighten her arousal. I knelt in front of her, and slowly sucked at her pussy; louder groans this time. Then gasps as I attached two pegs to each of her pussy lips in quick succession. Her legs quivering as I did so. I stood up.

"Lie on the sofa on your back."

She walked a little uncertainly and sat down. I pushed her down and pulled her forward, so her bum was on the edge.

"Hold your legs open, Sally."

"Yes, sir."

She wrapped her forearms behind her knees. I felt my cock jerk at the sight. I went and got the flogger, and let the fronds run over her again. She looked at it, then at me, her gaze vague. I started lightly flogging her thighs, every stroke caused a reaction. I started twirling it slowly, and moved up to her breasts, the fronds brushing over the pegs. This caused a much stronger response.

When I increased the speed, the pegs started moving, and finally, they started flying off. She let out a cry as each one came away. I moved the rotating flogger and saw there were just a few left. I moved it so it was spinning between her legs. Her face was looking up to the ceiling, suffused with an intense expression. Eyes soft, unfocussed, mouth hanging open, allowing her to breathe deeply.

I lowered my hand and she felt the strands sting her exposed sex, flicking the pegs. The moaning became continuous again, rising and falling over time. One of the pegs flew off, and she cried out. Another followed. Another cry. I saw she was building again and knew I couldn't resist this time. Dropping to my knees, I removed the two remaining pegs between her legs, eliciting more cries, then buried my stiffness in her warm wet flesh.

This seemed to bring her back. She looked straight at me and let out a loud urgent grunt, like a rutting animal. Then she pulled her legs further back towards her, raising her hips and widening her thighs, allowing me to penetrate more deeply. Looking down, and seeing the view, I happily did so, and she was gone again. Closing her eyes, she let her head fall back.

I started to fuck her, urgently. Trying to time each stroke with her rapid breathing. She soon started to come, this time in a series of small waves. I brushed my hand across her breasts a few times, knocking the remaining pegs away; a cry each time one flew off. I felt myself reaching the point of no return, and grabbed her shoulders, driving my cock into her, while pulling her body onto it. She screamed, and I felt her body tense up, shortly followed by me emptying myself into her heat.

My orgasm was strong, my body suddenly heavy, my muscles tingling. I slowed and released her shoulders. Started lightly stroking her, allowing her to come back. I unhooked one of her hands from her leg and lowered it to the ground and repeated it for her other leg. Her body had now slumped back onto the sofa. Her eyes were still closed, but her breathing was beginning to slow. It was now deep and heavy. Sweat glistened on her breasts, tummy, and forehead.

I leaned over her. As I did so, she opened her eyes, and slowly focussed on me. I put my hands behind her neck to undo the collar, but she reached up and held my hand. A weak smile crossed her face.

"Thank you, sir."

Her hand dropped, and I took the collar off, showed it to her, and threw it on the table. She put her arms around my shoulders and pulled me in.

"Are you okay?" I asked.

"Fuck, yes."

"I love you."

"More every day."

We lay there, both of us too exhausted to do any more. Our bodies pressed together, both of us now leaking onto the carpet. We didn't care.

"What's the time?"

I turned to look at the clock and laughed.

"Quarter to twelve."

She kissed me and gently pushed me off.

"Come on, there's still time."

She got up unsteadily and headed for the bathroom. I followed. We cleaned ourselves up as best we could and went into the kitchen. I grabbed some champagne out of the fridge, she grabbed a few bags of nibbles, and we went back to the living room and opened the lot. Turning over to the radio, Big Ben was winding up, and I poured two glasses as the first chime struck.

"Happy New Year!" we both said together and took a long slow drink.

By the time we returned to the music, we were both famished, so spent a while munching on lots of salty snacks. We looked at her bum; red, lots of little marks. Her thighs, less so, but still pink. The peg marks were still clearly visible on her breasts and she could still feel their effects on her pussy lips. I offered to kiss them better.

"Maybe later?" she replied.

"But don't expect another performance from me."

Her eyes opened wide.

"Ooh, I love a challenge."

We lounged on the sofa, Sally lying across my legs. More champagne, more salt. Talking about the evening. Yes, she had been to that place again. Calm, serene, able to accept – no, wanting - a level of pain and pleasure higher than she could take at other times. The feelings were different. She still didn't understand it and wasn't sure she wanted to. She teased me about the new orgasm rule but was happy for me to use it when I wanted to. I told her how it had been for me, how I'd picked up some of her different responses this time.

"Good," she said. "That means you'll know when you can push further."

"Whoa. I pushed quite hard at times tonight."

"I know. But I could have taken more, honestly." She gave me a gorgeous, cheeky grin. "Now, didn't you say something about kissing me better?"

"Yeah, make yourself comfortable, and I'll see what I can do."

"Hang on …"

She got up and left the room. When she returned, she held up a couple of cock rings and came over and kissed me.

"Fancy a challenge?" she asked.

"Go on."

"Sixty-nine. No restrictions this time. I bet I can get you hard before you make me come."

I knew I was on to a winner there; my groin was dead.

"The prize?" I asked.

"The winner has a slave for tomorrow."

"You're on!"

I couldn't lose.

The next day, she turned out to be quite a demanding Mistress.

Chapter 20 – Sally

Getting back to routine in the new year wasn't difficult. I loved what I did. And the usual comedown after all the festivities was absent this year. It had been such a wonderful time; the happiest Christmas that I could remember, certainly the best New Year. Nothing had happened to break the spell. Perhaps it wasn't a spell, perhaps this was how it could be. But there was one thing that clouded the outlook; I had to sort myself out. Marcus knew it, Mary knew it, Lucy knew it. Now, I knew it. I had to deal with my shadow.

I had finally booked a meeting with Jenny. I had taken the first step, but all the conversations I'd had with Marcus and Lucy gave me mixed feelings. It had clearly helped them both, but it hadn't been easy. I wanted to sort it out, but it had been so hard to tell him, and I wasn't at all sure I wanted to go through the whole story again to a stranger. And then probably go over it again and again over the coming weeks and months. But as I drove to see Jenny, I kept one goal in mind; what Marcus had said. Just meet her, see if you can work with her; that's all the first meetings are about.

She lived in a rather ramshackle bungalow on the outskirts of the city, the garden a bit overgrown. Small piles of building materials here and there, clearly untouched for years. I parked in the drive and took a moment to compose myself. On the dot of seven, I rang the bell. Within moments, the door opened.

"Hello. Jenny?"

"Yes. You must be Sally. Come in."

I followed her into the hall, and she led me through the house. As we went, I looked quickly into the rooms we passed; an eclectic mix of colours, furniture, and styles. All a bit haphazard, nothing quite finished. A cat looked up at me from a chair, obviously used to all the intruders in its territory.

We finally came to a room at the back of the house; part-conservatory, part-consulting room. A desk on one side, a couple of tables, and two large chairs, almost opposite one another, but not quite. She offered me one and settled herself in the other. After a brief pause, Jenny went through the things we had discussed over the phone. What she offered, and what she didn't. How she worked. The practical stuff; sessions, cost, confidentiality, and so on.

As I listened, I studied her. She was probably mid-fifties, straggly grey hair, a slight hippy look. Plump and maternal, but I detected a keen intelligence and a serious approach. As she wrapped up the introduction, she asked if it was okay for her to take notes.

"What can I help you with?"

The question threw me. I knew why I was there but wasn't ready with a short answer. I waffled for a bit, talking about my work, Marcus, Lucy, Mary, losing my parents, losing my sister, shadows. She just listened, didn't write anything down. When I finished, I realised I hadn't been making much sense. She smiled.

"Well, there's a lot there. But you've come to see me. People usually only do that when they've made the first breakthrough. That's accepting you want to resolve something. Have you come because you're at that stage, or because other people have persuaded you to come?"

I thought about that, I hadn't considered it before. Yes, others had encouraged me. But not forced me.

"They've encouraged me, but I'm here for me."

"Good. Because you need to be. Otherwise, you're not ready for this."

Over the remainder of the session, she began to gently tease things out of me. Very easy questions; how I was feeling, how was work, how my relationship with Marcus was. Little things, and by the end, I wasn't sure what we'd achieved. She asked if I wanted to move forward. I was happy to; I'd felt as comfortable as I thought I could under the circumstances, and she'd put me at ease and been patient. We booked in the next session, and she showed me out. Driving home, I was relieved; no great dramas, no confessions. I'd made a start.

I wondered if Marcus, Lucy, and Mary had been talking because before I started, they'd all told me more or less the same thing. They weren't going to ask me how it was going; just wanted to check I was okay every so often. They were there if I needed them.

I'd agreed with Marcus I'd send him a text after each session; just 'OK Good', or 'OK tough', that sort of thing. He'd told me sometimes I'd want to unload afterwards, and he was always ready to listen. But he'd also said I'd mostly want to think on my own. It wasn't Jenny who would resolve the issues. Her role was to help me resolve them myself. That meant working as hard between sessions as during them.

Even after the first one, I saw what he meant. When I got home, I poured myself a drink and went through it in my mind. I felt I could work with her; first goal achieved. But what had we actually done? I hadn't told her everything, hadn't told her what the problem was.

Over the next two or three sessions, I did, slowly. I talked, she listened, just the occasional question or nudge. It felt strange at first. I wasn't used to telling people about me, about my life. The shadow had made me wary, turn inwards. She'd picked up on 'the shadow' early on, and I'd eventually told her the story. Everything I'd told Marcus, everything I knew. Strangely, I managed it dispassionately, no tears, no drama. After that session, I felt quite good, almost proud.

The following weekend, Lucy came around to Marcus's for dinner. Zoe had come back after her family visits, but they weren't seeing as much of one another now. She was due to return home in a couple of months, so there were things she wanted to fit in before she went. They did sometimes end up in bed together but didn't do much else. Lucy didn't seem bothered.

"Well, I told you we weren't compatible – except in bed. I didn't think I was ever going to fall in love with her."

"So, you've just used her, you hussy!" Marcus said.

"Something like that," Lucy replied, smiling. "Although she isn't exactly innocent."

"When does she go back?"

"End of April, but I probably won't see her after Easter."

"Will you miss her though?" I asked.

"Yes and no. Sex, yes; otherwise, not much."

"You're a hard woman, Lucy," Marcus said, giving her a frown, which immediately broke into a grin.

"No. Just a realist. If I can't find love like you two, at least I can find someone to have as much fun as you two do."

Marcus gave me a questioning look, but I played the innocent. In truth, I didn't tell Lucy much about what we did. Well, told her how good it was, but not about what we got up to.

"How's the figure drawing going?" he asked.

"I'm feeling quite good about it. I've been getting lots of practice, and she's been a willing model. I've got a much better feel for the human form. I've done hundreds of drawings."

"If you want to get rid of any, I'll be happy to have a few more."

"Oh, most of them are thin sketches. Not finished, just practise."

"Still wouldn't mind some, I love that one." The one Lucy had given him for his birthday was hanging on the wall.

"I'll see. Some have got a bit … explicit."

"Oh well, if they're obscene I couldn't possibly see them," he joked, putting on his plummy accent. I made a note to pop in and see those.

"Are you still taking commissions?" Marcus asked.

"I'm open to offers."

"Portraits?"

"Possibly; depends what you want."

"I want Sally to sit for you."

"What?" I said, taken by surprise.

"I don't have one picture of you. I thought it would be good for Lucy to do one. Would you sit for her?"

"What would you want though?" Lucy asked. "My earlier attempts at portraits weren't a great success."

"But your work with Zoe is really good," he said. "Do whatever you feel comfortable with, entirely up to you. Whatever takes your fancy. Up for it?"

"Yeah, you Sal?"

"I guess so."

We talked into the evening. We hadn't caught up since Christmas for one reason or another. But we avoided my counselling and Lucy's family.

When she left, she asked me if I was all right. Just checking. I was, but we made a date to meet up in the week for a few drinks. When she'd gone, I felt the time was right to tell Marcus about my first few sessions. No long details, but about what we'd done. He listened, not saying a word until I'd finished my brain dump.

"That's about it so far."

"Thank you for telling me," he said simply. "Is it helping?"

"I don't know, too early to say. But I've been able to talk about these things without breaking down. That's progress in itself."

The next evening, I was feeling like a change, so Marcus let me tie him up; we'd done it once or twice. It wasn't about pain this way around, that didn't do it for either of us. Perhaps the odd slap or over-tight squeeze or bite. But I'd tease. Dress up in his favourite outfits, display myself, do the things I knew drove him wild. I was good at it, but I didn't have his patience. He could overcome his desire to prolong mine, but I couldn't. Once I got to a certain point, I needed to finish the job. But it was still good to have that control; he was helpless under me, and I got to use him. He never seemed to mind.

***

"Have you talked about it?"

"I've raised it once or twice, but carefully."

"And?" Lucy asked.

"I think he's thought about it, but he's wary."

"Well, look what he'd be taking on."

"Thanks."

"Sal, you're working things out yourself at the moment. Wait and see what happens there."

"Yeah, that's what Marcus said. It's right I suppose."

"And where would you live? Wouldn't make sense for you to move in with him in a rented place, and would you want anyone to move into your flat?"

"I don't know."

"So, don't rush. You already spend half the week with him. How much energy have you two got?"

"It's not all about that."

"I know. Only joking but take your time. You haven't known each other a year yet."

"A year next week actually, that was the first time he came to the book club."

"That's hardly an anniversary."

"No, I know, but just want you to get your facts right."

She laughed. But mention of the book club had given me an idea.

***

We started our own book club. We were still going to the monthly one where we had met, but this one was just Marcus and me. We would pick a book to read and spend some time each weekend discussing it. Only these were books the club would never have chosen. It was fun. Some of them were terrible, and we giggled at the semi-literate nature of the worst. But some were good; a few, very good. We got some new ideas too. We often ended up trying to copy one scene or another, usually abandoning the idea partway through to follow our own desires.

The sessions with Jenny were getting harder now. The facts were out in the open. Now it was more about my feelings. As they came out, they simply prompted more questions. I spent a few hours with Mary. We hadn't talked much about it over the years; I guess she thought I didn't want to, perhaps she didn't want to either. But she listened patiently, answering questions when she could, confirming most of my memories of the events of fifteen years ago.

Jenny gave me a safe space, never judging, never offering quick solutions. I was the one who had to solve this. Sometimes when I got home afterwards, I was exhausted, but with so much still going on in my head. I began to realise it was having an effect on me and Marcus. Weekends were still fine, but I began to pull out of the mid-week meetings. I needed time to think, so I was honest with him and he seemed to understand. Then he found a novel solution.

When I was about to leave one Monday morning, he handed me a DVD case.

"If you feel good one evening, try putting this on. There are two options to choose from. Don't watch it unless you're in the mood. Promise?"

I was intrigued and gave him a quizzical look.

"Promise?" he repeated.

"Okay, promise."

On Wednesday evening, I got home and made dinner. The session the evening before had been worrying, making me realise the issue wasn't as simple as I'd thought. What had my mother known? What had Wendy known? Had Mary told me everything she knew? I sat after dinner thinking but got nowhere.

A few weeks ago, I would have been with Marcus tonight, but he was giving me space, and I was grateful. I thought of him and remembered the DVD. Was I in the mood? I knew I soon could be, and I wasn't going to get anything else tonight. I poured myself another drink and put the DVD in the player and turned the TV on.

As I sat down, I got a shock; Marcus's voice came out of the speakers.

"Hello, Sally." I sat there puzzled. "There are two options coming up. I suggest you choose option one tonight, as the other requires you to put your collar on, so you'll need to do that when you feel ready. Have fun."

The screen changed, and a large '1' and '2' appeared. I selected '1'. His voice again.

"You'll need your phone and your wand; pause the disc, and restart when you have them." I paused and went and got them. It felt strange, but I restarted as soon as I sat down. "Now I want you to strip completely."

I removed everything quickly. It was a weird feeling. When I was at home, I never did this in the living room, only ever in bed. Now I was naked on my sofa listening to Marcus's disembodied voice. There was a certain thrill to it.

"Now I want you to watch," he continued, "watch closely. Imagine the girl is you. Concentrate on what you see, and no touching. That'll come later, don't worry."

A film started; a girl, naked, bent over, being punished by a man. Spanked, whipped. I guess it only lasted ten minutes. But it was working. I rarely used porn to masturbate, I'd watched enough when I'd been researching my new-found fantasies in recent years, but generally, my imagination was enough. This situation was different. He'd put this together; for me. That was a good feeling. I found myself watching intently, enjoying her pain. A lot. When the film ended, his voice came again.

"Now, text me. All you need is one two followed by yes or no, depending on whether this is working for you. Pause the DVD until you get a reply."

[12 YES]

I waited, wishing he'd hurry up. A minute or two later, my phone pinged.

[GOOD RESTART]

I did. His voice again.

"Another film for you, Sally. Watch closely, imagine the girl is you. Concentrate. This time, you can touch. But only your fingers."

The film was similar to the first, but this time, the girl was being punished by a woman. As I watched I could feel my arousal growing. Well, he'd given me permission, so I spread out on the sofa, and started exploring my body. This film was longer than the first, and I was again enjoying the girl's moans and cries, but also found myself watching the domme. Watching her obvious pleasure in what she was doing. The film ended before I brought myself to orgasm, but I was very worked up now. His voice again.

"Now text me. One three followed by yes or no to tell me if you've come or not, and m or f, depending on which film you enjoyed most. Pause until you get a reply."

Rather frustrated, I started typing; then stopped. Which had I enjoyed most? Oh boy, I couldn't decide. I shrugged.

[13 NO F]

Moments later, the reply came.

[INTERESTING RESTART]

I smiled; he knew my fantasies about women and sometimes played girl/girl films and pleasured me while I watched. He saw my reaction. I started the DVD again.

"Last film, Sally. A bit of a compilation, a bit of everything. Quite long. This is all yours. Leave it playing as long as you want. Take all the pleasure you want. Use the wand. Satisfy yourself completely. Let yourself wander into the scenes you see. Feel yourself part of them. When you're satisfied, skip to the next chapter."

The next hour or so was rather good. He was right, there was a bit of everything. Solos, Twosomes, threesomes, moresomes; rough, gentle, bizarre. I was lost in it. Lost in my pleasure, the most I'd had on my own. I let myself come down, then remembered his last instruction, and skipped to the next chapter. His voice.

"Welcome back, Sally. Now text one four followed by the number of orgasms you gave yourself."

Oh God, I didn't know. I was enjoying myself; I hadn't been counting.

[14 DIDNT COUNT SORRY]

Then I sent another.

[ANYWAY YOU GAVE THEM TO ME]

I was still recovering but smiling. The response came.

[JUST HELPED A LITTLE LOVE YOU SEE YOU FRIDAY SWEET DREAMS]

I smiled; I suspected I might have one or two.

At the weekend, he asked me about it. He'd had fun putting it together and wanted to know if it had worked for me. I told him it had. I asked him what else was on the DVD, but all he said was it needed me to be in the mood to put my collar on and act as if it was a real submission session, so I needed to wait for that moment. I wanted to submit that weekend; I'd done it once more since New Year, and it had been even better. But annoyingly – perhaps deliberately – he declined. We still had a lot of fun.

***

The next session with Jenny was hard. I was digging deep now, dragging feelings from deep inside me. But I could see the progress I was making. I even sometimes saw my mother and sister now without that shadow looming as large. I was interested to see Jenny hardly ever mentioned my father or the money. She was encouraging me to talk about everything else; those I wanted to remember fondly, I guess, rather than the things I didn't. He inevitably put in appearances, but he wasn't the focus. I had a bad night though, memories floating above me.

The next night, I wanted to relax and take my mind off the therapy, so I decided to play the other track on the DVD. After all, the first track had given me the desired results, and I was intrigued by the second. How could I submit when we were in different places? I knew some people did it but couldn't see how it would work. The whole appeal for us was the closeness, the touch, the physical and verbal contact. Oh well, let's find out.

In the beginning, he asked me if I wanted to submit to the virtual Marcus. Then he told me to get ready by dressing in any way I'd like and get a butt plug, lube, and the wand. I paused and got ready at my leisure. I showered and put on a full set I knew he loved. It made me feel good and the situation was turning me on. A new experience. I sat down with toys and my phone. Restarted the DVD; his voice.

"If you wish to continue you need to put your collar on. Remember, I will expect the same obedience, same rules. I will expect you to be honest and not break those rules. Obviously, you will be able to stop at any time given the situation, but if you do, I'd like you to tell me. If you're ready, put your collar on. Restart when it's on."

I picked it up and put it on myself for the first time; he'd done it for me up to now. It was a bit fiddly, but I fastened it up. Restarted.

"Sally, I still expect responses when I tell you to do things, even though I can't hear them. Is that understood?"

"Yes, sir," I heard myself saying to the empty room. It felt surreal.

"Right. Text me two two to tell me you're ready. Pause."

[22]

After a couple of minutes, the reply came.

[GOOD GIRL RESTART]

"Stand up." I did.

"Bend over the sofa." I did.

For the next hour or so, he moved me around; got me to stand in several positions and hold them. At first, it felt silly, like a game. But I gradually focussed on what I was doing, on listening for his voice and obeying his instructions. Saying 'yes sir' after every command. I let myself be led, wanting to follow. I obeyed and texted him as required. When I restarted after one pause, he told me to bend over my coffee table facing the TV, and a film started.

Another punishment session, this time quite fierce. A girl in the same position I found myself in, but tightly bound, being whipped and caned. I was worked up, and it turned me on more. I knew I couldn't do anything about it. Not without being told. Strangely I never even thought of disobeying. I watched as the girl's bum took more and more punishment, then the guy used her; mouth, pussy, ass, finally coming over her face, as always in these films. I was breathing heavily now, desperate for some relief.

His voice returned, text time.

[31 PLEASE MAY I COME SIR]

[NO RESTART]

The next film featured two girls in sixty-nine. I watched, wanting someone to do that to me right now; man, woman, I wouldn't have cared. In the middle, his voice came over the film.

"Put the plug in, Sally."

I reached for it and the lube, pulled my briefs down and inserted it without much difficulty, I was used to it now. Pulled them up again. All whilst keeping my eyes glued to the TV. I wasn't sure of the time now. Just lost in the moment. The film came to an end, and I tried again.

[32 PLEASE MAY I COME SIR]

[NO RESTART]

"Lay back on the sofa, Sally. During this next film, you can play with yourself any way you like. But only through your knickers, and you must not come until I give you permission."

The next film nearly blew my mind. One of my darkest fantasies; abduction. I'd told him. Two men snatching a girl, driving her to a deserted place; taking their time, stripping her, tying her up, toying with her, spanking her. But boy, given my mood, it was so hot. I was playing with myself now, my fingers rubbing my nipples and pussy over the material of my underwear.

They were whipping her now, her cries loud under every stroke. I looked several times at the wand but was worried once I used it, I wouldn't be able to control my need. When they started caning her, I succumbed. Putting it on low, I used it on the less sensitive areas, but even they were pretty responsive now. I avoided the obvious places. Couldn't trust myself. I was his. Couldn't disobey. The girl was being fucked now; mouth, cunt, ass. Two men together, using her. Suddenly his voice came through.

"What do you want, Sally?"

I put the wand down, and unsteadily composed a text.

[U SIR]

[TRY AGAIN]

[TO COME SIR PLEASE]

[NO KEEP GOING SEE HOW LONG YOU CAN BEAR IT]

I wasn't sure myself. I was getting close to my special place. The world was outside. But even so, I was finding it hard to control myself. I was watching the girl and imagining how it would feel to be in her place. To be beaten, to be used, to be fucked senseless. At that moment, I wanted to be her. I carried on, not thinking to slow down, let alone stop. I was his. Time slowed; I was lost. I vaguely heard a knocking sound. I carried on.

Another loud rap brought me back towards reality; someone at the door. Shit. Not now. Probably my elderly neighbour wanting one of her chats; that would bring the evening to a frustrating halt. I found the remote, paused the DVD, and walked a little unsteadily to the hall, still in a daze. Grabbing a coat off the rack to cover myself, I turned the handle.

Before I could fully open the door, it was pushed firmly, forcing me back.

"Marcus!"

A wicked smile crossed his face as he saw my wide-eyed surprise. As I began to realise the possibilities, he grabbed me, pulling the coat off. My head was spinning, still high on the earlier virtual activities, now desperate for the real thing. He held my arm tightly and pulled me into the living room. Pushing me against the sofa, he came close.

"Be careful what you wish for, Sally. It might come true."

Hearing his voice for real sent shivers through my body. He removed my bra, and pinched a nipple, squeezing it roughly between his fingers. Then moved to the other. Pain. Pleasure.

"Yes, sir," I managed to say. Virtual submission had instantly become real; I was still reeling from this sudden change. He was pushing against me now, his face inches from mine.

"Need to come, do you?"

"Yes, sir, please."

He turned me around and threw me over the back of the sofa, bent almost double. I was breathing hard now, almost ashamed at how much I needed him. He ripped my knickers off.

"These are wet, Sally. I hope you haven't come without permission."

"No, sir. Honestly. I haven't. I—"

Before I could finish, he stuffed my soaked knickers into my mouth. I struggled to breathe; had to make a real effort to take air in through my nose. Had to concentrate on that. I could taste myself in my mouth. Suddenly he started to strike my bum with his hand, hard. Spanking rapidly, remorselessly. I felt my legs flick up, but he carried on, holding me firmly over the sofa. I was whimpering, moaning, but my knickers muffled most of the sound.

Then my body convulsed as he entered me. I felt his cock rip into my pussy, driving hard to the hilt. Colours. I saw colours. Heat. I felt heat. And I was gone. I was aware of him pounding in and out, but my body had taken over. It was almost as if I was flying around looking down on us. I was well above the peak; sensations I'd rarely felt. Wasn't sure when it began, wasn't sure when it was over.

I was vaguely aware I wasn't bent over anymore. I was being pulled around to the front of the sofa and pushed onto my knees. When I landed, I was staring at his beautiful cock, glistening with my own juice. Before I knew it, he pulled my knickers out of my mouth and replaced them with his hardness, his hands holding my head firmly, as he slid vigorously in and out. Again, I was gone. Just allowing him to use me, to fuck my mouth. Very soon, I was rising again and lost myself to another round of ecstasy.

I was aware of being moved again. Pushed forward over the sofa. Felt the plug being removed. A sudden feeling of cold, then fierce heat, as he pushed himself firmly into my ass. Strong, rhythmic strokes, occasional sharp slaps on my bum. I lost it again. My hands gripped the sofa, my body writhing in response to his pressure. I wasn't fully aware of what he was doing, just its effects.

They ripped through my body and my mind. A sensation overload, seeming to come from my pussy, my ass, everywhere. Overwhelming me. I was only vaguely aware of him coming. I heard him grunt and felt the change in rhythm as his cock jerked to release his cum in me. Then conscious of his stillness, his hand on my back, stroking. Interrupted by my uncontrolled shaking. Nothing else. Spaced out. Then suddenly still.

The next thing I was aware of was peace. A feeling of exquisite peace. I slowly opened my eyes and took in what I saw. My house; the living room. Then breathing, soft breathing and my body gently rising and falling. But not my breathing, not my movement. Marcus. I was sitting on the floor, my bum by his thighs, my legs over his lap, and he was holding me to his chest, arms around me. As I slowly raised my head, he kissed my brow.

"Okay?" he whispered.

"Yes," I murmured. "I—"

"Ssh," he said. "Rest."

I don't know how long we stayed like that. But I finally came down to earth. He caressed me, talked to me, held me. I gradually replied. Giving each other little snippets of our feelings. It had been so intense. He finally got me something to eat and drink as I was feeling a bit lightheaded, and after a while, I began to feel normal again. Although after that experience, I wasn't sure I wanted to. He told me we'd finished over an hour ago. That

I'd cried quite hard during and after our joint orgasm. I didn't remember but saw it on my face when I looked in the mirror. It had worried him. His original idea had been to come in, do the deed, and disappear as quickly as he'd arrived. But when he saw my reaction, he changed the plan. I was glad. It felt good to have him there. I saw the collar lying on the table and picked it up, running it between my fingers.

"This is quite powerful, isn't it?" I said.

"No, it's what it means to us that's powerful."

I smiled at him.

"Thank you."

"For the collar?"

"No. For what you mean to me."

He stayed. We went to bed and talked into the night about the experience. The virtual element, the distance, the surprise. He worried about 'violating' my space, the amount of force he'd used, the tears. Confirming with each other it really had been as good as it felt. Somewhat to our surprise, we ended up making love again; slowly, softly, sensually. At two in the morning.

Then again at seven. More vigorously.

Chapter 21 – Marcus

I could see the counselling was affecting Sally. We still spent weekends together; still enjoyed being together. But there was a difference, a slight distance. If we spent some quiet time, I'd look over at her. Yes, she might have a book on her lap, but she wasn't reading. She'd be looking at the ceiling or out of the window, clearly deep in thought, and I guessed it wasn't about the book. It didn't lead to arguments or real problems, but it was noticeable.

It made me realise how my counselling years ago must have affected my then-partner. As now, I hadn't told her much, just a few words after each session. Seemed okay at the time, but I now saw how I'd kept it all to myself. She must have felt the exclusion. By the end, I had opened up to her and told her what I'd found. I hoped something similar might happen with Sally.

It was affecting our sex life as well. She was unpredictable. I found it harder to read her mood. Sometimes, she needed things to go slowly, at others she demanded urgency. She wanted to take control more often. Most weekends, she wanted to tie me up. And what she did became more assertive; giving me a spanking a few times, using a dildo in my ass. She seemed to be getting something out of it, and I enjoyed the result, but at times it seemed a bit mechanical, a bit cold.

While we were still having fun, I noticed her pleasure was less, more difficult to attain. And this seemed to reflect her mood generally. If she caught me looking at her in one of her thoughtful periods, she'd quickly flash a smile or blow me a kiss and come back. But she was less communicative, more reserved. I wished there was something I could do to help, but I knew there wasn't, other than be there if she needed me.

One weekend, she arrived late and was very quiet. We had dinner, and she made the effort to talk. But it was questions and answers, not conversation. We spent a slightly awkward evening and went to bed early. She was keen enough to make love, but it lacked our usual passion, our usual playfulness. Afterwards, she went to sleep almost straightaway, and I lay there conscious of my inability to help.

When we woke up in the morning, she had changed again. She woke me up, wanting to be taken. Tempting me, taunting me, until I did what she wanted. I was happy to oblige, but it was unusual for us in the morning. She was brighter during the morning but had a set expression a lot of the time. We went out for lunch, and walked around afterwards, window shopping; not buying anything, except some steak for dinner.

"I'm sorry, I'm not very good company," she said, pushing food around the plate.

"Tough time?"

"Yeah. I'm more confused than I've ever been."

"It's all right. Do what you need to do. I'm here if you need me."

"I don't know if I can go on."

"With the counselling?"

"Yeah."

"What happens if you give up now?"

"I put it all back in the box."

"And do you really believe that'll work."

She looked up at me for a while, then lowered her eyes again.

"No."

I wasn't sure whether to soothe or challenge.

"Is it painful?"

"Yes, at times."

"If you give up, what will that pain have been for? What will you have gained?"

She shrugged.

"Nothing," I said. "But if you carry on, you can sort this. I'm proud of you for doing it; you should be too. You will be by the end. And you'll be able to deal with this shadow."

I hadn't mentioned it to her since the start of her therapy, and she looked sharply up at me as I did now.

"I don't think I can beat it, Marcus."

"I'm not sure that's the point, Sal. Your father will always be there, you can't erase him."

"I wish I could."

"But you can't. You need to find another way. Give it time."

"But I've got more questions than answers. More suspicions than before. What if—"

"Sally, are you sure you want to talk about this? I don't want to get in the way of the work you're doing with Jenny. That might get even more confusing."

"Sorry."

"I'm not pushing you away, but I want you to be sure it will help rather than hinder."

She returned to pushing the fork around for a while, eating the odd morsel. Quietly, she did tell me about her progress. Questions, thoughts, feelings. Dispassionate at first, almost cold. But getting worked up at times, particularly when her father was involved. I listened, saying nothing. I let her get it out of her system. By the time she finished, she was leaning back on her chair, wine glass held between her hands.

"Don't you think that's progress?" I said. "That you can sit here and tell me all that?"

She looked thoughtful for a while.

"Yes," she said finally. "But I'm no nearer a solution."

"How much of what you've told me could you articulate before you started?"

"Not much."

"You're still finding the questions. Don't you want to go on and work out some answers?"

"I suppose so. Better go on then, hadn't I?"

We cleared the table and settled down to watch a film. It wasn't good. About an hour in, she sat up and turned to me. A strange look in her eyes.

"Marcus, can I tie you up?"

"If you want to."

"Yes. I feel like using you. Sorry."

"Sally."

"Yes?"

"Promise me one thing."

"What? I'm not going to hurt you."

"No. Promise me you'll stop apologising. You've been doing it all night."

She grinned for the first time since the morning, and just stopped herself saying sorry again.

"I'll try."

We went through to the bedroom, and she stripped me. Made me sit on the bed while she slowly stripped herself in front of me, and then tied me to the bed face down. After teasing and caressing, she started to slap me gently, building up until she was spanking me firmly. Then she asked if she could use the flogger. She'd never used it before, so it was mainly trailing it over my body, rather than flogging, but she tried it a few times, enough for me to feel some pain. I could hear her breathing in between; it seemed to be working for her.

She turned me over and tied me down again. Now she did use me. Holding the headboard, she lowered herself onto my face and used my mouth to bring her to orgasm; straddling my chest, I watched as she did the same for herself, and finally riding me slowly, pausing a couple of times to frustrate me, until she brought me to a climax.

After she untied me, we lay there in silence for a while, arms around each other.

"Was it okay?" she asked. "The spanking."

"Yes."

"And the flogging?"

"I certainly felt it."

She looked at my bum.

"There are one or two red patches."

"Did it work for you?" I asked.

She looked at my bum, and then up at me.

"It satisfied a need. Yes."

***

The text after her next session consisted of one word.
[BAD]

***

I didn't see her until the weekend. Lucy had persuaded her to go out the night before; I was pleased. She needed to let her hair down and have some fun. She'd enjoyed it at the time; got drunk. But Saturday morning the hangover had added to her melancholy. By the time she arrived at lunchtime, she was delicate and quiet. I fixed her something to eat and made her drink. Gradually, she began to feel better.

We sat in the afternoon, doing nothing, watching some rugby. She fell asleep. Apologising when she woke up; I told her not to. By dinner time, she was recovered, from the alcohol, at least. She asked if my bum was okay, even though I'd told her during the week it was fine, she'd seen there had been no marks the morning after.

"Why? Want to do it again?"

"Yes."

"Okay. You're in charge tonight."

She reacted straight away, taking over. Going to change, she told me to strip to my underwear, and wait. When she came back, she was wearing a chemise and stockings; what else I couldn't tell. Her hair was tied in a ponytail and she had a handful of toys.

"Lie on the floor."

I laid out flat on my back. She put the stuff on the table and stood at my feet. Slowly, she walked around me, allowing me to look up and catch glimpses of thigh. Then she walked up over me, one foot either side until she was standing above me. I could see she wasn't wearing any knickers; better still when she opened her legs more.

Moving back slightly, she pulled the chemise over her head; nothing but hold-ups. Looking down, she started caressing herself, teasing me. It worked. Quite quickly moving her fingers between her legs, spreading herself for me to see. She bent down and placed two of her fingers in my mouth; I sucked them. Lowering herself to her knees, she again placed her pussy over my mouth and invited my touch.

This time my hands were free, and I could hold her bum and move her around as I started to lick and suck her. She was soon uttering evidence of enjoyment. As she built, she became more assertive, pressing down on me, rocking her hips to rub herself onto me. As she neared orgasm, she started telling me what to do, quite aggressively for her. Where she wanted my tongue, what she needed. When she came, she dropped harder on to me, and I stopped most of my movements, as she gently rocked, twitching. I could smell her, taste her; hardly breathe. Getting off me, she bent and gave me a kiss.

"Good boy," she said seductively and smiled.

"Thank you, mistress," I joked back.

"Good boys deserve a reward, just a little one."

She moved around and removed my briefs. Bending by my side, she proceeded to lick and suck my cock, whilst playing with herself gently between her legs, making sure I could see what she was doing at both ends. I wondered how long I'd last. She knew; she stopped well before I was in danger of coming.

"I want you over the cubes."

My original cube had been joined by a couple of others. The combinations and possibilities were endless. She arranged two next to one another with a gap between them.

"Lie over them, cock in between."

She started running her hands over my back and legs, occasionally reaching underneath, and stroking my hanging cock. One hand ended up resting on my bum, squeezing. I felt her hand lift off, and then come down with a glancing blow. Not hard, but firm. She repeated the stroke, then again. Moving around, maintaining a steady rhythm. She was still holding my cock with her other hand, her grip tightening slightly with each slap on my bum. The strokes got harder and started to sting.

This was the hardest she had spanked me. I could feel the warmth spreading. She moved her other hand up to grasp my balls, and again her grip tightened with each impact. I was beginning to move in reaction to each hand fall, and my breathing was catching. I heard her chuckle.

"Too much?"

"No, not yet," I replied. I was wondering how far she would go. She stopped, and stood up; going to the table, she picked up the flogger, and stood in front of me, letting it trail over my face, head, and neck. She squatted, legs open, knowing I was looking straight at her open sex.

"Your bum's quite pink. I want to make it red."

It was a statement, not a request.

She got up again and trailed the fronds down my back and along my legs. The touch parted from my skin, and I waited for the first strike. Last time, she'd given me a few light blows on my bum, not practised enough to be effective. I felt the contact with my cheeks; gentle, almost a quick drag across the skin. She repeated this for a while, moving up to my back a few times. Stopping, she reached under me to stroke my cock, laughing slightly. I felt her stand up, and she started again, firmer this time. Still concentrating on my bum, but with the occasional contact with my lower back and thighs.

"Open your legs."

I hesitated slightly, not sure whether I fancied exposing myself to her inexpert flogging, but seeing my hesitation, she stopped and eased her hand between my thighs. Without orders from my brain, my legs opened to allow her access, and she started massaging my scrotum and working her fingers down my cock.

Then the suede hit again. Still gentle, but regular and accurate. It wasn't yet really painful, but it was the most I'd ever taken, so I was absorbing this new sensation. She stopped, and used her hand between my legs, before squatting in front of me. Her pussy wet. She pushed two fingers inside and drew them out, licking them herself, a fixed grin on her face. Reinserting them, she placed them at my lips, and I licked them clean.

"Time for the next step."

Again, a statement, not a question. She went to the table, and I saw her pick up some lube and a plug. Behind me, she pulled a cheek to one side, and I felt the cold gel hit my ass, then the tip of the plug push into me. She often played with me there, so it wasn't unusual, and I raised myself slightly to allow the plug easier access. It slipped in.

In this calm, I briefly considered how I was feeling. My cock was stiff, and my ass felt good. My bum was stinging; I wasn't getting turned on by the pain itself, just from the situation. She played with the plug, and massaged my sex again, before standing up. I waited for the pain to begin again and I didn't have to wait long.

She restarted with the same intensity. I was feeling it now. She continued with slow regular strokes, only every ten seconds or so. And my body was responding to each one now. I noticed her breathing for the first time, a little grunt every time the fronds came down on my flesh. I gradually felt the force increase, my body tensing with each stroke to deal with the pain.

But she didn't slow down; still regular, but steadily increasing in force. I knew I might need to use a colour soon. I wasn't used to this, and it didn't produce the simultaneous endorphin rush it did in her. For me, it was just pain. Every so often, I felt a frond catch my perineum or the base of my scrotum; that stung, made me yelp. If she noticed, it didn't stop her. Her grunts were clearly audible now on every stroke. Suddenly, the force increased, and all I had now was pain, severe pain.

"Yellow," I finally said. Another stroke. The pain intensified.

"Yellow, Sally," I repeated, louder. I was struggling now. Searing pain with each stroke.

Nothing. Then an agonising pain shot between my legs, as a frond hit something delicate. I cried out, my breath catching in my throat. But another stroke followed, hard across my bum, and again a severe pain from my right cheek.

"Red, Sally. Red!" I shouted, as loud as my breathing would allow. Another stroke landed almost immediately. Then nothing. I let my body relax and tried to get my breath back. I heard her breathing heavily. Then scream. A piercing shriek. I managed to look around in time to see her drop the flogger, a look of horror on her face. She raised her hands to cover her mouth, looking at the results of her work. She dropped to her knees and burst into tears.

I was hurting; my bum was burning, and something between my legs was throbbing. But I slowly got up and turned around. She was staring at me, eyes wide open. Distraught, sobbing, shaking. Hands still over her mouth. I went over to her, and knelt down, putting my arms around her. She didn't respond, just leaned towards me, rocking slightly. My pain was gradually settling, but I could still feel throbbing in my groin, and a sharp stinging on one cheek. I tried to soothe her, but she carried on crying.

"Oh, God!" she mumbled. "What have I done?"

"Ssh, it's okay."

I stroked her hair, pulling her close. Her body slowly softened into me.

"I'm sorry. So sorry. Oh, God. What have I done?"

I held her. I wasn't sure what she'd done, but I needed to calm her before I took a look. After a while, she started to quieten. I pulled away from her. Her face was wet with tears, her expression still one of distress. I kissed her.

"It's okay, it's okay."

"No, it's not. I've hurt you."

"It's nothing, I'm not used to it. Don't worry."

"Show me," she demanded.

"It's okay."

"Marcus, show me. Turn around."

I got up on my knees, turned around and bent forward. Another shriek.

"You're bleeding!"

This started her sobbing again. I went back to hugging her, and she resumed her rocking.

"I'm sorry. I'm sorry." Over and over again. In the end, I kissed her to stop her saying it.

"Ssh. Stop apologising. Remember?"

"But …"

"Accidents happen. It's nothing, it'll have gone by the morning. You sometimes have your marks for days."

"But you've never made me bleed."

"It's just an accident, Sal."

"Oh, Marcus."

She pushed against me again, and I held her. The tears gradually subsided. I eventually pulled myself away and went to look at the damage. She was right, she had broken the skin. But only a little nick on my bum, and the more painful one between my perineum and scrotum; that was the bugger that hurt. Neither was going to be anything other than a bit sore for a day or two. I took the plug out, cleaned the cuts, and went back. She was kneeling in the same position I'd left her, in a daze. She looked up at me. I reached down and helped her off the floor. Leading her over to the sofa, I sat her down and asked if she was okay.

"How can I be? I've hurt you. I'm so sorry."

"Sally. Listen to me. It's nothing. Don't worry about it."

"Oh, Marcus."

I got her a drink, not sure if it was a good idea, but she gulped it down, coughing as the alcohol met her dry throat. I sat beside her, and she leaned on me. The occasional single sob shook her. We stayed like that for some time, except when I got her another drink. She kept on apologising; I kept on reassuring her.

Eventually, I suggested we go to bed; to cuddle and to sleep. Our desire had long since gone to bed anyway. I led her through to the bedroom, she was in something of a trance. I took her stockings off, and climbed in beside her, cuddling up and holding her. Kissing her shoulders gently and telling her I loved her. I didn't get much back. Hopefully, a good night's sleep would put it in a clearer perspective. It didn't.

When I woke in the morning, she was gone.

Chapter 22 – Sally

What a difference to Christmas. Slumped in a pair of old PJs on the sofa, not watching the TV glowing in the corner. Drinking coffee, eating chocolate. At seven in the morning. Specifically, the big, thick egg Marcus had had delivered. When it arrived, I'd been pleased, then ashamed. Put it on the table, and it had stayed there ever since. Until half an hour ago. I'd ripped it open and smashed it into chunks.

Now I felt sick. Coffee, dark chocolate, feeling shit. A bad combination. Every bite I took reminded me of him; I hadn't seen him for three weeks. Hadn't spoken to him, couldn't. Just replied to one or two of his texts with a monosyllable. I couldn't face him. Memories of that weekend still whirled around in my head …

I'd managed to get out of his flat early in the morning; I hadn't slept at all. I lay there for a few hours while I thought things over. For the first time at Marcus's, my shadow appeared. I made my decision and making sure he was asleep, I'd crept out of bed, grabbed the minimum clothing I needed and slipped out to my car.

Driving home, the tears started again. I felt so low. By the time I got in, I was exhausted, but knew I wouldn't be able to sleep. The shadow had come with me. I spent Sunday ignoring his calls; sometimes wondering why he didn't come around, but grateful he didn't. I eventually answered one of his texts asking if I was okay.

[NEED TIME SORRY]

He responded.

[I LOVE YOU]

Then no more messages.

Going to work on Monday had at least allowed me to concentrate on other things. But David asked me if I wasn't feeling well, so I obviously wasn't managing to hide it. The session that week was horrible. I told Jenny I'd hurt Marcus; not how – I couldn't be that honest - but enough for her to understand. She asked me how I felt, and it all came out.

I didn't deserve him; I didn't deserve anything. I wasn't worth his love or trust. I'd lied to him, misled him. Now I'd hurt him. I felt guilt. Perhaps it would be better if I let him get on with his life. After allowing me to dry my tears, she'd asked me how Marcus had reacted. I told her.

"Why don't you believe him?" she asked.

The question stunned me. I hadn't thought of it like that. I was silent for some time; she just sat there. I trusted him completely, so why couldn't I accept what he'd said, that it was an accident. Nothing more. When I got home, I poured myself a drink and thought it through. I didn't come up with an answer.

I was struggling to function; felt miserable all the time. In the end, I did tell David I was having a few problems with things from my past and was getting help for it. He was great about it; offered any support I needed. Every evening, I sat at home, going through everything time and time again. The shadow, my constant companion.

I didn't get anywhere and usually ended up in floods of tears, mainly of frustration. Lucy had rung a couple of times and I'd tried to hold a normal conversation with her. Didn't want her fussing about, couldn't handle it. But on Saturday, she appeared at my door, took one look at me, and took over. Despite my protests, she pushed me into the shower, and told me in no uncertain terms not to come out until I was 'in a fit state'. By the time I reappeared, she had tidied my bedroom, cleaned up the living room, and made me some coffee and breakfast. When I'd had some, she was her usual self.

"Right you," she said. "What's going on? You look shit."

"Oh, Lucy, don't. I don't need this."

"Yes, Sal, you do. What's going on? Marcus is worried sick."

"You've spoken to him?" I was shocked.

"Yes, he called me yesterday. Asked if I'd seen you. If you were all right. Then I was worried."

"What did he tell you?"

"Enough to know I needed to come and sort you out."

"What did he tell you?"

He'd told her that in our 'passion' I'd accidentally hurt him, and then felt guilty about it and disappeared the next morning. Well, at least he hadn't gone into detail.

"Is he okay?" I asked.

"He's fine. Just worried about you."

"He hasn't come around."

"Would you want him to?"

"No," I finally admitted.

"And he knows that; knows you better than you know yourself."

We sat in silence for a while. When she restarted, her tone had softened.

"Is this the counselling, Sal?"

"Yes."

"Tough?"

"Yeah."

She came over and hugged me; I hugged her back and burst into tears. She let them come. They stopped eventually, and she broke away.

"Right," she said. "We're going out, time to get ready."

I resisted; didn't feel like it, wanted to hide away. But she won. Taking me through to the bedroom, she made me do my hair, put some makeup on, talking about God knows what whilst she watched. We went into town, wandered around the shops, and had some lunch. Afterwards, we came home, and she stayed with me for the rest of the day. She didn't ask any more questions, but I did tell her things. Sometimes unconnected phrases, sometimes ramblings. She just listened. We got a takeaway and opened a bottle of wine, then another. By the time she left, I was shattered. I hadn't slept all week. I went to bed and drifted off almost immediately.

The session that week was more productive. I'd been thinking hard about what my life would be like without Marcus; it was horrible. I missed him. I'd hurt him and was becoming aware I was probably hurting him now too. That made me feel worse. But I didn't know what to do.

Jenny asked me how I felt about him. I told her; she knew how we'd met, how much I loved him. But I added a bit more detail about what else we did, enough for me to think she understood me. She seemed cool about it; asked a couple of questions about the relationship, perhaps checking it wasn't abusive. I told her I'd physically hurt him, about leaving, about not seeing him.

"Why don't you call him? Go around?" she asked eventually.

"I can't. I don't know why. But I can't face him."

"Are you frightened of him?"

"God, no. More frightened of myself. I don't want to hurt him again."

"What happened, Sally?"

I looked at her, sighed, took a deep breath. And told her.

***

Over the next few days, I tried to answer her parting questions. Why did I do it? Why didn't I hear him say yellow or red? I hadn't thought about it. But now realised it was the crucial element, more important than the actual pain I'd inflicted. What must he be thinking? I was certain he wouldn't have ignored me if the situation had been reversed. Trust; we trusted each other. But now?

At the weekend, Lucy appeared again; I'd thought she might. I knew I couldn't fob her off either. We spent the day at home this time, reminiscing. Boys, girls, holidays, arguments. Everything. Laughing, joking, melancholy. I asked her if she'd spoken to Marcus. Yes, they'd spoken a couple of times, him checking I was okay. Hesitantly, she passed on his love, although he was still texting me every day, telling me. I rarely responded, almost embarrassed now. I loved him but couldn't tell him.

Another takeaway, more alcohol. When I went to bed, I felt better than I'd felt for many days. I thought about Marcus; images of some of our adventures filtered into my mind, and I felt aroused for the first time since I'd hurt him. And I finally did something about it. But immediately afterwards, the tears came. He wasn't there to hold me, to hug me to sleep. I missed that. The shadow seemed to laugh, quietly.

By the next session, I had an answer. It had come to me in the night. The shadow had appeared, and I had shouted into the darkness, telling it to go away. And I had the answer. I told Jenny.

"I was taking my anger out on him. Releasing that pent-up rage on Marcus."

"Possibly."

"I was, Jenny, I see it now. I've relived it in my head."

"How does that make you feel?"

"Dreadful. How could I have done it? I love him."

"He was there. You needed to release that energy."

"But I wasn't angry with him."

"No. But anger isn't easy to control. Can you explain your anger?"

I tried to, stuttering, rambling. Anger about what I didn't know about my father and his money, my mother's death, losing Charlie, about Wendy. Back to my father again. About the effect it was having on me. By the end, I was quite agitated. Almost shouting. Jenny let me spout, left me to tire myself out, handed me the tissues. She asked me if I saw a common factor.

"My father. I hate him."

"Perhaps. Why?"

I started recounting the story, but she stopped me.

"No, Sally. What is it that you actually hate about him? Where is the rage focussed?" I couldn't tell her; it was too general. "You need to think about the focus, the point your rage is centred on. This hatred is hurting you, not him." I thought about the time Marcus had said that. "Then, we need to give you a way of neutralising it."

"How?"

"Do you feel better for getting all this out tonight?"

"Yes."

"We need to find a safe release for it." She paused. "Other than whipping your boyfriend half to death." I felt myself blush slightly. "Think about it. For some, it's as easy as a new hobby or exercise; running, going to the gym. For others, it might be meditation or yoga. Some might want to go into the middle of nowhere, and shout and scream until they're exhausted."

Over the next few days, I did think about it. Some of her suggestions made sense, but it seemed most were just a way of coping, not a way of solving. I still wanted a solution. But Jenny had got me thinking. Why did

Sally

I hate my father? I'd never really analysed it, just knew I did. And what was my release? Easter weekend was fast approaching. I had nothing to do. Plenty of time to think …

So here I was. Alone. On Easter morning. Almost snorting caffeine. I'd been thinking for two days; hadn't washed, hadn't changed. On Friday, I had laid photos out on the tables, on the floor. Pictures I normally hid away. Mum, Charlie, me; and my father. I only had two or three of him. I didn't have family photos on display. Now I'd got them out I'd realised Marcus didn't have any either. Just two of the dogs he had had with his last partner.

But now they were all around me, bringing back memories, good and bad. Holidays, family gatherings, fun in the back garden. I had ended up with the ones of my father on the table in front of me. I'd spent hours staring at them, trying to read the face looking back at me. But the strange thing was it spurred little reaction. I wasn't afraid of them, or the man in them. Where was the hatred?

I eventually got some breakfast and more coffee. I forced myself to sit down and drag up every memory of him I could, everything I could remember about him; his short visits, his presents, holidays together. My dislike was evident, but I couldn't find any single thing that had sparked my hatred.

I tried to work out when I'd first recognised it. But I couldn't. I didn't remember it being there after he died, just a numbness. We'd never been close. After the will, I'd been more mystified than angry. When did it start? Slowly I worked it through; it had grown slowly, over the years. Without me realising it. As I had pushed him more and more into the back of my mind, so the shadow had grown.

After grabbing a sandwich, I thought about the money. How did I feel about it? Again, the more I'd tried to forget it, the more it burned away at me. I thought of all the things I could have done with it. All the things I could do with it now, *we* could do with it, Marcus and me. Give it away, that's what he'd said. Give it away. Would it help? I doubted it. It was too tied up with my father. I had to resolve both. Getting rid of one wouldn't help, would it? I fell asleep in the afternoon, all this swirling around in my dreams. I woke up sweating.

Opening a bottle of wine, I started to drink; slowly, but steadily. I was going to get drunk, perhaps it would allow me to see something I'd missed. After all, we can all solve the world's problems if we're drunk. But it didn't help, I simply started to get angry. Started talking to the pictures. Asking questions they couldn't answer, calling them names, throwing accusations. More alcohol; the last of the chocolate. Tired, melancholy now; tears. I managed to crawl into bed, bleary and drunk. Asleep.

I awoke with a start. Sweating, feeling terrible, feeling sick. Just made it to the loo before throwing up. I was crying before I'd emptied my stomach, retching, gasping for breath. I slumped down on the bathroom floor, vaguely aware I needed to stay there for a while. The room was spinning; I wasn't sure what time it was.

Then it appeared, my shadow. Hanging over me. I called out, shouted, pleaded with it to leave me alone, to go away. I tried to stand up; vomited again. The shadow was gone. I half-stumbled, half-crawled into the hall, and staggered through the house, calling out to it. My arms waving, vaguely aware of bumping into things as I searched. Didn't find it.

I swept the photos around, poking them, talking to them. Holding a picture of my father, blaming him for everything, for everything that had ever gone wrong in my life. For Mum's death, for Charlie's death, for landing me with his dodgy money. For all my failed relationships, for ruining my relationship with Marcus. It was all his fault.

I managed to get back to the bathroom before retching again, but there wasn't much left to bring up. I went back to bed and pulled the duvet over me. My head hurt, my throat hurt, my gut hurt. I lay there, half comatose. Crying dry; the tears were all gone. As I finally felt myself giving in to my exhaustion, the shadow appeared. Looking up at it, I saw a face staring straight back at me.

***

I was dimly aware of a heavy thumping; I turned over. Then aware of my phone ringing somewhere in the house. It stopped, then rang again. I tried to lift myself up, but dropped again, as nausea overtook me. It rang again. This time I struggled to get up, and holding anything I could reach, I made my way down the hall. As I passed the door, a loud rapping shocked me into consciousness, and I was confused for a minute, before looking through the spyhole. Lucy. I slowly unlocked and opened the door. She took one look at me.

"Sally, are you all right?"

"No. I … feel … terrible. I …"

The nausea rose again; she manhandled me into the bathroom, and I threw up. She sat by me, passing me tissues when I'd finished. Her arm around me.

"Okay. Let's get you sorted out."

She stripped my PJs off and made me get in the shower. I felt the warm water flowing over me. She handed me some shower gel and let me get on with it. Sitting on the loo seat to make sure I didn't fall over. When I came out, she handed me a towel and went to get me something clean to put on, and a robe. Leaving the messy stuff on the floor, she led me into the kitchen, sat me down, and gave me a glass of water.

"Drink it. Slowly."

I tried; it caught in my throat, but it went down. She said nothing, just told me to keep going. Then she took me through to the living room and put me on the sofa. I curled up. Clammy, headache, nauseous. And fell asleep. When I opened my eyes, she was sitting on the other sofa, with a book on her lap.

"Feeling better?"

"Uh … Well, I can see you clearly now. I'm hungry."

By the time I followed her into the kitchen, Lucy was buttering some toast.

"Try this. Don't wolf it down."

We sat at the table, and she drank some coffee while I ate. It seemed to stay put. She made some more.

"What happened, Sal? This place looked like a bomb hit it." I looked at her frowning. "I've spent the morning clearing up. Broken ornaments, overturned furniture, photos all over the place. Empty bottles."

I was baffled; broken … overturned … I didn't remember any of that. I remembered the photos, though, they'd been the key. And my drunken revelation.

"Broken?"

"Yes. Your green vase, glass bowl, a couple of other things I couldn't recognise."

"God, that must have been last night."

"What happened?"

"Got drunk; had a bit of a meltdown."

"How are you feeling now?"

"I think I've cracked it, Luce."

"Cracked it?"

"Yes. It's not my father. It's … me."

***

Jenny noticed a change straight away. I told her about the weekend, about the photos, about the binge. About the meltdown. And how, when I finally recognised a face in the shadow, it wasn't him. It was me; my own face staring back at me. As if I was looking in the mirror.

"How does that make you feel?"

"Well, I don't understand it, but I get the feeling it's a big part of the answer. I'm not sure how to deal with it, not sure what it means. But when I was looking at the photos, I was puzzled by how I felt when I looked at my father's picture."

"What did you feel?"

"Nothing. No anger, no hatred. No feelings at all. I couldn't figure out why."

"And now?"

"Still nothing. I've been thinking about him ever since. No hate. No love either, but no anger. He's just my father."

"And the rest of the family?"

"It's early, but I remembered them yesterday without the usual heaviness, even Wendy."

"You had quite a weekend, Sally."

"Not one I ever want to repeat."

"No. I suggest we find some ways to make sure you never have to."

We talked some more about my feelings; what I wanted to do moving forward. She made some suggestions, and we agreed to work on some of them. She still wanted me to think about a release mechanism for any stress or emotion, but I'd already come up with an answer for that. Lucy had somewhat reluctantly agreed to join the gym with me.

"What about Marcus?" Jenny asked towards the end. That was the one cloud. I'd asked Lucy not to tell him what had happened at the weekend if she spoke to him. I was desperate to go back and try and make it up to him; if he wanted me. But I was scared about how it had affected us. Could we go back to how we'd been? Could he forgive me?

Over the next couple of days, it felt as if I was awake again. Some of the pain lifted. I knew I still had a lot of things to put into place, but I was happier. I felt I was over the worst of it. At night, my desire had returned, and I'd satisfied it thinking of Marcus. Still too nervous to talk to him, to see him.

I wanted us to go straight back to how we were, but I knew that wasn't going to happen. I'd missed his signal. I'd hurt him, both physically and by running away, and then avoiding contact for nearly four weeks. I still felt guilty. That wasn't going to be easy to overcome. I just needed to find a way to do it. I came up with a dozen ways to deal with it, not happy with any of them. Perhaps I was over-analysing, that would be ironic. I decided to keep it simple.

Chapter 23 – Marcus

Well, that was Easter. What a difference to Christmas; another weekend without Sally. That was three in a row. I felt helpless. I also missed her; missed her like crazy. I missed her smile, her laugh, her smell, her company, her humour, her love, and her body too. I'd texted and e-mailed her but got few replies. Lucy had agreed with my decision not to just turn up. But the silence was depressing.

I tried to get on and write, and some stuff came. Odd stories about the past, about despair, about loss. All quite dark or melancholy. It didn't stop me thinking about her. I knew she might come out of this with new goals, new ambitions, and they might not include me. I tried not to think about that. I was something of a realist; if it happened, I would have to deal with it, but it was going to hurt. Badly. When Lucy told me Sally hadn't been too well over Easter, I wasn't sure what to think.

[NEED TO TALK. FANCY A DRINK? CHECKERS 6?]

I breathed a huge sigh of relief.

[YES]

Checkers was a small bar around the corner from her. It had a nice roof terrace, and the weather was just about warm enough to get a bit of privacy if we needed it. I put on a few layers and got there early. Waiting outside, I wondered what to expect; how would she be? I hadn't spoken to her for nearly four weeks, had no real idea how she was or how things had been going. When she walked around the corner, my heart skipped a beat. As she approached, I looked at her. Baggy jeans, jumper, jacket. Hair up. She stopped a few paces from me.

"Hello, Marcus."

"Hi, Sal."

She had a serious look; a bit more make-up than usual, but it highlighted those green eyes. My beautiful Sally. I let her go in first, and we went to the bar. It was quite busy, mostly people who'd met up straight from work by the look of it. We took our drinks onto the terrace and walked to a free table at the far end. Taking our coats off, we sat down. I smiled at her, and she eventually returned it. It struck me how nervous she was, and I wasn't sure that was a good sign.

"How are you?" I asked after a minute or two of silence.

"Quite good. You?"

"I've missed you."

I saw her flush, that delicate flush.

"I've missed you, too." She looked away. Silence again. She fiddled with her hair.

"So," I said. "You wanted to talk."

"Yes. But I'm not sure where to start. It's been a bit of a rollercoaster."

"You said you were feeling good. Does that mean you've made progress?

"Yeah, I think I've worked it out, well part of it."

"That's good, Sal."

"In a way."

Slowly, she told me what had happened with the counselling. She avoided any mention of our last weekend, of our weeks in limbo. Her voice was matter of fact, not angry or sad. I became keenly aware she was talking about her family and her father without any emotion. That was progress. She told me how she now felt about them all, about the legacy. When she got to her realisation that the problem was hers to solve, and how that had been something of an epiphany, I smiled inwardly.

"That's where I am."

"How do you feel about all this?"

"Lighter; I haven't felt the shadow all week. That's good, isn't it?"

"Of course it is."

We lapsed into silence again.

"Marcus, I'm sorry …"

My heart sank. I waited for the 'but'. It didn't come.

"For what?"

"For what I did."

"It was nothing, Sal. Healed in a day."

"Not that, though that was bad enough. But for running and hiding."

"Seems to have helped."

She looked thoughtful.

"Perhaps."

Silence again. We both returned to our drinks.

"Come on Sal, spit it out." I waited for the gentle let-down. She took a deep breath, and for the first time, those eyes looked straight at me.

"Will you give me a second chance?"

I felt myself relax, breathed an inward sigh of relief.

"Second chance?"

"I don't want to lose you."

I smiled and stretched my hands across the table; she hesitantly put hers in them.

"Sal, I'm not going anywhere, I thought *I'd* lost *you*." She closed her eyes and let out a heavy breath; I squeezed her hands. "I love you, still do. I missed you like crazy."

Her eyes opened again. "But I feel so guilty, I took my anger out on you."

"Come on, don't replace hate with guilt. Otherwise, you'll be in therapy for years."

"I broke our trust. I didn't stop when you called red. I've been trying to think how I would react if it had been the other way around."

"Yes, that bothered me. I've thought about that quite a bit. But I know more now about what you were going through. In truth, you weren't in the right frame of mind for play."

"No. I know that now."

We fell silent again.

"Sally, do you still love me?"

"Yes."

"And I still love you. Nothing's changed."

"It has, you need to trust me again."

"Possibly, but that means lots of practice."

She grinned. "Thank you."

"What for?"

"For being you."

I lifted one of her hands across the table and kissed it.

"I told you, I'm no good at being anyone else."

She had visibly relaxed now, her face lighter, brighter, the smile returning. I suggested another drink.

"No. Come home," she said. "Let me get you dinner."

"We could find a restaurant."

"No. I'll cook."

By the time we got to her flat, we were easier together. We had walked hand in hand, talking about trivial things. When we got there, she led me into the kitchen and sat me at the table in the window. I soon realised she'd planned for this, most of the ingredients were already prepared in the fridge.

"Nothing special, I'm afraid; I'll get it going, and it'll be half an hour or so."

"How fortunate you had all this food prepared."

"Yes, wasn't it," she replied, kissing my forehead.

When she'd done what was needed, we went through to the living room; she got us something to drink, and we chatted. A while later, she went off to the loo. I relaxed into the sofa and looked around. I noticed a few photos on a bookcase I didn't remember seeing before, but I had only been here a few times. I got up and crossed to them as Sally came back. She'd changed; that must have been prepared as well, she hadn't been gone five minutes. Hair still up, face bright, eyes sparkling, and a green dress I couldn't help following as it traced her curves.

"Oh, God, Sally. You look good."

"Thank you. I feel good, for the first time in what seems like ages."

She walked slowly towards me and laid her arms on my shoulders, and for the first time in nearly a month, we kissed. Gently at first, teasing each other. Then with more passion, arms around each other. Tasting each other again before coming up for air.

"That's better," she said.

"Isn't it?" I looked at the photos. "Are they …"

"My mother, Charlie, and my father."

"Were they here before?"

"No. They came out over Easter. They helped me solve the problem." A timer went off in the kitchen. "Let's eat. I'll tell you about it."

"Are you sure?"

"Yes. I want to. I want you to know."

Over dinner, she told me more about the last few weeks, and particularly about the Easter weekend. It made me wince but telling me seemed almost cathartic for her. Even the worst bits seemed to amuse her, and hearing about Lucy's part in it made me realise the extent of the bond between them.

"How much did she tell you?"

"Nothing," I replied. "She told me you hadn't been well over Easter."

"Don't be angry with her."

"I'm not. She did what you asked. That's what friends do."

She toyed with some food on her plate.

"I didn't know how to start again," she said. "I knew I wanted you, wanted to get back to where we were. But I couldn't work out how. I didn't know if you still wanted me. The longer we weren't talking, the harder it got. I dreamt up all sorts of ideas to make it right." I sat quietly and listened. "Eventually, I decided what I was going to do. I wanted you to punish me, *really* punish me. I had it all worked out. I felt I deserved it and was going to take whatever you wanted to do to me. No limits, nothing. But last night, I was in bed, and suddenly realised you wouldn't do it, would you?"

I smiled back.

"No Sal, I wouldn't. I'll turn your ass red when you want me to, give you purple stripes if you want, use you when we're both up for it. But I'm not punishing you for anything … real. For something you think you've done. That's not what either of us wanted."

"So, I decided to talk to you. Should have done that in the first place."

"Simple is normally best."

Once she had told me the whole story, we let it rest, and she started flirting. I had been watching her, the old Sally appeared to have returned. Bright, sassy, gently animated. Green eyes flaring and expressive. I realised it was having an effect. She brought some fruit in, and passing me, bent down and gave me a long sensual kiss. I placed my hand on her back and allowed it to slowly slide down to her bum. As it reached one cheek, she peeled away and resumed her seat, a wicked grin on her face.

"Miss Fletcher, anyone would think you were trying to seduce me."

"Is that a problem, Mr Foxton?"

"No, Miss Fletcher. Not at all."

"Good … Ooh, I've got something for you."

She went out into the kitchen again, and on her return, handed me an Easter egg.

"Better late than never," she said. "Fancy some now?"

"Never say no to chocolate."

"I'll feed you."

She came to my side, and gently lowered herself onto my lap, laughing and wriggling her bum when she felt the effect of her seduction. She gave me a kiss and opened the egg. Hitting it to break it up, she took a piece and held it between her teeth. Moving her face towards me, I attacked the other end, and we met in the middle, lips finally touching. It was a tasty combination, our lips smeared in chocolate, licking each other clean.

She picked up another piece, and we repeated the process. I put my hand on her leg, stroking her stocking, while she continued to move her bum on my lap every so often. I moved my hand up her leg slowly, under the hem of the dress, finally reaching the top, and feeling the smooth skin above.

She snuggled in towards my ear.

"I thought I was doing the seducing?" she said in her most seductive voice.

"Shall I stop?"

"No. Keep going."

I didn't go far; yet. We weren't in a hurry. I concentrated on stroking her thigh and could hear her little sighs as I did so. She used her fingers to put a long piece of chocolate in my mouth, then sucked her way down it towards me, finally licking it out from between my lips. I looked into her eyes; bright and alive. Beguiling. Smiling. Gorgeous.

Finally, she stood up and held out her hand. I took it, and she led me towards the sofa. I pulled her the other way, and she followed, a questioning look on her face. I led her out into the hallway, and through to the bedroom. When we got there, I drew her towards me, putting my arms around her and our lips met, soft and sensual. My fingers found her zip, and slowly eased it down. I slid my other hand into the open back, and ran it over her skin, causing her to shiver slightly.

When the zip was undone, she took a step away, and put her hands into the shoulders, slowly sliding the dress down her body. Revealing her stunning sheer underwear. She loosened her hair and shook it out, then came towards me. Reaching up, my shirt buttons gradually came undone, and she eased it off. I pulled her towards me, and this time, my hands travelled down her back and rested on her bum. Gently feeling her cheeks; stroking them, squeezing them.

I felt her undoing my belt and trousers and letting them fall to the floor. With some difficulty, I managed to lift my feet out of them and kicked them away; she giggled at my clumsiness.

We caressed and allowed our hands and fingers to explore each other again. Still kissing softly. I undid her bra, and she released her arms from behind me so I could add that to the clothes strewn on the floor. She pushed in again, her erect nipples pressing into my chest. I stroked her back and allowed my hands to drop to her bum. Easing my fingers under the top of her briefs and massaging her cheeks. I pulled out of our kiss, and dropped in front of her, taking her underwear with me, and she stepped out of them when they reached the floor.

My head was now level with her sex, now lightly covered with a mat of short hair. I raised my hands again, and laying them on her bum, brought her towards me and started lightly kissing her thighs, moving up to her abdomen, and slowly dropping. Her hands were resting on my head. I kept moving down until I allowed my lips to softly suck her hood. She let out a little gasp. I carried on to her entrance, already wet. I passed my tongue across it a few times and then stood up to kiss her again. She met me more forcefully this time, tasting herself on my lips.

I guided her back onto the bed, and she lay in the middle, head dropping onto the pillow. Just stockings and suspender belt. I got on and knelt between her legs. She was smiling up at me. Running my hand up her leg, I reached a stocking top, and unclipped the suspender, then another, and did the same for the other leg.

"Don't you like—"

"Yes. But right now, I want you. Stripped. Bare. Naked."

She lifted slightly to allow me to undo and remove the suspender belt. I slowly peeled one stocking down, and kissed her raised foot, moving slowly up her leg, as I placed it back on the bed. Repeating it on the other leg.

"I'm naked," she said. "You're not."

I knelt up and slid my briefs off, my cock glad to be finally free. She looked at it keenly. I started to move over her, kissing her tummy, on up to her breasts, licking around her nipples, the occasional gentle bite causing a little flinch. Her hands again resting on my head. Then our lips met, sensual, loving, soft. I lowered my hips, allowing the head of my cock to make contact with her body. I used a hand to lay it along the length of her pussy, gently splitting it apart as my weight pushed it down; again, little sounds. Rocking gently, I rubbed it up and down, the underside of the shaft rolling over her clit.

I moved back down her body, kissing as I went until I was back sitting on my heels between her legs, a hand on each thigh. I eased her legs apart and brought them up until she was wide open. Trailing my fingers over her skin, I placed one hand on her tummy above her sex, using the other to continue working on her thigh. She was looking at me, occasionally closing her eyes.

I leant forward and started to massage the sides of her pussy, stretching and relaxing it, thumbs feeling their way along her perineum. More little sounds now, contentment mixed with pleasure. I changed position to stretch out on the bed, bringing my face into her. I watched the soft folds move under the pressure of my fingers, pink and glistening. I could smell her, inviting me to taste. I kissed the tops of her thighs, moving up to her groin, then finally, reaching the outside of her lips.

Running my tongue down the edge, moans getting louder. Down under her pussy, her lifting her knees higher to allow me easier access, fully exposing her tight little ass. I could reach that now too, and ran a finger around it, causing little twitches. Nudging it, pressing the tip into it, toying with it. I worked my way back up to her pussy, and nudged it open to let me lick inside, my fingers gently pressing her lips.

Her hands came to rest on my head; little nudges to guide me where she needed me. I moved up to her clit, now swollen. Kissing it, I softly put my lips around it. She pushed me down slightly to find the right spot. I used a couple of fingers to trace around her entrance, and I felt her legs stretch a little more. I eased them inside and heard a groan.

Turning my hand palm up, I curled my fingers slightly and sought that sweet spot. Pushing gently, her clit came up to meet me under the pressure. Immediate response. I let her guide me, the occasional pressure on my head, but mainly the response of her body. Twitches, moans, groans. She was building up now, breathing uneven, body snaking sinuously on the bed.

I loved feeling that response, seeing her pleasure. As she moved more, I tried to maintain the same pressures, to take her over the peak. She soon reached it. Her body froze for a few seconds, then a loud, long groan, as she jerked and twitched gently, her climax playing out all over her body, her breathing unsteady, mixed with whimpers. A close connection with each other as we shared that most intimate moment. I withdrew my fingers and lifted my mouth. Gently kissing the inside of her thighs again.

Her hands dropped away from my head, and I watched as she placed one over herself, gently exploring her own folds. She ran two fingers across her open entrance, and I followed them as she drew them up to her mouth and licked and sucked them, looking into my eyes as she did so. She let her legs relax, and I moved up and laid half over her, one leg between hers. She wrapped her arms around me, and we lay there, almost motionless.

"Oh, I've missed you," she whispered.

"Missed you too. God, you taste good."

I heard a deep throaty chuckle.

"I seem to remember you do too."

She gently pushed me and rolled me over onto my back. Kissing me, she lifted her leg and straddled my hips. Lowering herself, she guided my cock between us, sandwiching it between my tummy and her slit. Leaning down, with her elbows on the bed either side of my shoulders, she let her hair fall over my face, and slowly rubbed her pussy up and down the underside of my shaft. She started giving me faint kisses, pulling away each time I raised my head to meet her.

Then suddenly dropping her head, and almost smothering my mouth with hers, forcing her tongue between my lips, and licking and sucking. All the time rubbing herself up and down on my cock. It was intoxicating. She lifted her mouth, allowing me to breathe, and moved down my neck, kissing as she went, finally settling on her knees between my legs, and gently pushing them wider apart, bringing them up towards me. She placed one hand on each of my thighs, tight to my groin, and I watched her head drop, felt her mouth touch me below my balls, and her tongue ran up and down, making me shiver.

I felt her mouth reach my balls, slowly sucking one into her mouth, and massaging it with her tongue. Swapping to the other, her hand finally reached for my cock, and she slipped a couple of fingers around the base of the shaft, pulling to allow a little more skin to loosen my tight sac. Just enough to let her take both into her mouth and close her lips around them.

I gasped as a finger invaded my ass, and inched in, slowly twisting and turning. She let my balls slide out of her mouth, and looked up at me, smiling. Pressing a hand over my balls, she flattened it, pushing one either side of my cock, which was now pointing straight at me, flat against my tummy. Staring into my eyes, she firmly massaged my cock, while still fingering my ass, pressing her finger into my prostate. The feeling was intense. She released the pressure on my cock, and as it stood up, she dropped her mouth onto it.

Not her delicate touch, a stronger, more forceful movement. Taking long deep strokes, her tongue pressing against the shaft as she did so. That, combined with her fingering, was almost too much. But I didn't want to come yet. She didn't want me to either. Sensing it, she slowed, sliding her mouth off, and retaining the tip between her lips, removing her finger.

She was gently massaging my head with her lips, still holding my eyes with her gaze. Her fingers were now playing with my balls. I knew she was good at this. I knew she could read me; do this for ages while delaying my climax. I relaxed, and took the pleasure; the feeling, the sight, the sounds we both made. I let my head settle back on the pillow for a while, let the sensations fill my body. Every time I looked down, she looked up at me, love in her eyes, passion. I closed mine for a while; I was moaning now, letting my feelings escape, allowing her to read my responses.

I felt a finger exploring my ass again, and her mouth go deeper over my shaft. She attacked it vigorously for a few strokes, then stopped. I looked down to see her resting her arms on my thighs, a hand stroking me slowly but firmly. She was beaming, her eyes wide. She kissed the very tip of my cock and climbed slowly up over me. She moved her legs outside of mine, and lowered her hips, pressing my cock to my tummy, rubbing her pussy against it.

Lifting herself slightly, she guided my cock towards her entrance, and slowly dropped onto it, taking the head inside her, moving slowly up and down. Teasing me by never going as far as I expected her to, wanted her to. I felt it nudge into her, felt the heat even before it fully enveloped me. She was looking down at me, tongue between her teeth, enjoying this at least as much as I was.

With every slow rise and fall, she went slightly lower, gradually taking more of me into her. I felt her skin against me as she reached the base, and felt her weight finally rest on my hips. She dropped down, and we kissed; she teased at first, but then the kisses became stronger and deeper. She began to move her hips slowly in circles, rubbing her clit against my pubic bone, and feeling my cock move around inside her.

She was near to orgasm; her breathing was strong but often catching as she moved. She was using me. God, it felt good. I reached down and grabbed her thighs, just able to reach the edges of her bum. She moved slightly so I could extend my reach and started squeezing her cheeks. She could still rub herself on my bone, and now stopped kissing me, concentrating on her own pleasure.

Her eyes closed, and I watched as she constantly adjusted her position to achieve her goal. I felt her pussy grip me tighter, she let out a couple of loud gasps, and her breathing became heavy and rapid. Her thighs and bum cheeks quivered as the pleasure returned, and I stroked her skin as she came. Whimpering, sighing, her weight slowly settling back on me, as she passed the peak. When she opened her eyes and looked down, she had a slightly glazed look, but it quickly turned to a smile, and then to determination. I knew what that meant.

She started to rock backwards and forwards on my hips, my cock sliding in and out. Then she moved back slightly and began to rise up and down, slowly at first, pausing at the top to again tease the head. I was now getting to the point where I needed to come; my balls were aching, needing a release. She knew. She dropped down hard and started to ride my cock, long deep strokes, then a few shorter ones, then longer again.

I surrendered; she knew how to milk me, better than I did sometimes. These alternating rhythms were wonderful, my own hardness enclosed in her warm, wet softness. I felt myself beginning to tense up, so did she. She settled on a firm, steady movement, and looked down at me, concentrating on my reactions.

My body tensed and I held my breath, as my cock erupted, then disjointed exclamations came from my mouth. My hips rose involuntarily to spear her, but she pushed her weight down on me, forcing me deeper. I could feel my cum pulsing out, deep inside her, filling the narrow spaces between us. My whole body jerking with each contraction. She felt it too, letting out a little gasp with every spasm.

My body slowly relaxed, going limp on the bed. She let her arms slide under the pillows either side of me, dropping down until her head joined mine to one side. Both of us breathing deeply.

After a beautiful pause, I brought my arms up around her, and slowly stroked her back and shoulders. She let out some gentle moans.

"I needed that," she said.

"So did I."

"I love you."

"I know. You know I love you too, don't you?"

"Yes." She paused, then laughed as she wriggled her hips. "I can feel it."

"Oops," Sally said, looking at me innocently. "Dropped another one."

After we had recovered and whispered sweet nothings for a while, we both felt in need of sustenance, so had come out to the living room, and were finishing off the fruit and chocolate, along with a drink. I was sitting on the sofa, with her sitting between my legs, her own resting over mine to one side, leaning her body against me.

We'd had fun feeding each other, and a surprising number of grapes had dropped between her legs or mine. This time, I reached to pick it up, and her thighs closed, gripping my wrist. I found the grape, and moved my hand towards her groin, pressing my closed fingers against her sex, and pulling them out across her new short bush, prompting a little giggle.

"Would you like me to shave it off again?"

"You know I don't mind."

"I've neglected it for the last few weeks. But I think I'll grow it a bit, then start again. Might even get waxed. Luce does, but I've always chickened out. What shape would you like it to be?"

"Whatever you want, I'll still love it."

"What do you want to do for the weekend?" she asked. I looked at her, eyebrow raised. "No, apart from that. Shall we go over to yours tomorrow?"

"You still not comfortable here?"

She looked around.

"It's not that; I'm not sure if the shadow has gone for good or not, but I'm not worried about it anymore. It's just most of our toys are at yours. I might want them."

"We can always improvise."

"I think Lucy might pop around tomorrow. She doesn't know I was meeting you tonight, so she'll still be fussing."

"She's looked after you, Sal."

"I know." She became thoughtful and still. "It's her birthday next month. I want to do something special for her to say thank you."

"Got anything in mind?"

"No, not really. Any ideas?"

"Why not take her away? Have a girly weekend."

Her face slowly broke into a smile.

"That's a brilliant idea, I'll ask her tomorrow. Thank you."

She kissed me and we both realised we were recovering. Her hand slid down my tummy and reached my groin.

"What did you mean by improvise?" she asked.

"Depends what you want."

"There's nothing here to colour my cheeks."

"I always bring my hands with me, and I guess you probably have a leather belt."

Her eyes opened wide, a wicked look on her face.

"Shall I get one?"

"No. Not tonight."

She put on her best pout. Her hand was slowly working around my cock and balls, which were rapidly responding. I had my hand between her legs, and she was slowly spreading them allowing me greater access.

"What else do you want to do then?"

"You."

"How do you want me?"

I kissed her and moved close to her ear.

"Bend over something and hold on," I whispered. "I'm going to fuck that horny little devil in you until she squeals."

She let out a deep chuckle.

"She's all yours ..."

Chapter 24 – Sally

I looked at Marcus asleep on the pillow beside me. Breathing slowly, peaceful. Last night was still replaying through my mind. It had been such a relief, and then such a wonderful evening. I felt so contented, happier than I'd been since Christmas, I suppose. I'd gone a long way to sorting myself out, and we were together again.

Last night had shown two sides of our passion. First gentle, intense, loving, then raw, powerful, him taming the dirty little minx in me, her loving every minute. What had he said? *'until she squeals …'* Boy, did I squeal! By the time we finished, we were both sweating and exhausted. The thought of it was making me horny all over again. I studied him, wondering if he would mind me waking him up.

Nah, he wouldn't mind at all.

The rap at the door echoed down the hallway, stirring us from our restful reverie. I kissed him, and slid off the bed, wrapping a robe around me. Suddenly reminded of the evidence of our passion between my legs, I grabbed a pair of knickers and pulled them on. Looking through the spyhole, I saw Lucy outside. Smiling, I opened the door.

"Hi, Luce. Come in."

"Morning slug-a-bed. It's nearly ten."

"I know, we went to bed late."

She stopped stock-still.

"Oh, God, Sal. Is Marcus here? I'm sorry, I didn't know."

"Of course you didn't. It's fine."

"Morning Lucy," Marcus called down the hall.

"Uh, morning Marcus. Sorry, I wouldn't have interrupted if I'd known."

"You didn't, we were taking a break." I stifled a giggle; Lucy noticed. "Give me a minute or two to put something on, and I'll join you."

By the time he came into the kitchen, I'd assured Lucy she wasn't imposing and set about getting some coffee. By now Lucy was smiling.

"It's good to see you two together."

I put my arms around his neck and kissed him.

"It is, isn't it? Anyone fancy a bacon butty?"

As we ate, we chatted. Trivial stuff, all of us happy, for slightly different reasons.

"What did you have planned to keep me occupied today?" I teased Lucy.

"Well, I had thought about getting some gym gear for our assessment, but I guess that can wait now."

"Gym assessment?" Marcus asked, a curious smile on his face.

"Yes, I thought I'd give it a go and Lucy volunteered to go with me."

"Volunteered?" Lucy replied.

"Okay. I twisted her arm. We used to go running."

"That must be more than five years ago."

"We need to get back to it. Do you mind if we pop into town, Marcus? We shouldn't be long."

"No, not at all. I'll go home if you like."

"No, you won't. You stay here. I'm not finished with you yet."

Lucy laughed.

"Making up for lost time, Sal?"

I noticed Marcus looking slightly embarrassed.

"Something like that. Right, I'll have a quick shower and get dressed. Won't be long."

When we got back, I noticed he had changed.

"I popped home for a few things." He looked at me knowingly. I knew. "Did you get what you needed?"

"Yes. Enough to start with anyway. We got some things for lunch. Are you hungry?"

We settled down to eat, and I told him we'd agreed a weekend away just before Lucy's birthday but hadn't decided where yet.

"Just what did you bring from home?"

"A few things."

"What exactly?"

Lucy had gone and I was curled up beside him.

"A few bits and pieces."

I gave up, I knew I'd find out. We spent a contented afternoon with each other, cooked dinner together and settled down. After a while, I turned to him.

"You know that horny little devil in me?"

"Yes."

"I think she needs to be taught a lesson."

"Do you?"

"I think she needs you to take her in hand tonight, show her who's in charge."

"Really?"

"I have an idea she's feeling naughty, very cheeky. Think you can handle her?"

He looked me straight in the eye.

"Oh, yes."

"Good. I'll go and get her ready for you."

The next day, I finally raised the subject I wanted to resolve.

"Marcus, have you thought any more about us living together."

"Yes."

"And?"

"It's a lovely idea …"

"But?"

"I'm still not sure."

I stayed calm; I didn't want him to hear my frustration.

"What's stopping you?" I asked him.

"It's difficult to put into words. It's not us, we're good."

"Is it about the man being the provider?"

"No, you know that's not how I think. But I would like to feel I'm making an equal contribution to the relationship."

"And why wouldn't you be? Is the money the issue?"

"I'm very aware of it."

"Don't want to be a kept man, eh?"

"Not sure, look what happened with Claire."

"Oh, Marcus. Yes, that situation was hard on Claire. But this is different. We're never going to be short of money."

"Are you sure you don't want kids?"

I had to stay calm again, we weren't getting anywhere.

"Yes. Absolutely sure."

"Where would we live?" he asked.

"Ah, now that's more positive."

"Well?"

"I propose we look for somewhere new. It wouldn't make any sense me moving in with you, and, if I'm honest, I wouldn't mind leaving this place behind. We don't move into your place or mine. We find a home for us."

I didn't point out that having started to come to terms with the money, we could look for somewhere better than either of our current flats.

"Yes. That's what I'd thought."

I decided not to force the issue. I felt we both wanted it to happen; that it was when, not if.

"Promise me you'll think about it?"

"Promise."

Well, we'd made some progress. I had a bit of an agenda. I'd been thinking about the money, and realised I'd finally accepted it. It was mine, now to do something with it. For me, and for those who were important to me.

***

I went to see Mary. She knew the progress I'd made; I'd probably told her more about my counselling than anyone else, at least until I'd opened up to Marcus. Simply because she had been a part of it all, knew what had happened. But there was something I wanted to do. For her. I dropped in and set out my stall.

"No, darling," she said when she'd heard me out. "I don't need it. It's yours."

"But Mary, you've done so much for me. You've supported me at the toughest times of my life. I wouldn't be where I am without you."

"I've done what I could," she replied, smiling.

"I want to do something for you. I feel some of this should be yours. Let me help you out. You had to give up your job when you were ill. It can't be easy."

"Sally, I'm fine. I'm back working now anyway, part-time. Decided to slow down a bit. Enjoy life. Have fun again. I'm doing all right."

"Then let me pay off your mortgage or something."

"Haven't got one dear. Paid off long ago."

I was surprised. Mary's house wasn't grand, but it was large, in a nice area, and although she'd had a career, it wasn't that highly paid. She'd never married, so anything she had, she'd earned.

"Oh. Well, take some for a rainy day, something to fall back on. It's as much yours as mine in a way."

I was suddenly aware she seemed a bit uneasy. Possibly embarrassed at my persistence, but I felt there was more to it.

"I don't need it dear, honestly."

Something unsaid made me feel uneasy too.

"Mary … What is it?"

"Are you sure you want to know?"

"Yes, might as well."

She looked out of the window, pondering whether to continue. I wondered what new revelations were about to appear. Eventually, she turned back to me.

"I've already had some of your father's money."

I took this in slowly; surprised, turning it around in my mind. Couldn't make sense of it.

"How? When?"

"You really want to know?"

Too far now, I needed to hear.

"Yes, no more secrets and ghosts. Tell me."

I listened as she filled in a blank I didn't even know existed. She'd had an affair with my father, when she still thought he was on the level, before the doubts set in. When they had, Mary had stopped it, but Mum was trapped; married to him, and pregnant with Charlie, by then. I let it sink in, shocked but bemused rather than angry.

"Is that why you and Mum were distant?"

"I don't think she ever found out, she never said anything to me, anyway. No, we were just different. I think she saw me as the black sheep."

"Black sheep?"

"She thought I was … loose. That would have been her word. I enjoyed life, went through the boys." She chuckled to herself. "Then the men. None lasted long, I got bored with them. Had too much fun chasing new ones. Your mother didn't approve."

"Perhaps she was jealous?"

"Possibly. I didn't care at the time. She'd chosen her life, I chose mine. Then she met your father. There was something captivating about him; handsome, charming. Just the man I expected your mother to fall in love with. Me? I saw him as another challenge. Sounds cruel now, I suppose."

"What happened?"

"Sometime after they got married, he started giving me things. Little things at first, a bracelet, a brooch, chocolates. I knew what he wanted, but I did respect your mother. I didn't want to disrupt things. But he persisted, and eventually, I caved in."

"How long did it last?"

"About a year, on and off. I wouldn't see him for weeks, then he'd appear one day, and we'd spend a night together. More presents followed, increasingly expensive. Jewellery, even envelopes of money."

"What did you think?"

"I started to feel uncomfortable; wondered if it was … payment. I didn't like that. That was when I started to back away, and it fizzled out. He tried to keep going, but I knew by then I was probably one of many. I didn't love him. In the end, I told him it was over. He paid me off. To keep quiet, I suppose. Who was I going to tell? My own sister? Hardly. But I took the money. I suspected by then it wasn't legit. With everything he'd given me, it almost bought my first house."

My mouth dropped.

"Then when your Mum died, I offered to come and look after you. He wanted me to marry him. I knew he didn't love me, just wanted a housekeeper. He knew it, I knew it. I refused. I was happy to come and look after the two of you, but I wasn't going to get involved with him again. He tried his old method, gave me presents and money. Rightly or wrongly, I took them.

"Finally, his patience ran out, and Wendy appeared. I couldn't hang around after that, not even for you and Charlie. He paid me off again; guilt, probably. The rest you know. But it means I own this house, and I've got more than enough to give me a comfortable semi-retirement. I don't need any more, darling."

She fell silent as I ran all this through my head. If I'd heard this six months ago, I wouldn't have believed it, it would have made things much worse. But now? What did it matter? My view of my Mum and Dad was so different now. I'd accepted him and had stopped idolising her. Who was I to judge? Finally, I laughed.

"Mary, you old tart!"

She looked at me. "Yes, I probably was. I'm sorry, darling."

"Don't apologise. I think it's quite funny we've both ended up with his bloody dodgy money."

"Yes, I suppose it is. I promised myself never to tell you, but I think now it's right you should know. Complete the story, so to speak."

I went over and hugged her.

"You've been my surrogate Mum for twenty-five years; a bloody good one. This doesn't change anything. I love you, Mary, always will."

"I love you too darling; proud of you."

"Thanks."

We hugged for a while, and then she got us a drink.

"Are you still being an old tart, then?"

"Oh yes, plenty of life left in me yet!"

"Ken?"

"Yes, for now. He's keeping up. A bit naïve; he'd only ever been with his wife, and she died six years ago. He's keen, but I am having to educate him a bit. I do hope Marcus has some imagination, darling. That's the key."

I smiled.

"Oh yes, Mary. Imagination is something Marcus has in abundance."

***

"I've told you before," Marcus said after he stopped laughing. "Be careful what you ask for."

I'd told him Mary's story, still not completely sure how to deal with it. Part of me was amused, but part of me thought I should be angry, or at least upset. I wasn't. He suggested I throw it into the mix with Jenny. I was still having regular sessions. There was still a lot of work to do. But it did add the final pieces; at least, we both hoped they were the final pieces.

***

I took Lucy to London for a long weekend. When we were younger, we'd often gone on holidays together, and they'd been a scream. Somewhat debauched, as I remembered. This was much more civilised, and probably the better for it. But we'd had an argument before we even booked it.

"Sal, I want to go halves."

"No, Luce. I'm paying. Consider it a birthday present. I want to go somewhere special."

"But we always paid our own way."

"That was before I … Well, you know. Think of what I could have done with the money over the years. I want to make up for some of that."

"Yes, but …"

"No buts. Marcus is going to have to accept it, and so are you."

She let me book the hotel. A suite; two bedrooms and a sitting room. After her initial shock, we soon got used to the good life, and the weekend was a joy. Friday night, we had dinner at The Thomas Cubitt, before going to see Wicked. After a leisurely breakfast in our suite, we spent Saturday wandering around the shops.

"Luce, I haven't bought you anything for your birthday."

"Apart from a weekend at the Connaught."

"You know what I mean. If you see anything today you like ..."

"Oh, Sal."

"I mean it."

"I know. That's what worries me."

After a couple of hours, we ended up with a few bags each. Lucy finally decided we'd finished.

"That's enough, Sal. Anything I say I like, you want to buy for me. It's too much."

"Sorry. It's fun. I wasn't thinking."

She hugged my arm.

"I'm not complaining. But I think I've got several birthday's worth here."

"Right. One more stop. Come on."

I dragged Lucy into Victoria's Secrets with me. She watched, amused, as I looked around, spoilt for choice. I settled on a few things and even persuaded her to let me treat her one more time.

After lunch, we took our bags back to the hotel and then spent the afternoon being pampered in the spa. We passed the evening in Covent Garden, watching the street performers, and grabbing some food in a really good little restaurant.

Sunday morning found us viewing an exhibition at the V & A, followed by a river cruise, and tea at the Ritz. By the evening, we were both shattered, and spent the evening relaxing, having dinner in our suite, along with plenty of wine.

"Do you miss Zoe?"

Lucy thought for a moment.

"No. We both knew it was only fun. Avoided the painful split."

"I guess she learned a few things."

"I think she probably did!"

We reminisced about bad break-ups, now able to laugh about them, however painful they'd been at the time. She told me how lucky I was with Marcus, how happy he seemed to make me. I told her how lucky he was to have me, but knew she was right. She asked me what made him so different.

"It's difficult to explain really. We have a connection. Similar interests, same outlook on life. Happy in each other's company, even if we don't talk for hours. Marcus calls it quiet companionship."

"And good sex?"

"Yes, there's that as well. He's very … imaginative."

"Imaginative?"

We'd had a few glasses of wine by now.

"Yes. We … explore our fantasies."

"Want to tell me more?"

"No."

"Spoilsport."

"You don't tell me what you do in bed, so I'm not either."

"Dare you …"

I guess it was the drink, but by the end of the evening, we both knew considerably more about each other's experiences. I was sober enough not to go too far in my confessions, but far enough for Lucy to suggest we should change 'quiet companionship' to 'kinky companionship'. Which I rather liked.

Sober enough too for the stories to make me horny. Lying in bed later, enjoying the touch of my fingers between my legs, I found myself thinking about Marcus. But also thinking about Lucy, wondering if she was doing the same as me. Imagining her standing at the edge of the bed, naked, watching me. I saw her climbing onto the bed …

***

"Lucy says the portrait's nearly finished. She wants to bring it over next weekend."

"Do you like it?" Marcus asked.

"I don't know. She won't let me see it."

I'd sat for Lucy a couple of times. She'd taken loads of photos and done a few sketches. A few days after one of the sittings, I had given Marcus two framed pictures of Zoe – well, parts of Zoe. They were beautiful, but he'd given one back to me. We had hung them in our bedrooms, a link between us whenever we were home alone. Which wasn't often now. I spent most weekends at his, he spent most weeknights at mine.

When Lucy arrived at Marcus's on Friday evening, she dithered.

"I think I've finished it; not sure. I've put it in an old frame, but obviously, you'll need to put it in one to match wherever you want it. That's if you want it."

"Lucy …" he said softly, amused by her nervousness.

"Yes?"

"Just show us the picture."

"Oh … okay."

She unwrapped the blanket she'd put it in to bring it over, and placed it on the sofa, resting against the back. She stood behind it, watching us as we viewed it for the first time. Her face was a picture of nervous pride. But I wasn't looking at her face; I was looking at my own, staring back at me from the paper.

I couldn't tell if it was pencil or pen and ink, but it was stunning. Some light shading; on skin, on hair. I was leaning forward slightly, one hand resting on the opposite shoulder, my chin tucked into the gap between shoulder and wrist. Hair up, a few strands hanging loosely here and there. But the focus was clear; the only colour, staring straight out at the viewer. Two amazing, brilliant green eyes.

"Oh, Lucy …" Marcus whispered.

"I can change it. Start again?"

"No. Don't touch it. It's perfect. It's Sally."

"Wow," was all I could manage.

We stood for a minute or two, looking at it.

"Sal mentioned you loved her eyes."

"I do. Get lost in them sometimes. Sal, what do you think?"

"I love it. But it's very flattering."

"No. It's you. Just you. Thanks, Luce."

"You're welcome." She had relaxed a lot. "I'm really glad you like it. It's a gift, from me to both of you."

"Thank you," Marcus said quietly. I went around the sofa and gave Lucy a hug, before returning to his side.

"But there's only one picture," I said. "Where are we going to hang it?"

He knew what I was asking, and I was holding my breath. He looked back at me, smiling.

"We'd better find a new home for it; somewhere we both see it every day."

I threw my arms around his neck.

"I love you."

"I know."

Epilogue – Lucy

I was happy with the portrait. I thought I'd captured the Sally I knew. But you never can tell. Unveiling it to both the subject and Marcus had been nerve-wracking. But they both seemed to like it. Genuinely like it. And it somehow prompted their big decision; to move in together. I knew Sal had been wanting to for months, and now Marcus had agreed.

I made ready to leave, but they insisted I stay for the evening. Sally volunteered to go and pick up a Chinese, so Marcus opened a bottle while we waited for her.

"Are you happy with it?" I asked. He had put the portrait on the floor in front of the fireplace, for now.

"It's perfect; it's Sally. Are you?"

"Yes. I am."

We both sat, looking at the picture.

"Sal's so excited about you two moving in together, you know," I said.

"We both are. I guess I don't show it as much."

"No, probably not. You two are so perfect together, it's sickening."

"Still no one, Luce?"

"No. I'm fed up with all the hassle."

"Know what you're looking for?"

I paused, thinking.

"Not sure I do anymore. I'm beginning to think I might prefer living on my own. I can do what I want, please myself."

"I know what you mean. I was like that before I met Sally, but I'm so glad I did."

"I wouldn't mind finding someone like Zoe again." I thought back to what Sally and I had shared on our London weekend. "You know, to share a few fantasies."

"Oh?"

"I gather you're helping Sal fulfil some of hers."

Marcus was wary now.

"Well, possibly a few," he replied.

"Only a few?"

He thought for a moment.

"I can't help her with all of them."

"God," I replied. "They're not that extreme, are they?"

He looked lost in thought, as if deciding what to say.

"No. But they don't all involve men."

I looked at him, slowly digesting what he'd said. A faint smile was etched across his face. Then it dawned on me. Realisation. Had I been that blind?

Before I could say anything, the front door opened, and Sally arrived with dinner. For the rest of the evening, my mind mulled over this new information. Even if true, did Sally want to do anything about it? Some fantasies are just that, fantasies. And would Marcus be happy for her to explore that side of her nature? But if not, why did he tell me?

Things had just got interesting. And incredibly complicated …

* * * * * *

The story continues in **New Temptations**.

Author's Note

I would like to thank all those involved in helping me bring this story to the page. You know who you are, and I will be eternally grateful.

The adventures of Sally, Marcus and Lucy continue in New Temptations, the second book in the Kinky Companions series. I hope you'll join them.

To keep in touch with my writing, you can visit my website, where you can subscribe to my newsletter, blog or follow me on social media.

Website: www.alexmarkson.com
Twitter: @amarksonerotica
Facebook: @amarksonerotica
Goodreads: Alex Markson

Alex Markson
February 2020

Printed in Great Britain
by Amazon